“Wow, what a story! Written wr, this gut-wrenchingly honest no e road trip to the land of Growin Todd and Jedd!”

—MELODY CARLSC ing author of more than one hundred books, including the teen series TRUECOLORS and DIARY OF A TEENAGE GIRL

“I started reading *Bad Idea* out of curiosity; by page three, I was hooked. When it comes to writing, The Brothers Hafer know what they're doing, exuding a confident command of style, tone, and wit that had me eager to see what was on the next page, and the next, and the next. At long last, a modern novel that refreshes as it challenges. Here's hoping they get an even worse idea in the future.”

—ADAM PALMER, author of *Mooch;* coauthor of *Taming a Liger: Unexpected Spiritual Lessons from Napolean Dynamite*

BAD IDEA

a novel {with coyotes}

TODD & JEDD

Hafer

TH1NK
P.O. Box 35001
Colorado Springs, Colorado 80935

Published in association with the literary agency of Alive Communications, Inc., 7680 Goddard Street, Suite 200, Colorado Springs, CO 80920 (www.alivecommunications.com).

TH1NK is an imprint of NavPress.
TH1NK and the TH1NK logo are registered trademarks of NavPress. Absence of ® in connection with marks of NavPress or other parties does not indicate an absence of registration of those marks.

ISBN 1-57683-969-9

Cover design by Studiogearbox.com
Cover image by CSA Archive
Creative Team: Nicci Hubert, Cara Iverson, Arvid Wallen, Kathy Guist

CIP DATA APPLIED FOR

Printed in the United States of America

1 2 3 4 5 6 7 8 9 10 / 10 09 08 07 06

A Note to Our Readers:

Easy answers. Perfect, pious people. Storybook endings. These are just three of the things you won't find in the novel you're about to read. What you will find are true-to-life characters with true-to-life problems, interpersonal conflicts, and struggles with faith. In creating this book, authors Todd and Jedd Hafer drew from their experiences of working with thousands of teens, from runaway street kids to those raised in the church. Todd and Jedd also drew heavily from personal journals of their own coming-of-age years. The result is a compelling, gritty story, free of clichés and pat answers. *Bad Idea* offers no gratuitous content, nor does it shy away from the real issues that today's millennial generation faces. And we at TH1NK believe that you can't present real issues and then try to hide them behind unrealistic façades.

We respect our authors' commitment to be real with their readers; we trust you will, too. And if you or someone you know is struggling with any of the particular challenges faced by the novel's lead character, Griffin Smith, please take a look at the list of ministry resources at the back of the book.

Thank you for reading,

Terry Behimer
Editorial Director

To Jody,
These are dark times, but I write in your light.
—T.H.

To the memory of my beloved friend H. Rodney Johns III, who dove into life, who feared nothing, and who left this earth too soon. I'll see you in heaven, Rug.
—J.H.

Acknowledgments

From Jedd:

With all my heart, I thank:

My Savior, Jesus Christ

My big brother and hero, Todd Hafer

The Hafer family

The Casteels

My brother in Christ and writing, Scott Degelman

Danny Oertli—your words and music move me every time

Dr. Charles Fay—you have more wisdom about kids in pain than anyone

Nicci and all the great folks at NavPress/TH1NK

Beth and the Alive Communications family

The Children's ARK family

And my beautiful wife and amazing children—you are gifts from God, and you inspire me daily

From Todd:

Writing a book is like cutting a record. And just as recording artists make a point of acknowledging their bands, the people who make the music possible, authors should do the same. So, please, let me introduce the band—and more . . .

Harmony Vocals: Nicci Hubert. Nicci, you helped harmonize our book with TH1NK's mission and artistic vision. Thanks for believing in *Bad Idea* as strongly as you do. You can sing with me and my brother anytime.

Backing Vocals (e.g., our voices of encouragement and support): Toby Mac, Tricia and Melissa Brock, Nichole Nordeman, Sigmund Brouwer, Bruce & Stan, Melody Carlson, and Danny Oertli. Thanks to all of you for your kind words. We won't forget that a LOT fewer people (like about 17 total) would read our books if not for the halo effect of your good names.

Rhythm Section (e.g., our creative foundation at NavPress and TH1NK): Terry Behimer, Cara Iverson, Arvid Wallen, Kathy Guist, Melanie Knox, and the aforementioned Nicci. You are a great creative team. Thanks for making this book possible.

Management/Booking (and part-time Crisis-Management Counselor): Beth Jusino, at Alive Communications. Jedd and I are deeply grateful for an agent who "gets" our quirkiness and isn't scared of weird ideas (or Bad Ideas). Also, thanks for your patience with two guys who suffer from Attention Deficit—hey, wanna go ride bikes?

Technical Advisor/Equipment Manager: T.J. Hafer. Thanks for being a great Web master for haferbros.com—and for answering advanced technological questions like, "Hey, I got me a big FATAL ERROR message in the middle of this here computer screen; is that gonna be a problem?"

Lead Guitar/Co-Lead Vocals: Jedd Hafer. My bro, it's a privilege—and childhood dream—to write books with you. Thanks for being the best brother and friend a guy could hope to have.

Soli Deo Gloria

Prologue

I learned five key life lessons as a result of my first real, multi-day road trip, and I know I should list them chronologically or in order of spiritual magnitude. At least alphabetize them. That would make this a lot easier for all of us.

But I guess I have to start with this lesson, the one that stands out in my mind right now. **Key Life Lesson #1:** If you're going to grab an ostensibly dead coyote by the paws and attempt to drag him someplace, you should confirm the death first. If one fails to learn this lesson, the result will be traumatic and dangerous—for him and for the coyote.

The coyote incident occurred approximately a third of the way into the road trip, on a solo leg that flung me off the course of my final destination. I had left my dad, his young cliché—I mean fiancée—and my best friend back in Denver so that I could drive two hours to southeastern Wyoming to see my mom for the first time in almost two years.

She and her new husband, Maxwell the Mediocre, live on a nonworking farm (nonworking in oh so many ways) outside of a little town called Wheatland, where he writes mediocre suspense novels and she . . . must do something, I suppose. I have no idea what. I know only that she's "really and truly happy" for the first time in her life, because she tells me so when she sends me a birthday card every October. (My birthday, just for reference, is September 21st.)

Anyway, at 8:38 on an August Friday night, I was bouncing across the 1.7-mile stretch of corrugated dirt road that led to the nonworking farm when a coyote decided to bound into my path. I didn't have time to swerve or pray or swear. I felt a series of thumps under my dad's Durango. It sounded like the start of a really great rock 'n' roll drum solo, but then the drummer suddenly dropped his sticks—or perhaps died.

When the thumping ceased, I mashed the brake pedal to the floorboard and stuttered to a stop in the middle of the road. My first thought was, *I really hope it rains buckets tonight so I won't have a bunch of coyote blood and entrails dried on the family vehicle.* (I am not vain about our SUV. It is seven years old, two years older than my little brother. It's racked up more than a hundred thousand miles and has a dent about the size of a bowling ball in the driver's-side door. Confession: The dent is *exactly* the size of a bowling ball because my mom held my dad's sixteen-pound Brunswick over her head, like Moses with one of the stone tablets, before she used it to smite the family vehicle, just before she drove away in Maxwell's Lexus almost four years ago.)

Thus, the Smith family vehicle (and I use the word "family" loosely) holds no aesthetic or sentimental value for me. I just had no desire to drive to some high-pressure car wash called The Whale Spout or something and try to rinse Coyote McNuggets from the front bumper and grille. That task would be tedious and unpleasant, but if I failed to do it, someone might think I downed a couple cans of malt liquor and ran over some little kid's Great Dane. I didn't want some kid's mom to walk by our parked SUV, stare at it and then at me, then hurry her child away, saying,

"Don't look at that bad young man or his big nasty automobile, Blaise. He's not a Friend to the Animals!" (Yeah, go ahead and judge me, lady—at least I'd never name my kid Blaise.)

Anyway, I checked my rearview mirror and saw the coyote sprawled on his side in the middle of the road. He seemed to be intact, internal organs still internal, which brought me relief. I sat in the SUV for the duration of an Eric Clapton guitar solo, studying the coyote for any signs of movement. I hoped he was dead rather than just mortally, painfully wounded.

Before you decide Blaise's mom was right about me and report me to PETA, let me explain myself. I hoped for the coyote's demise only because if he was injured and suffering, I couldn't face the prospect of a mercy killing. To me, "mercy killing" is an oxymoron, like "Republican party" or "Free-Will Baptist." By that point in my life, I had never killed anything larger than an insect, and I had no desire to fetch a tire iron and crack a coyote's cranium.

I have long admired coyotes. And no, it's not because of those Road Runner cartoons where the bumbling Wile E. Coyote perpetually fails in his efforts to capture his prey. I never cared for Wile E. and his pathetic overreliance on Acme gadgets. I favor real coyotes, mainly for their running ability. They can zip along at about thirty-eight miles an hour, if I remember correctly a wildlife film I saw in second grade. They are lean and agile and graceful. But misunderstood. The coyote and I have much in common.

And here's the main reason I like coyotes. In seventh grade, I returned kickoffs and punts for the Clear Creek Middle School football team. In our first home game, I scooped up a low, bouncing kickoff at our twenty-three-yard-line and returned it for a touchdown. It was the only touchdown I would score in organized football. It was a decent return. Sure, I had great blocking, but I had to reverse my field twice and juke the kicker at the twelve. When I got to the sideline, after my teammates finished smacking me on the shoulder pads, I heard Janine Fasson say the following to her friend Tracy Miles, who was sitting next to her in the first row of bleachers: "Who is that number eighty-four? He runs like a coyote!"

Janine Fasson was easily among the three hottest girls in our entire middle school, which explains why she had to ask a classmate who *I* was. But from that point, I had my "in" with her. I was no longer just another skinny twelve-year-old who didn't exist in Janine's World o' Hot Guys; I was Coyote Boy. I dashed, darted, and danced like a lean canine predator whom women admired and farmers, and their sheep, feared.

As soon as those words spilled from Janine's mouth, the coyote replaced the cheetah as my favorite animal. Yes, I know that cheetahs are much faster, but Janine Fasson didn't liken me to a cheetah, did she? So now perhaps you can imagine my angst over the prospect of killing my brother the coyote.

I clicked off Clapton and shifted into reverse. I looked over my shoulder and slowly backed toward the prone coyote. When I was close enough for my taillights to illumine my way, I stopped, drew in a deep breath, and got out of the Durango. I crept toward the coyote, circling him as if I were a high school wrestler facing a much-superior opponent. Then I said this: "Hey, you okay, buddy?" (I know, I know. But what was I supposed to say? "Boo!"?)

The coyote was, as they say in the medical dramas, nonresponsive. So I grabbed him by the back paws and started to drag him off the road. Not exactly an honorable burial, but at least it showed a measure of respect.

I'm not going to give what happened next the big dramatic buildup. You have a general sense of what transpired. We're all intelligent, reasonable people here, so there's no need to indulge in cheap literary-suspense devices. I'll leave those to Maxwell. However, it is worth noting that it wasn't the coyote's sudden recovery and the fact that he made me scream like a schoolgirl that unsettles me to this day. I don't blame the coyote for jerking to life and hurling that guttural snarl at me. It was the look in his eyes and the way he snapped his jaws twice at me before bolting away. It was pure hate.

Rhonda, my dad's aforementioned cliché/fiancée, told me later that the coyote was just scared and upset and didn't act out of malice. I don't buy it. I have been scared and upset before every math and science exam I have ever taken, yet I've never growled at anyone because of it, nor have I tried to bite anyone. (And don't think I haven't been tempted. Dividing polynomials makes me hostile, man.)

Anyway, aggression born of instinct or fear, that I could forgive. But this coyote acted with personal acrimony. It destroyed the almost-six-year bond between us. In fact, I distrusted the coyote so much that, even though he quickly put several football fields' worth of yardage between us, I sprinted to the SUV, scrambled inside, and locked the doors. I feared he might return, revenge in his heart.

I realize now that it was probably excessive to lock the doors, but you had to be there. I had a vision of the coyote breaking through the high wild grass that flanked the road and flinging himself against the driver's-side door like that Saint Bernard in the movie *Cujo*. Later I would chuckle at the thought of a 60-pound animal ramming a 4,600-pound steel automobile, but on that dark Wyoming road that night, it was no laughing matter. I turned on the CD player. "I Shot the Sheriff" brought me a measure of comfort as I drove slowly away, checking my rearview mirrors every several seconds.

As Clapton asserted that he "did not shoot the dep-u-tee," I determined that, until further notice, the cheetah had leaped back to the top of the Griffin Smith Favorite Animal List. "The coyote is so over, man," I whispered with resolve.

At that moment, I began to question the Wyoming leg of the road trip and, consequently, the journey in its entirety. I wished I had trusted my better judgment, which told me, "Simply fly from Kansas City to Southern California." If I had, I would already have been settled into my dorm. I would have met my colleagues on the Lewis College cross-country team, and I would have met my Secret Girl Pen Pal, The Carrot.

I *wouldn't* have experienced the first fistfight of my eighteen-year-old life. I wouldn't have seen a shockingly gruesome death. And I would already have said goodbye to my best friend, Cole, instead of wondering how, exactly, I was going to do that without hurting so bad that I'd go into shock.

But I had only myself to blame. If I had wanted to veto this whole ill-conceived "journey of bonding and discovery," as Rhonda called it, I could have done it four weeks previously.

"We should totally drive!" Rhonda said, wagging a limp french fry for emphasis.

I clenched my teeth. I hate it when adults try to talk like teenagers. Rhonda does it all the time. Her efforts are particularly grating to me because she does, in fact, employ the teen vernacular, but always, *always* at least one season too late.

Thus, my father's twenty-eight-year-old fiancée didn't say "Congrat-ulations!" when I was inducted into Quill & Scroll (the National Honor Society for high school journalists) early in my senior year. She said, "Big ups to you, G!" And when I was named Honorable Mention All-Area in track and field (small-school division), she didn't say "Way to go!" She said, "Big respect, G-Man! You got the mad wheels, homey!"

If she says, "I'm feelin' you, dawg," during one more of our Dad-initiated dinnertime theological discussions, I'm going to puke on her shoes.

Fortunately for Rhonda, and all of the people at the Big Bear Diner on the night the road trip was conceived, I didn't barf when she said, "We should totally drive!" I raised my eyes to the ceiling and said, "I don't think we should *totally* drive. I don't even think we should partially drive."

I looked across the booth to my dad to accept the disapproving glare I knew he would be offering. I smiled at him. It was my infuriating, smug smile. I practice it in the bathroom mirror. It's so irritating that when I see my reflection doing it, I want to punch myself in the face.

My dad didn't hit me. That wasn't his style. He just nibbled his bottom lip for a while before saying calmly, "I think we should give the idea due consideration rather than reject it out of hand."

"Okay," I said, sipping my bitter iced tea, "let's hear why we should cram ourselves into a car and drive for, what, three or four days to Southern California, stomping on each other's raw nerves all along the way and probably breaking down somewhere near the Kansas-Colorado border. Or maybe getting in a wreck."

Rhonda looked at my dad, giving him her Wounded Face, all droopy eyes and puckered chin and poofed-out lower lip. You know the look.

He looked at her, then at me. "Griffin, please . . ."

"Okay, okay, okay—you're right, you guys. Yeah, you know, now that I consider The Rhonda Eccles-Someday-To-Be-Smith Plan carefully, it's sounding better. I mean, why would I want to enjoy a quick, economical, and stress-free flight when we could all cram into a tired old vehicle and *drive*? Let's go with the option that means more time, more money, more risks, more headaches."

Rhonda tried to smile, but she couldn't get the corners of her tiny heart-shaped mouth to curl upward. "Well," she said quietly, "I just thought it would be bomb to make a road trip of it. See the country. Stop at mom-and-pop diners like the Big Bear here. Maybe spend a day in Denver—hit an amusement park or catch a Rockies game. Griff, please be more open-minded. Think of the time it would give us to kick it."

"We talk now," I observed.

"Yessss," she said, drawing the word out as though it had sprung a slow leak. She wrapped her long, slender fingers around her coffee mug and took a sip. "But in the car, you wouldn't be able to run away from the convo whenever it got too intense for you."

I pushed my chair back from the table and popped up like a piece of toast. I was ready to wad my napkin and spike it like a football on the table before marching out of the Big Bear. Then, only a half second before the Great Napkin Spike, I realized that would be proving her point.

Rhonda was studying me. I scrolled my mind for options on saving face, because since she had unofficially joined our family, I had lost more face than Michael Jackson. But I scrolled in vain. My brain was nothing but blank screen.

Now other patrons were watching me too. I could feel their stares. An idea began to emerge. It wasn't a good idea, but it was all I had, so I went with it. I said, with an air of dignified indignation, "Well, I'm going back to the buffet for another muffin. Would anybody else care for one?"

This is why I'll never be a politician, a courtroom litigator, a public speaker—or a success in anything that requires more than a modicum of human interaction. I have my moments, but rarely can I think on my feet when I'm around people. Half the time, I can't think off of 'em either. Maybe this is why track is the only sport I'm good at. All you must do is keep alternating left foot, right foot, left foot, right foot, and turn left every once in a while. I found football and basketball too taxing mentally. They say Larry Bird was a hoops legend because he could foresee plays unfolding before they actually happened. So he always executed the perfect pass, put himself in position for nearly every rebound, stole inbounds passes at will. The game didn't take him by surprise. Not the case with me. I played organized basketball in junior high and the first two years of high school. And every time I got a jump shot swatted back in my face or ran into a hard pick, it was like a new, albeit unpleasant, experience. So I became a track man. I run the 1600 and 3200 meters—that's the mile and two-mile for those of you still holding strong in the anti-metric resistance.

I should note that I'm also adequate in cross-country. I often panic before races, though, because many of the courses are complicated. Even after reading the maps posted near the starting line, I don't understand where I'll be going. And you know those diagrams at big malls, the ones that assure that YOU ARE HERE? I study them, stare at them. Then I look around the actual mall and become convinced that the diagram has no concept of where I am. The diagram is mighty presumptuous, if not outright cruel and dishonest. How can it purport to know where I am? Half the time, I don't know that myself.

Luckily, at a mall I can always find some low-rise-jeans-wearing Mall Girls to lead me to the Food Court, and in cross-country I can follow the other runners. If I'd ever lead a race, I'd be in trouble, but this was never a problem in four years of high school, so there's no chance it will be a problem in college. Assuming I can even make the team. Sure, I did receive one of Lewis College's supposedly prestigious Scholar/Athlete scholarships, but I suspect it was part of some Be Kind to Kansas White Boys quota system. I'm not convinced I won't fold like a beach chair during my first college race—or first final exam.

Anyway, I give Rhonda credit (or in Rhonda-speak, "mad props") for not snort-laughing at my pathetic muffin excuse. She said she could "totally go for another blueberry" and smiled at me as I left the table.

When I returned, she waited as I carefully peeled the pale yellow corrugated paper away from my muffin, then hers, being careful not to break off the stumps. I hate when that happens. Destroys the integrity of the muffin.

"Before you dis the driving idea," Rhonda said after buttering her muffin, "there's something you should know."

I looked at her and arched my eyebrows.

"I talked to Cole yesterday. He's totally down with the plan. We can drop him off at Boulder on the way to So-Cal. Think of the time you guys will have together. You'll really be able to kick it, ya know."

I nodded toward my little brother. "What about Colby?"

"Yeah," he said, wiping chocolate milk from his upper lip with his shirtsleeve. "What about me?"

"You'll stay at Aunt Nicole's crib in Topeka, my little dude," Rhonda said cheerfully.

Colby crinkled his nose. "Crib? I'm not a stinkin' baby! I'm five. I won't sleep in a crib!"

"Her *house*," I clarified for Colby. "'Crib' is what they call houses back in da 'hood where Rhonda is from. Rural Wisconsin."

"Oh," Colby said.

I looked to Dad for a scowl again, but he was busy patting Rhonda's hand and whispering reassurance to her.

"I'm just kidding, Rhonda," I said without looking at her. "Don't get all sentimental. Hey, it was a good idea to call Cole. And if he's 'down widdit,' so am I."

Rhonda's eyes were moist, but now they were shining-hopeful moist, not somber moist. "So it's a road trip then?" she said.

I sighed. It sounded like one of my dad's sighs. Too long and too loud. Heaven help me. "Sure," I said, "why not."

I was quiet on the drive home. All I could think of was how I was going to talk Cole out of the trip. First, of course, I'd need to find something to calm myself down so I wouldn't go Rant City on him. He tends to shut down when I do that. I hoped I hadn't exhausted my supply of vodka, that I still had a bottle or two tucked away in my sock drawer. Otherwise I'd have to resort to NyQuil and Peppermint Artificial Flavoring again. And let me tell you, that's a rough way to get yourself mellow. (Of course, it does provide the side benefits of the clearest nasal passages and freshest breath in town.)

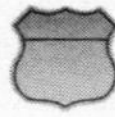

"What kind of Midwest mojo did Rhonda use on you?" I asked Cole as soon as I heard his flat "Hullo?" on the other end of the phone line. "A road trip with my dad and his cliché? I mean, this is a joke, right?"

I watched the seconds morph by on my LCD watch. After eighteen of them passed, Cole said, "You need to relax, dude. The trip will be cool. It's more time together before we have to go our separate ways. And it's a real road trip—not just some one-day, there-and-back thing. We've always talked about doing something like this, remember? To be honest, I thought you'd be all over this thing."

"But this isn't a *normal* thing, Sharp. This isn't going to St. Louis to see the Cardinals at Busch, before they tore it down, with a bunch of guys from school. There is a bona fide adult in the equation—one-point-five if you count Rhonda. So it's no longer a road trip; it's a chaperoned ordeal. You understand that there will be no hard music on the CD player? No Hatebreed. No Gwar. Dad listens to only classical and old-school rock. And Rhonda likes those guys who are like twenty years old but sing like sixty-year-old opera stars. That crap freaks me out, man. And there will be no mooning busloads of girls' volleyball teams along the way."

"It's not volleyball season yet," Cole said. This was no attempt at a snappy retort on his part. The way he said it, he was just pointing out a fact, such as, "Augusta is the capital of Maine."

I sensed I was losing the argument. "You won't be able belch in the car, or swear. My dad 'abhors profanity.' You know that." I wondered if I sounded as shrill and desperate as I felt.

"His ride, his rules. Besides, you like old-school rock, and it's kinda starting to grow on me."

"Okay, but consider this: Before we go, my dad will make us circle up and hold hands while he blesses the stupid SUV before the trip. And since we'll probably have to rent one of those small trailers to haul all our stuff, he'll probably get on a roll and bless that, too: 'Father God, please bless this little U-Haul and all of its contents.' Those words probably have never been uttered in the history of the English language. And he'll make a plea for 'traveling mercies.' Traveling mercies! That sounds like the name of a really bad folk-rock group. Are you understanding how all of this is going to go down?"

"Praying for our trip—I'm cool with that."

"Did you hear me say we'll have to hold hands?"

"Dude, I would hold hands with Rhonda any day. She's a fly honey."

"What about me? Or my dad?"

"The team held hands in football huddles all the time. It's only a problem if you're insecure in your masculinity."

I did my involuntary Dad-sigh again. "Okay, man. I guess it's on, then."

It's on, then? I wagged my head in disbelief. That was something Rhonda would say. I don't talk like that.

The pre-trip prayer meeting was all that I feared it would be, and more. I stood between Colby and Rhonda, holding the former's small sticky hand and the latter's unsettlingly soft hand. (I wanted to ask Colby why his hand was so sticky, but I have learned from experience that it's much better not to know such things.) Anyway, the Colby/Rhonda height disparity required me to hold my body at an awkward angle. I felt like a marionette waiting to have a puppet master jerk it to life. Cole served as the link between Dad and Rhonda in our little half circle of supplication.

Dad prayed that Colby would have a "fine time" at Aunt Nicole's house in Topeka. He prayed that Aunt Nic would demonstrate "long-suffering." Then it came: "And we pray, Father God, that you will grant us traveling mercies for our journey."

I looked at Cole, but his eyes were sealed tightly. They popped open, however, when my father began to sing the doxology. In our driveway. Right in front of the Jacksons, the older couple next door, who were sitting in Adirondack chairs on their porch, enjoying the morning. At least, they were enjoying it up until Dad's atonal assault. Dad had transformed the doxology into the unorthodoxology. This musical piece seems short when we sing it at Grace Fellowship Church. It barely gives the ushers time to bring the silver plates from the rear of the church to the front for the post-offering prayer. But on this August morning, it seemed longer than "Bohemian Rhapsody." I made a mental note to look for a For Sale sign in the Jacksons' yard when I came home for Christmas break.

I think Rhonda might have joined Dad for the last couple of words and the "Ah-ah-men," but she might have been just moaning in embarrassment. I couldn't know for sure because shortly after the singing began, I closed my eyes and tried to pretend the whole thing was a dream.

Once Dad had coaxed our Durango onto westbound I-70, he announced, "Since we don't have too long before Topeka, let's each share what we're most looking forward to on this trip, okay?"

"I'll start," Rhonda piped up as though she were trying to beat out fellow competitors on *Jeopardy*: "I'm looking forward to kickin' it with my homies, getting to know each of you better. You don't often get this kind of face time with your peeps, you know."

"I'm not lookin' forward to nothin'," Colby grumbled from the middle of the backseat. "I don't know why I can't go on the *whole* trip."

"Colby," Dad said evenly, adjusting the rearview mirror, "I have explained this more than adequately. This is a long, long drive. You would end up going stir-crazy. Besides, your Aunt Nicole practically begged me to let you stay at her house."

Colby crossed his arms. "I wouldn't go stir-crazy," he said. "I don't even know what that means. How can I go something if I don't know what it is? It's not fair!"

I put my arm around him and told him, "It'll be okay."

Then I started thinking about how I really didn't know what stir-crazy meant either. I mean, I grasped the basic concept, but *stir-crazy*? Stir. Crazy. What does sitting in a car have to do with stirring? And I doubted that this trip could make anyone truly crazy, even Colby. Sure, I already wanted to lower the window and throw myself under the tires, but that wasn't crazy. At the moment, it made perfect sense.

Cole's voice snatched me from my suicidal fantasy. "I know where Colby's comin' from," he said. "There are a lot of things I'm not looking forward to, including saying goodbye to all of you. But I do want to see if I can really walk on and play football in Boulder. I've always wanted to play college ball. Challenge myself, you know?"

I could see Rhonda's head bobbing in the front passenger seat. Then she corkscrewed herself around and flashed me one of her toothpaste-commercial smiles. "And . . . now . . . let's hear from the Griff-dawg!"

I yearn to unfasten my seat belt and have Dad stomp on the brakes and fling me from the vehicle to an immediate, merciful end, I thought. *Come to me, sweet death.* But I said nothing. I wondered if I would ever be able to do a brain-wipe and rid myself of the memory of being called the Griff-dawg by an adult quasi-Mom figure. I'm convinced that *this* is the kind of thing, not peer pressure or the movies or hip-hop music, that turns young men to drugs.

I crossed my arms, matching Colby's pose. Then I sat back and enjoyed the uncomfortable silence.

Eventually my dad sighed heavily and Cole jumped to the rescue. "I don't want to speak too much for Griff," he said, "but

I can think of one thing he's looking forward to: meeting The Carrot in person."

"Oooh," Rhonda cooed, "that *will* be bomb. Griff, have you imagined what she looks like? Do you think she's a hottie? Hotter than Amanda Mac, even?"

I looked at Colby, who slitted his eyes at me. But he didn't need to worry; I was not going to sully the name of Amanda Mackenzie by revealing to him my interest in The Carrot, my mysterious West Coast pen pal. He was too young to appreciate the allure of someone who finds out your address and sends you real mail, not just e-mails, for a whole summer—someone whose main goal in life seems to be "to meet Griffin Smith, up close and personal."

I couldn't tell Colby that I *needed* The Carrot to be the woman of my dreams, which at this point meant she practiced basic hygiene, was not bisexual, and would at least consider the possibility of going out with me. And I was flexible on the bisexual thing. It wasn't necessarily a deal breaker. Moreover, I had recently begun to wonder if I had been too rigid on matters of hygiene. After all, so what if a girl had B&O Railroad, hobo-power body odor? Could that really stand in the way of true love?

Here's *why* I needed The Carrot to be the woman of my dreams: so that she could chase Amanda Mackenzie out of them.

I could list seventy-something reasons why I love Amanda Mackenzie, assuming I have some clue what love is. If I applied myself, my Amanda Mac Love List could even creep into the low eighties. There is the straight dark hair, the light spray of freckles across her nose (you don't see them at a distance, but they absolutely kill me when we're talking close up), the fact that she's honest—dead honest.

But maybe it's better to show you one vignette that captures the quintessence of Amanda Mackenzie. (And I know "quintessence" is pretentious, but Mr. Ross, my lit teacher, loves those kinds of words, so I peppered my every paper with quintessences, verisimilitudes, and juxtapositions, and I never got less than an A-minus. I dropped a "vis-à-vis" on him once, and he wrote in the margin, "Griffin Smith, you're my hero!" So if we're gonna play ball here, you're just going to have to indulge me.)

Anyway, back to Amanda Mac. It's one week after graduation. I e-mail a pizza order to Lorenzo's Pizzeria and bring Colby with me to pick it up. Amanda is working the counter, and a couple of other recently departed Talbot High seniors are making the pizzas. One is a spliff-head named Kinkade; I don't know the other guy's name, but he has a propensity for wearing a T-shirt declaring FAT CHICKS NEED NOT APPLY. (Apparently, chicks with any taste would be out of luck too.) The two pizza makers are complaining loudly about the rote nature and low wages of their job, and I've witnessed Christmas cantatas in which Jesus' name was invoked less often.

I look down at Colby and notice he's wincing with each Messianic reference-as-expletive. For a moment, I get nostalgic for the time when I used to wince at that kind of thing, too.

I look at Amanda and shrug as if to say, "What are we going to do, Ms. Mackenzie? Our generation just doesn't respect the Lord."

She narrows her pale blue eyes at me, then spins gracefully around like she's doing tai chi. "Hey," she says matter-of-factly, "Jesus *loves* you guys. Why do you disrespect him by using his name like that? It hurts him when you do that. Did you know that?"

I look down at Colby; his mouth has formed a perfect O. Then I look at Kinkade and his cohort. I fear they'll do more than roll their rodent-beady eyes, which they are doing at the moment, and that they'll start screaming at Amanda. I decide I'll give them a "beeyotch" or two. But anything worse than that, and I know I'll have to vault the counter like it's a pommel horse and defend her honor. Pepperoni and mozzarella will be scattered. Blood—and pizza sauce—will be spilled. Bones might be broken. I can only hope that Kinkade and company's chemically altered reaction times will be sufficiently slow so that none of the broken bones will be mine.

But it soon becomes apparent that no Griffin Smith heroics will be needed. There is only one sheriff in this town, and her name is Amanda. "I know this is a free country," she's telling them, "but I'm a Christian, and so are Griffin and his little brother. Jesus' name *means* something to us. We wouldn't disrespect your religion; please don't disrespect ours. Now, get this man's pizza out of the oven before it burns."

She turns her attention back to me and Colby. She gives me a long, severe look, then smiles at my little brother. "So Colby, you're how old now?"

"Five," he says, and then, painstakingly and one by one, holds up every finger on his right hand — just in case Amanda needs a visual to confirm the information.

"So that means you'll start kindergarten in the fall, right? At Shining Star Elementary?"

Colby nods proudly.

"Do you know the school song? The Shining Star song?"

Colby dips his head. "Well, kinda. My friend Andrew's big sister has been trying to teach it to us."

Amanda nods sympathetically. "Well, it's been a while since I went to Shining Star, but I think I can remember it. You wanna try to sing it together?"

Colby turns to me, and I give him a reassuring pat on the top of the head.

Amanda leans over the counter. Her hair almost touches Colby's face. She starts singing in her cotton candy voice,

Shining Star, much brighter than the rest
The students help each other so we all can do our best
Shining Star, we're glowing bright and true
It's a place where I can shine, and so can you.
(Yes, so can you)
Shining Star!

Then she high-fives Colby and hands me the pizza. “Will there be anything else, men?” she asks.

Except for the part when you clamber over the counter and kiss me and we drive over to Grace Fellowship and get married right now, that’s about it.

“I guess we’re good,” I mumble to her, nodding.

Colby smiles and says, “Thanks for the pizza,’Manda. And for helping me with the song. You rock my socks!”

“You rock my socks too, Colby. Enjoy your pizza and come back and see me again soon, okay?”

In the parking lot, after I buckle Colby into the backseat, he looks at me and wags his head. “Dude,” he says, “if you don’t marry ‘Manda someday, you’re a idiot.”

So that’s Amanda Mackenzie. Charmer of little boys. Thwarter of blasphemers. The closest thing to a saint I’ll ever see. And her faith is so natural to her. It seems I have to remember to put mine on all the time — usually for special occasions. And every time, it seems progressively tighter and itchier and more out of style. I can’t help worrying that people will point and giggle and say, “You’re still trying to wear *that*? Seriously, man! Do you know what year it is?”

Not Amanda. When she called out Kinkade and his friend, she never raised her voice. She never affected a holy tone. She was just so measured and sincere that she rendered them speechless. Sure, it probably helped that they have about nine working brain cells between the two of them, but you see my point.

Amanda is the same person at school as she is at Grace Fellowship Church. And I’m sure she’d be that same person on a date. Unfortunately, I never managed to ask her out, even though that was No. 1 on the list of Five Goals for High School, which

I completed on Day 1 of my freshman year at the bequest of Mr. Saunders, one of the Seminar teachers. He told us, "Goals are dreams with deadlines. Therefore, you must dignify your dreams by holding yourself accountable for their fulfillment."

I was tempted to put To Be Able to Dream, Free from the Pressure of Oppressive Deadlines as my one and only goal, then volunteer to share my "list" with the rest of the class. But I ultimately decided not to reveal what a jerk I was so early in my high school career, so I just did the assignment as instructed. The rest of my list, just in case you were wondering, went like this:

2. Be all-state in track
3. Graduate with a 4.0 GPA
4. Bench-press two hundred pounds
5. Earn a scholarship—any scholarship

Graduation is well behind me now. Any guesses on how many of these Dreams with Deadlines I achieved?

How about one? *Uno. Un*. The aforementioned Lewis College Scholar/Athlete partial scholarship. I think it's given to incoming freshmen who aren't smart enough to get a real academic scholarship and not talented enough athletically to earn a ride on the sports gravy train.

I'm not sure if something's wrong with my dreams, or if I'm just lousy with deadlines.

Amanda shared her list, unprompted, at youth group early in the frosh school year. It went something like this:

1. To represent Jesus in all that I do
2. To be a true friend
3. To be a loving person

4. To make my parents proud
5. To always, always be real

Clearly, Amanda kicked my butt in the setting of her goals and also in the all-important accomplishment portion of the competition.

She takes a lot of garbage for being a lamb among a herd of swine. Some of the jerks at school (Jerk exhibit A; see Tucker, Carlton, more on him later) would fold their hands like nuns when they passed her in the hall. And sometimes after she would make an emphatic point in a class discussion, those same knuckleheads would start humming the Hallelujah Chorus or mumbling, "Amen."

I asked her once if the harassment bothered her. She told me, "It does hurt sometimes, but I'm not going to change who I am, even if the whole school starts making fun of me. That would be very, very lonely, but I have to be real. You understand that, don't you Griffin?"

I wanted so bad to say yes, but that would have been lying, and that would be a too-ironic way of answering a question about authenticity.

So instead I said, "Mmm." Let's pause for just a moment to honor "mmm," the greatest noncommittal vocalization in the history of spoken language. I can imagine Trog, the Neanderthal, returning to his cave, only to be confronted by his cave wife, Blanche. Through a series of tongue clicks and grunts, she asks him, "Were you really out hunting saber-toothed tigers all day, or were you over at Olga's place, dragging her around by the hair and looking at erotic cave paintings? What about it, big boy? Have you found another sharply sloped forehead against which to rub your matted beard, or do you still love me?"

Trog, of course, would give his wife a severe look and say simply, "Mmm." Conversation over.

I wish I could have outdone my brain-the-size-of-a-walnut predecessor. I wish I could have given Amanda more than a monosyllabic response. I wish I could have told her this:

"No, Amanda, I don't understand your compulsion to be real. Most of the time, all I want to do is keep my profile low, my GPA high, and my mile-repeat workouts under six minutes. Sometimes I find myself trying to be real, but isn't *attempting* to be real the same thing as *pretending* to be real? Thus, Ms. Mackenzie, I feel like a fraud pretty much everywhere. At parties, I nurse my one beer, ever wary of anyone who looks like he or she might take a swing at me or vomit on my shoes. 'I'm a designated driver tonight,' I explain to anyone who offers to refill my red plastic cup or hand me a bottle of Jack or a flask of whatever.

"'Huh,' I'll hear sometimes. 'Weren't you a designated driver *last* party?'

"Then I'll chuckle and say, 'Nope, that wasn't me. Besides, what do you know? You were too wasted to remember!'

"And that will always earn me a laugh and a clumsy but hearty pat on the back. It's the emptiest kind of congratulations you can get—except, perhaps, all of those envelopes Dad gets in the mail, informing him, YOU MAY ALREADY BE A WINNER!

"I feel like a fraud at Sunday school and youth group, too, among the mostly smiling teens who probably don't have small airline-portion bottles of vodka stashed in strategic places in their bedroom. (And lest you think this bit of information contradicts the whole one-beer-per-party rationing, let's just say that my public and private drinking rituals are two entirely different critters. More on that later.)

"Also, to the best of my knowledge, my church peers' families are intact, or at least not stained by scandal. You know that 'Kid Whose Mom Has a Torrid Affair with a Crappy Novelist and Abandons Her Family and Then Whose Dad Becomes a Midlife Crisis Man by Falling For an Uncomfortably Attractive Woman Eighteen Years His Junior' Club? I'm sure I'm the only member. I'm president, secretary, treasurer, sergeant at arms—the whole nine.

"I'm sure, as well, that none of my church peers cusses like a stevedore every time someone passes them in a cross-country race.

"If I could go back to Old Testament times, Amanda, I am relatively certain I could find lepers more comfortable in their own skin than I am.

"Maybe that's why I let four years of high school slide by without asking you for a date, opting instead for a dismal series of ill-fated, morally compromising, and ego-stroking relationships, few of which had better shelf life than warm buttermilk. Now, I know that you might counter that you're an accepting person and you'd love me as I am, so I wouldn't feel all that pressure to be something I'm not. But there's a bigger reason we couldn't be a couple, even though I have wanted that so bad it makes my bones ache.

"To be blunt about it, Ms. Mackenzie, I am a mess. For example, I drink. A lot. Not at parties so much, but like my role model, Mr. Thorogood, I drink alone. And no beer. Just hard liquor. Why? Well, I know you think I am smart, given my almost-perfect GPA. My parents thought that too. But it's not true—and that is not false modesty. I know how to get good grades, but that's not the same thing as being smart, like Miss 4.0 Nina Majors is. Most people our age download their favorite songs to their iPods. Know what I listen to most of the time on my car speakers and earbuds? Myself. Reading my school notes and textbooks out loud.

"And that's in addition to the Red Bull–fueled late-night study sessions, the checking of teachers' websites like they contained the keys to the meaning of life—or naked pictures of Kate Bosworth. It got to where I couldn't even read *Sports Illustrated* without the haunting feeling that I was going to be tested on it. Why the obsession, you ask? Well, it's not really about the quest for knowledge for its own sake, or even for an academic scholarship or to see my name on the honor roll all the time. Here's the real juice: It was during my freshman year that my parents started getting loud and proud with their fighting. The screaming. The threats. Mom tossing glass plates like Frisbees, and Dad bobbing and weaving and Riverdancing to keep from getting hit.

"They fought about everything, eventually. They even got into a near-shoving match over what street that used-furniture store was on. The only thing they could *agree* on was that their son Griffin was smart, an ace student. They could be smacking the D-word around like a volleyball—and getting painfully specific about each other's physical shortcomings—and I could enter the room with a straight-A report card, and it would be like delivering the paperwork for a temporary truce. All the harsh stuff melted away. It was like a magic trick: 'Ah, Griffin, we're so proud of you. Our smart boy. Let's go to Lorenzo's and have some pizza to celebrate! You want to drive, Mr. A-Student?'

"So I studied and wrote papers and attacked essay tests like our family depended on it. Because that was the truth. School wasn't an Opportunity for Learning and Discovery for me; it was a J-O-B. And I had to be the best at this job, or the most important people in my life would, in essence, get fired. So just a wee bit of pressure there. And after a long day of feigning smarts, staying informed, taking notes like a court reporter on crack, and generally being "on" all the time, there is no refuge like being able to be drunk and slow and stupid in the privacy of your bedroom. Nothing like trying to quote T. S. Eliot and hearing yourself sounding like that old fat drunk guy on the Andy Griffith reruns.

"You should know, too, that eventually I was able to consume enough vodka to knock out a Cossack. And for those rare evenings when even the good people at Stoli couldn't make the pressure go away, I discovered painkillers. Yes, Stoli and Vicodin, a match made in addictive-substance heaven.

"The alcohol and pills, incidentally, are not my biggest problem, not my worst vice. That should give you some perspective on the train wreck that is my life. And while train wrecks can be intriguing to look at as one passes by them, they are not exactly where you want to spend date nights."

I don't know how Amanda would have responded to that speech. But I do know this: My friend since fourth grade would have listened—to the whole sorry thing—and she would have cared. Maybe she would have talked me into changing my mind about college, perhaps staying closer to home, Kansas State or KU, where my dad and people from the church had a better chance of keeping an eye on me. I know she would have discouraged me from going off to someplace where I knew no one. Maybe she would have even talked me into going to the little Christian college in Oregon with her. Maybe out of the fishbowl, away from the pressure, we could have finally become a couple.

Instead, I'm riding to California, harboring the hope that some apparition named after a vegetable is going to take away the sting of years and years' worth of regret. Good luck on that one, Griffin Smith!

I don't even like carrots. Colby is right. I am a idiot.

Halfway to Topeka, I looked at Colby and saw his nose twitching. He turned to Cole. "Aw, man," he whined, "is that you, dude? Did you SBD?"

I knew that would bring Rhonda's head poking around the seat. "SBD? What's the what with that, my little man?"

Colby rolled his eyes. "Silent but deadly, Rhonda. And I know it wasn't Griff. His don't smell like that."

I had to smile, wondering if this was the kind of "for-real sharing" that Rhonda craved.

Rhonda was grinning at Cole. "Well?" she said, raising her skinny eyebrows.

I would be squirming in my seat under this kind of scrutiny, but Cole nodded dismissively, tapped the side window, and pointed at the trailer load of livestock pulling up next to us. "Cattle," he observed.

"Are you sure?" Colby asked. "'Cause it's okay if it's you, but we need to roll down a window or something."

"It's not me," Cole said, "so lowering the window will only make things worse."

He didn't sound defensive at all. That's one of the cool things about him. He doesn't take things personally—even being accused of producing a livestock-quality stench.

Once we were out of visual and olfactory range of the bovines, Colby amused himself by shooting imaginary terrorists with a crooked chicken tender. This is something I love about kids Colby's age: Any object can be anything. A banana is a telephone (and often a gun as well). A speckled rock is a bald-eagle egg. A couch cushion is a hammerhead shark. A boot can be a submarine, but, in Colby's case, it's most often a gun, like its cousins the chicken tender and the banana.

"Die! Die! Die-die-die-die!" Colby shouted as we neared the edge of Topeka.

"Colby," Dad said, his voice sounding wounded, "I wish you wouldn't talk like that. And I wish you wouldn't pretend to be shooting a gun."

"It's okay, Dad," I noted. "He is shooting terrorists, after all."

"I so *don't* think that's okay, Griff," Rhonda interjected. "I don't want Colby to grow up thinking violence and bloodshed are ways to solve problems, even problems like terrorism. Whatever happened to diplomacy, huh?"

Dad's head began nodding so emphatically that he looked like a bobble-head doll. I slid down in my seat and shrugged helplessly at Colby. "Yeah, Colb," I whispered, "lay down thy chicken tender and learn the Way of Diplomacy. And once you've learned it, you can call the Secretary of State and the President. Perhaps they would be interested in learning it as well."

My brother eyed me suspiciously. "You're so weird, big bro."

Once inside the Topeka city limits, Dad took only three or four wrong turns on the way to Aunt Nicole's house, thus preserving his average.

"I don't know why I invariably fail to simply *write down* the directions to my own sister's home," he scolded himself. "I mean, if I'm not going to apply the discipline to memorize the route, I must provide myself something for reference!"

"It's okay, B.T.," Rhonda cooed at him.

B.T.? I slid back up in my seat. *What's with the initials, Rhonda?*

My dad's first and middle names are Bryant and Thomas. It never occurred to any of us to call him by initials. Dad is not an initials kind of guy. Initials-names are for jocks, or fat ex-jocks, or rodeo clowns, or hip-hop artists. They are not for guys who wear white gym shorts when they exercise, and especially those who exercise by walking briskly around the neighborhood, swinging their pool-cue arms like metronomes and humming Fanny Crosby hymns and thus humiliating their children.

Some important background information: I was in seventh grade when I started seeing a school counselor regularly. (When you start crying every time you get anything less than a perfect grade on a test, the administration takes notice.) The counselor, Ms. Young-Thornton, tried to help me by playing a game called Worst-Case Scenario. She would talk me through situations, with the objective of showing me that even if everything went wrong, things really wouldn't be all that bad.

She gave up on this method after about two weeks. She severely underestimated just how bad my imaginary worst-case consequences could be. I think it was the time when she asked me what would be so bad about getting a B in Computer Applications that nudged her over the edge. I told her, "If I get a B in Computer Apps and ruin my middle school 4.0, I could lose so much self-esteem that I'll let a seemingly nurturing Internet predator lure me into a real-life meeting. He will then kidnap me, and he and his schizophrenic half brother, Ernie, will sexually abuse me for two years. Then, when they are tired of me, they will cut me into twenty-eight pieces and feed me to their rottweiler."

A week later, Ms. Young-Thornton told my parents she had done "all that a school counselor could be expected to do" for me. And I think she gave them the name of one of those high-priced industrial-strength psychotherapists, but I'm sure that was too expensive for a couple journeying down the pricey road to divorce.

I, however, have continued to play Worst-Case Scenario, for my own private amusement and torment. So, Ms. Young-Thornton, don't despair. Don't think I didn't learn anything from you.

Here's how I saw the whole B.T. thing playing out in Worst-Case Scenario Land:

1. Rhonda gives Dad a nickname that fits him about as well as one of Colby's hoodies.
2. Dad starts to think, Hey, I have a cool nickname; perhaps I am a cool dude after all.
3. Dad colors his hair. (He always describes it as "salt and pepper," but it's mostly salt.)
4. Dad spikes and gels his newly colored hair.
5. Heaven help us, Dad sprouts a soul patch and gets an earring.
6. Dad starts going to one of those fake 'n' bake tanning places, and the image of him lying there, naked and glowing in one of those freaky tanning pods, will burn itself into the accursed retinas of his elder son.
7. The elder son moves to India and joins a cult. It doesn't matter which one, as long as said son is allowed to renounce all remnants of his previous existence.

Ultimately, B.T. trial-and-errored his way to his sister's home. Aunt Nicole sling-shotted out of her front door and started hugging people like she was in a timed hugging competition.

Five minutes later, she was hugging everyone again. Goodbye hugs this time. I turned away when the teary-eyed Rhonda bent down to say goodbye to Colby. I knew it would either enrage me or make me impossibly sad.

I turned back around and watched from a safe distance as B.T. plucked Colby from the ground and my brother wrapped his arms and legs around his thin dad. I wondered if I had ever embraced Dad like that. It didn't seem possible.

Eventually, Dad lowered Colby to the ground, and he darted to me. I tried to smile at my little brother, but I wasn't sure if the correct facial muscles were working for me. Perhaps this is how Botoxed people feel.

He looked up at me, and his blue-green eyes showed an earnestness I hadn't seen before. "I'm real-gonna miss you," he said quietly. It's going to kill me when he outgrows saying this.

I nodded. "I'm real-gonna miss you, too."

I stooped down and grabbed him. He hugged me fiercely around my neck. You know the way little kids do. I'm not one of those people who likes to freeze moments in time. Mostly, life for me is something just to get through. I find myself constantly urging life, "Next, next, next! Let's hurry up and get to the good part!" (assuming there is one). But I could have stood there with Colby for a couple of days and not cared about anything else, except my neck started to cramp up after a minute or so.

When I felt my little brother's grip loosen, I lowered him until his feet lighted on Aunt Nicole's sidewalk.

He looked up at me. "I real-love you, Griffin. Don't forget that, okay?"

He looked and sounded as serious as a judge. And, thanks to cheery realities like Custody Hearings, I know how a judge looks and sounds. Believe me, you won't see one grinning and giggling when posing questions like, "Young man, tell me about the time you spend with your mother. What do you enjoy about that? What do you dislike?"

Colby was crying soundlessly by the time he said goodbye to Cole, who was squatted down like a baseball catcher in front of him.

"What's the deal with our names, little dude?" Cole asked softly.

"Our names are the same," Colby said, his voice trembling a little. "Almost."

"I'm driving," I announced, sliding my sunglasses down over my eyes, just in time. I could feel the big gloppy tears forming—the kind you can't merely blink away or attribute to ragweed. And my voice sounded ragged, like Springsteen's after one of his three-hour concerts.

I ejected Dad's *Classical Masters* CD and slid in *Blood on the Tracks*. That's the rule I had made for this trip: Driver selects the music. Although good old B.T. would never quibble over my choice of music.

Dad says that this is the first time ever when a lot of parents and their teen kids love the same music. He has no business sense, or sense of direction, as far as I can tell, but on this topic he's right. If you were to wander the halls of Talbot High, you'd see dozens of Led Zeppelin and The Who and Beatles T-shirts. And that's the kind of music you hear flying out of car windows in the parking lot too—that is, before it gets so cold that you have to roll up your windows and crank the heat to keep from becoming a life-size frozen entrée. (We don't get a whole lot of snow in suburban Kansas City, but we get ice storms. And we get these razor winds, so if you stay outside too long on the wrong kind of day, your bone marrow will turn to sorbet.)

Rhonda says I'm an Old Soul, because, as she points out, "All the artists you listen to are, like, old enough to be your parents!" And some of the guys at school call me Throwback. I don't care. I'm in the camp—and Cole has signed up too—that's proud to proclaim, "We prefer music that was created before music started stinking like a rotting hippo carcass."

If you disagree, please try this experiment. Tune in to your local "hit radio" station. Then, being as objective as possible, honestly consider if any of the eight or nine songs that constitute the playlist is not so pathetic and formulaic that you can almost hear your soul withering and your brain cells committing suicide as you listen. The worst song on *Blood on the Tracks* is better than anything on hit radio. Heck, the worst song on *Knocked Out Freakin' Loaded* is better.

Carlton Tucker, the biggest woman-getter at school (besides Cole), disagrees with me. You can always count on him to tout the latest release from the hip-hop thug du jour.

"Your problem," he told me after track practice one day, "is that you're just not street." (Carlton, by the way, is a mediocre high hurdler. Meanwhile, and I'm trying not to say this boastfully, I am a slightly-better-than-mediocre distance man.)

"Street?" I countered. "Tuck, you live on Candy Tuft Terrace in the richest subdivision in the whole school district. You drive a Lexus, which your parents bought for you."

"Yeah, but my Lexus is *pimped out*. You just haven't seen the interior. And I got a heata in the glove box."

"That's great, because I've seen some really gnarly-looking raccoons prowling these mean suburban streets. A guy can't be too careful. Best to arm yourself against the fearsome raccoons. Waste them before they waste you."

At that point, I thought Carlton might hit me, which would have been okay because it would have given me an excuse to hit *him*. It would be like the Lord Jehovah handing me a jackass's jawbone and nodding approvingly as I proceeded to use it, ironically, to break a jackass's jawbone.

But Cole appeared at my side, tossing his twelve-pound shot put in one hand, like an egg. "Griff," he said, "I need to get in some extra throws. You wanna be my shot fetcher?"

"It's what I live for."

Then Cole dropped the shot near Carlton's left foot. "Whoops," he said.

Carlton appeared ready to speak, but then he wisely edited himself and jogged toward the Wyatt brothers, who were lounging on the high-jump pit. The Wyatts constitute two-thirds of the African-Americans on our track team.

"There's goes Carlton, going to annoy Justin and Phil," Cole observed. "They tell me they don't want to hurt his feelings, but they might have to say something to him one of these days."

"But he wants so bad to be black," I said.

Cole nodded his head. "But he's very white."

"I know mimes less white than he is," I agreed.

Carlton Tucker would hate the music on The Smith Family and Friends Road Trip/Debacle. Even Rhonda, though she talks like she's a backup dancer for 50 Cent, doesn't listen to anything that would sound inappropriate oozing from the speakers of your local Target.

I stole a glance at her, sitting in the backseat. Her eyelids were at half-mast. How anyone could fall asleep during "Tangled Up in Blue" is beyond me, but most things about Rhonda are beyond me.

She's eighteen years younger than my dad. I know that's not a Rod Stewart– or Billy Joel–level age discrepancy, but rural Kansas isn't Hollywood, either. Not even close. A lot of people in my hometown don't believe in evolution, and they're a little skeptical about gravity and photosynthesis, too.

So you can probably imagine how the Smith family scandal — replete with deception, bitter divorce, adultery, destruction of property, a young hottie waitress, and some really crappy literature — provided endless hours of debate and hand-wringing and Old Testament-style judging from our entire community.

To be fair, I should note that Rhonda didn't start the fire of controversy and shame that ravaged what little sense of home I had. She just came along and nurtured some dying embers, then poured gasoline on those few parts that the original fire had somehow missed. She helped make sure nothing was left but scorched earth.

But the guy who deserves most of the credit is the hack writer Maxwell the Mediocre, who, before playing the role of an improvised explosive device on our family, lived on the Missouri side of the Kansas City metro area, cranking out a crappy "erotic mystery novel" every few months. Mom collected them all, like literary Beanie Babies or something, keeping each chubby paperback volume lined sequentially on our living room bookshelf. It nearly made me cry that her boxed Perelandra trilogy touched the front end of the Maxwell Row of Shame, and her Dorothy Parker anthology had to be up close and personal with the latest Maxwellian volume. I couldn't even believe Mom could read material of such divergent quality. It's like chasing down your Big Mac with a bottle of Dom.

But Mom loved the books of Maxwell to the max. She'd sit for hours with her nose tucked into *Murder by Moonlight* or *Curse of the Naked Raven*. (Aren't *all* ravens naked?) Sometimes I'd catch her studying Maxwell's photo on a back cover, his shaved head resting on the heel of his right hand. He looked about ten years older than Dad—and that was after all the airbrushing. I met him in person the summer before my freshman year at Talbot when my Mom dragged me to a book signing he did at our town's one and only bookstore. The real Maxwell looked like the guy in the picture's much-older brother—eyes redder, skin saggier, and a neck wattle like a prize rooster. Mom told me once that some entertainment magazine named him one of the 50 Sexiest Men Over 50. "Isn't that like being named one of the 50 Tallest Pygmies?" I asked her. She called me shallow and told me to get out of her face.

I responded by sprinting upstairs, grabbing my copy of *The Brothers Karamazov*, and bringing it down to the living room to read. I never read in the living room, but I knew that I couldn't enjoy the feeling of superiority I craved if I were reading Dostoevsky alone in my bedroom. As I read, I realized that I'd never seen a picture of Dostoevsky, but I would bet my college savings that he was a far-handsomer man than Maxwell the Mediocre.

"Won't it be cool to meet a real author?" Mom had asked me on the way to the signing. It was all I could do to hold back my response: "Real author? I thought this was a signing for Maxwell. Did he cancel, and the bookstore got John Irving to replace him?" Instead, I just offered the meagerest nod in the history of nodding.

"I hope we don't have to stand in line too long," she said. "But with this being front-page news in our paper . . ."

I closed my eyes briefly. Yes, Maxwell's appearance at The Book Nook, which is about the size of Carlton Tucker's three-car garage, had made the front page of *The Talbot Times*, our skinny, two-section weekly paper. Motto: "We're the only paper in town, so we can be lousy and you'll still read us. Come on, admit it: You're curious to discover if anyone you know died this week!" But the story was below the fold, dwarfed in importance by two above-the-fold features: (1) We were getting a new donut shop, and (2) REO Speedwagon had been booked for our annual Fall Festival.

Once at the signing, I promised Mom I'd clean all three of the Smith family toilets if she wouldn't make me stand in line with her. Then I found a paperback version of *The Catcher in the Rye* and read while I watched Maxwell sit behind a square table, armed with a Sharpie and a made-for-TV smile.

When Mom made it to the front of the line, Maxwell shook her hand and held it for a while—too long of a while, I realized later. They shared a joke about something. Probably about how you don't need talent, or even a soul, to be a successful novelist.

"Wow, that was something else," Mom said on the drive home. "To meet someone with that kind of literary track record . . . very cool."

This statement was, by my estimation, lie number 138 in a series of 500 Mom's Maxwellian Misappropriations of Truth. I would learn later that she had "met" Maxwell on many occasions before the local signing. She met him in St. Louis (I'll never be able to watch *that* play) when she was supposedly going to "visit a high school friend who recently moved there."

She met him at his condo in downtown KC. She met him down in Wichita at a writers' conference, which she attended, she told Dad and me, to explore the possibilities of becoming a freelance book reviewer.

To the best of my knowledge, my mother and Maxwell the Mediocre had been meeting since Colby was about a year old and I was barely fourteen. She didn't take off with him until almost a year after that.

After Mom had been gone a while, I heard Dad tell someone on the phone, "This whole thing kind of took us by surprise, like a tornado." He was wrong. We get tornadoes in our part of Kansas. They hit. They do their damage, tossing cars and tree limbs and mobile-home patios around like a kid having a temper tantrum. Then they move on and die out.

But that's not what happened to our family. It was subtle and slow and sneaky—like when a chemical plant starts dumping poisonous waste in the water and you get sick, little by little. It's time consuming but effective. See, after a tornado, you can clean up, rebuild your life. The poison, on the other hand, can stay in your system forever. And even if you don't die, you'll never be the same.

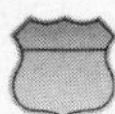

I started scanning the side of the highway for a sign revealing how many miles to Salina, Russell, or Hays. Recalling the book signing and everything else made me want to put as many miles between us and Talbot as possible. Soon a green sign noted that Salina was only ten minutes away. I glanced at the LED clock above the CD player. It was almost noon, more than three hours since the prayer half circle had broken. We had wasted too much time in Topeka. Also, Dad was a slave to speed limits, and he had cleared his throat disapprovingly every time I hit a speedometer number higher than Carlton Tucker's IQ.

I scanned the scene inside the Durango. Everyone else was asleep. I was hungry, but it was cool to have the vehicle quiet except for a best-of U2 CD over the speakers. I nudged the speedometer past eighty.

I passed by Salina as the rapid-fire drumming of "Sunday Bloody Sunday" began. I noted Russell as a possible next stop.

Via the rearview mirror, I let my eyes rest a moment on my dad, his arm draped around Rhonda. It freaked me out the first few times I saw him showing a public display of affection to someone other than Mom, but I was used to it now. It wasn't comfortable or natural to witness, but I could live with it. It was like the steamed broccoli Mom used to make me eat. Even after years passed, it didn't taste any better—even when she tried to trick me by covering it with melted Velveeta—but I at least got to the point where it didn't make me gag and nearly barf at the dinner table.

Rhonda was snoring softly now, and I was tempted to leg-press the brake pedal and see if a slight case of whiplash might shut her up. But that would just make her start talking, and her talking was exceedingly more nerve-twanging than her snoring. Rhonda Eccles: Was there anything about her that *wasn't* annoying? And to think that when she was just a harmless waitress at Mafia Marco's Italian Eatery, I actually thought she was cool. It's frightening to me how easily guys in my age group confuse being cool and being hot.

Some of my friends—not Cole, of course—call Rhonda "Rebound Chick," but that's not accurate. After my mom dashed off to Wyoming with MTM, just as my sophomore year was beginning, my dad didn't go out looking for a woman to ease his pain or to show Mom that he was still a good catch too. No, Dad poured himself into several unsuccessful business ventures, which allowed us to move from our four-bedroom, upper-middle-class house in Johnson County, Kansas, to a 938-square-foot apartment that was still in Johnson County, but just barely.

My favorite business bust was Pizza On the Move. The idea was that people would call POTM, and the friendly pizza experts would start baking their pie. Then, when the pizza was half-baked, it would be loaded into the attractive POTM truck, tastefully decorated with pepperoni polka dots and equipped with an oven that would complete the baking of the pizza en route. *The Freshest and Hottest Pizza. Ever.* That was the slogan Dad came up with as the enterprise's crowning touch.

Okay, *stop* stroking your chin thoughtfully and/or nodding. This was *not* a good idea. Think about it: Four-hundred-twenty-five-degree ovens are not meant to be hurtling down suburban roads at forty-five miles per hour. Do the math. Do the physics. What my dad invested his entire post-divorce financial remnant in was, essentially, a small fleet of mobile infernos. Pizzas became ablaze. Trucks filled with smoke, causing teary-eyed drivers to collide with trees and, in one case, a brick mailbox. There were lawsuits and rumors of lawsuits.

"Pizza On the Move turns out half-baked" sneered *The Talbot Times* headline after the business folded. "I can understand the paper covering the story," Dad had said. "It is newsworthy on its face. But why the sarcasm? Why the cruelty? Don't they understand that there were *people* involved here? Dreams? Hopes?"

Windshield repair came next. Dad printed brochures illustrating the various types of windshield damage a vehicle could sustain on the mean streets of eastern Kansas/western Missouri. There was the star, the dimple, the chip, and, my favorite, the hickey.

Three months after the first brochures were published and distributed, Dad trudged home one afternoon and sunk into the living room couch. "Either we're not doing a good job of advertising," he said, "or they're making automobile windshields much better than they used to."

Somewhere between seeking fortune via Internet-based Texas Hold'em and—have mercy—motivational speaking, Dad met Rhonda Eccles.

It was a year and a half after the divorce became final before Dad brought Rhonda over to swim in the Cheyenne Vista Apartment Homes pool and eat pizza (pizza that we bought *frozen* at the grocery store, then microwaved at *home*, the way God intended).

"Hey, dude!" Rhonda had said to me upon our first meeting, extending her fist. "Give me some dap!"

"Dap?" I said.

"C'mon, dawg," she said. "Don't leave me hangin'."

So I stuck out my fist and softly bumped it against hers. I've eaten half a pepperoni pizza right before bedtime, chased it down with a liter of Code Red and a cute little bottle of Stoli, and not had *dreams* that surreal. However, I reasoned that giving Rhonda dap was better than hugging her, as she was wearing a sparse white bikini at the time. I was sixteen. Hugging my dad's then-twenty-six-year-old bikini-clad girlfriend would have resulted in years of expensive therapy. And Dad and I couldn't even afford name-brand peanut butter. Still can't.

"Russell, Kansas, at last!" I announced, four hours into the trip. "This is the home of Bob Dole, so everybody wake up and show some respect."

"Griffin," Dad yawned from the backseat, "must you be so sarcastic and cynical about everything?"

"I wasn't being sarcastic. I meant what I said. After all, how many people have served their country in war, been U.S. vice president, *and* pimped Viagra to boot?"

"The service in the armed forces alone earns the man all the respect in the world, as far as I'm concerned."

"Your dad's got a point," Cole said, stirring in the passenger seat next to me.

Before Rhonda could pile on, I decided to take the conversation down a side road: "Hey, guys, you know how towns put up signs for residents who have accomplished something great in life? Like Mr. Dole?"

"Yes," my dad said warily.

"Well, what about the towns that spawn criminals? I mean, if we ever drove by wherever Mark David Chapman was born, would we see a sign saying CHAPMANVILLE, HOME OF MARK DAVID CHAPMAN, MURDERER OF JOHN LENNON. (SORRY 'BOUT THAT ONE, EVERYBODY)? And, hey, wasn't John Hinckley born somewhere in Colorado? We'll be passing through there before too long; maybe the Convention and Visitors Bureau can help us find his birthplace. Rhonda, would you take a picture of me posed by that sign? HOME OF JOHN HINCKLEY, OBSESSIVE STAR-STALKER AND WOULD-BE PRESIDENTIAL ASSASSIN. BETTER LUCK NEXT TIME, JOHNNY. Maybe that pic could be the family Christmas card, once you and my pops git yourselves all hitched and whatnot."

"Are you going to speak to your son?" Rhonda grumbled. But she didn't sound genuinely angry—only peeved. But that was okay. We still had lots of driving ahead of us. She'd be way past peeved before we hit the Utah border. To that end, I was committed.

We ate a late lunch at a Russell sandwich shop, and the cashier reminded me of Amanda Mac. Almost as thin, almost as level in the upper torso region.

Please don't get me wrong here: Amanda's build is just fine with me. It definitely keeps her off the radar of pervs like Carlton Tucker. He much prefers the build of the other Amanda at Talbot, Amanda Carlisle. Everything Mother Nature held back from Amanda Mac, she must have bestowed upon Ms. Carlisle.

"I would kill for Amanda Carlisle's body," class brainiac Nina Majors told me once before a National Honor Society meeting.

"Many people probably will," I responded.

Amanda Mac, however, doesn't pine for anything the other Amanda is packing. In fact, every now and then she came to school sporting a T-shirt that said "Yes, They're Real!" The first time she wore it, I could have kissed her—it was that freakin' cool.

I spent most of our lunch stop picking the outer crust off my Featuring Fresh Bread sandwich. I thought about how much Amanda Mac loved sandwiches. Once a month, our youth group met at the Big Bear, and Amanda always ordered the same thing: veggie sub with brown mustard instead of mayo. "Mayonnaise," she explained to me once, "is basically eggs and partially hydrogenated oils, served cold. Think about that." I did, and started holding the mayo on everything.

The more I thought about Amanda, the less I felt like eating my Russell, Kansas, FFB sandwich. But I didn't want to sit there, with everyone watching me *not eat*. So I asked my dad for a twenty and volunteered to pay the bill while everyone else finished up.

After paying the Russell version of Amanda, I felt the small portion of fresh turkey sub threatening to resurface. I told Dad to pull over to the gas station next to the sub shop and I'd catch up with him there.

Then I hurried to the sub shop restroom to throw up and/or read a letter from The Carrot. Anything to get Amanda Mac off my mind.

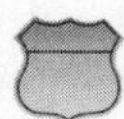

Back home, I kept The Carrot's letters stacked like dominoes in my top drawer, next to my athletic socks and vodka. The first one had arrived in June, about two weeks after I graduated. The return address read simply, "The Carrot, Somewhere, CA." The stationery inside was thick and artsy and cream-colored, littered with tiny brown specks, as if the writer was eating walnuts and sneezed all over the paper.

The Carrot favored printing over cursive. This is a good thing.

Rhonda always leaves me cursive notes, and I can't decipher half of them. One time she ended a note with a P.S. that looked like, "Don't forget the cabbage." I was nonplussed. I hadn't been aware that I was supposed to remember cabbage in the first place. Turns out that Rhonda had actually scrawled, "Down at Florence's for cribbage." Go figure. Also, *I* wouldn't admit in writing that I played cribbage, but that's just one more difference between Rhonda and me. She says that cribbage with some of the apartment complex's older women is part of her "ministry." If cribbage can be ministry, maybe it's time to change religions.

Anyway, The Carrot's penwomanship was big and loose and feminine. By that, I don't mean that she dotted her i's with hearts or interlaced her o's so that they looked like part of a geometry problem on the ACT, which I took three times. (And yes, I am an obsessive geek; thanks for wondering.) Anyway, The Carrot's writing was smooth and round, even her capital e's. Also, her thoughts were rendered in lavender pen. Best of all, I could read what she wrote.

"Dearest Griffin," the first letter had begun, "Hi! Congratulations on choosing Lewis College and for being part of the cross-country team! As a sophomore here, I commend you on a great choice—athletically and academically. I look forward to meeting you and cheering you on this season. Be watching your mailbox for more letters from me as the new school year draws closer. Have a great summer! Sincerely, Your Secret Girl Pal (The Carrot)."

A new letter arrived every week or so. The Carrot was unwaveringly eager to "meet face-to-face," and she always encouraged me to "keep puttin' in the miles." After I had collected a handful of letters, I decided to lay them side by side on my bed. I shook my head and said to Cole, "Look, the salutations change. We've gone from 'Dearest Griffin' to 'Hey, Dude!' But the body is almost the same thing every time. And she never writes more than a page. Still, they are letters from a girl, so I guess that's something."

"Yeah," Cole said.

"And check this out," I said, tapping my forefinger on the bottom of the most recent letter. "Her complimentary close is different here. She's transitioned from 'Sincerely' to 'Hugs.' That's significant, don't you think? And check this out: This time she doesn't even sign her name; there's just this little drawing of a carrot. It's like we're already graduating to *beyond* first-name basis. We're at icon level now. We've transcended names."

Cole nodded slowly. Ten seconds passed. "If she goes by 'The Carrot,' I wonder why she writes in purple ink instead of orange," he said.

"I don't even know if they make orange ink." I sounded irritated. I hoped Cole didn't notice. "Anyway, do you think I should pack these and take 'em with me to school?"

Cole answered immediately, very un-Cole-like. "I wouldn't. Best to travel light. Maybe just the most recent one."

I had thought a few times about showing the letters to Rhonda, to get her opinion about The Carrot. After all, she and Ms. Carrot were both in the same general age group, although The Carrot was no doubt more mature and well-spoken. But I knew that Rhonda would take that as a sign—a sign that I was accepting her place in my life. And the only sign I wanted to show her was one that warned Keep Out: Trespassers Will Be Prosecuted to the Fullest Extent of the Law.

The Carrot's last letter had assured me she was "literally counting the days" until we met face-to-face and that she was "so-so-so" eager to see me that she "could almost taste it." I don't know how you can taste seeing someone, and literal counting is pretty much the only kind of counting there is. But I told myself that sheer emotion can sometimes trump logic, and I shouldn't be so judgmental.

Standing on the sticky floor of the sub shop bathroom, I wished I hadn't listened to Cole. I should have brought more Carrot letters, or at least a different one. Maybe the one in which she said, "I saw your pic in the freshman directory. Your a cutie!" Perhaps sheer emotion can trump grammar, too. And to be honest, any girl who sees a picture of me and says that I'm cute can Freddy Krueger the whole English language, as far as I'm concerned. Sorry, Mr. Ross. Please don't be too disappointed in me.

I don't get a lot of female compliments in the looks department. Didn't even get them from my mom. It was always my report cards, not my class pictures, that she slapped all over our refrigerator/freezer.

I must note that Amanda Carlisle has called me a cutie and, on another occasion, a hottie. She was extraordinarily drunk both times. Her characterizations would never hold up under cross-examination in a court of law: "Ms. Carlisle, at the time you characterized Mr. Griffin Smith as, and I quote, a 'hottie-katottie,' how many cans of 3.2 beer had you consumed?"

"Ummm . . ."

"Ms. Carlisle, may I remind you that you are under oath. Now, as to the 3.2 beers—how many?"

"Ummm . . . about 6.4?"

"No further questions for this witness, Your Honor."

But in The Carrot I had found a woman who, based on her impeccable penwomanship, was as sober as a Mormon when she deemed me desirable based on solid photographic evidence. A picture of *me*. Not the picture of Cole that I almost sent in and claimed it was me. This could have been trouble in the long run, given Cole's wavy brown hair versus my lifeless Beaver Cleaver hair, his strong chin versus my weak, cowering chin, and so on. But I had concocted a plan for skeptics who questioned photo-enhanced Griffin versus actual Griffin. I planned to tell them I had become very sick during a missions trip to Guatemala, due to a water-borne intestinal virus, and lost a lot of weight. Or that I had been maimed in a motorcycle accident and, due to family financial constraints, had my face restored by a barely competent plastic surgeon, working out of a place called Crazy Dave's Discount Plastic Surgery Village (motto: We're CRRRRAAAAA-ZEEEEE About Giving You the Face of Your Dreams for a Low, Low Price! Be sure to ask about our organized-crime witness-relocation discount).

I studied my reflection in the filmy bathroom mirror. In the bad light, in a dirty mirror, with my vision blurred from lack of sleep, I deemed myself passable in the looks department. Still, I stood there, haunted by the fear that perhaps The Carrot's eyesight was as weak as her command of language.

Before rejoining my fellow travelers, I valiantly attempted to vomit in the sink but managed only a weak seal-bark.

Cole was intently trying to squeegee the remains of a bumblebee off the windshield when I caught up to him.

"We're making lousy time," I observed. "It will get dark soon, and Dad has lousy night vision; he won't want to drive. I'm feeling tired and sick to my stomach, but I definitely don't want Rhonda driving. There's no way I can sleep knowing all of our fragile lives are in her hands."

"I'm ready to drive," Cole said.

"But you get sleepy when you drive. Remember when we went down to Wichita for that tobyMac concert? You almost rammed into the back of a Winnebago on the way home."

"I think I'll be okay. And I promise to pull over at a rest stop if I feel myself getting groggy. Besides, it'll be okay if we don't make it to Denver today."

"No, it won't."

Cole shrugged. "Why not?"

"Because we *said* we were going to make it to Denver today! Don't you understand?"

Another shrug. "I guess I don't."

I got in the front passenger seat and slammed the door. It's times like these that I wish my best friend were as obsessive/compulsive as I am. It would make things so much easier for me.

True to his word, Cole dutifully pulled in to a rest stop, all of forty miles from Russell. "I'm sorry, everyone," he said. "I guess I shouldn't have had a double-meat turkey sub; I'm getting tired."

I swiveled my head around and looked in the backseat. Rhonda was out cold. She looked like a stuffed animal, the way her head was flopped on my dad's shoulder.

"I could drive again," Dad offered, yawning.

"Nah," I said. I could hear the irritation in my voice. "You look comfortable back there. And it's pretty obvious Rhonda's happy. I can drive again. No problem. But as long as we're here at this lovely rest stop, anybody need to use the facilities?"

Eventually, everyone, including a puffy-eyed Rhonda, tumbled out of the Durango to answer nature's call for the second time in the past thirty-eight minutes.

Waiting on Rhonda, Cole and I stood studying a topographic map of Kansas on the wall between the men's and women's rooms. "Lewis and Clark made better time than we are, and they were in a friggin' canoe a bunch of the time," I grumbled.

"It's okay, Griff, really. We're both gonna get to school on time, and what you see as delays are really just giving us more time together, you know?"

I rolled my eyes at him. "If you tell me to enjoy the journey . . ."

"Griff, enjoy the journey." Delivered in classic Cole-speak. One hundred percent sincerity.

"Yes, sensei. I shall try."

"That's good," he said. No irony, no sarcasm in his voice. The only other person I know who is as guileless as Cole is my little brother.

Earlier in the summer, I had taken Colby to the park, and he became addicted to going down this long, meandering circle slide. For a while, he had the slide to himself, but then this pudgy kid about twice Colby's size showed up and pushed his way past him at the top of the slide.

"*I'm* gonna go first," Pudgy proclaimed.

I got up from the bench where I was watching Colby and reading the same page of *Slaughterhouse-Five* for about the tenth time because he kept asking me to use my sports watch to time how long it took him to serpentine his way down the slide. I started rehearsing possible Pudgy speeches as I stalked toward the bully.

"Hey, dude, you look about eight years old; would you like to live to see nine?"

"Excuse me, slick, but the next time you push my little brother, I'm gonna send you down the slide *head* first. Then I'll send your body down a few minutes later."

I was trying to think of a good fat-kid joke, too, but then I started to feel guilty. Why did I feel guilty about a weight joke before feeling guilty about a threat to maim a little kid? I wish to God I knew.

Anyway, I climbed to the top of the slide, where Colby was still perched. I expected to find him crying, or at least fighting back tears. Instead, he just smiled at me as he watched Pudgy flop like a prize trout down the slide. "There goes a kinda-big boy who needed to be first," he said. "Hey, Griff, will you go to the bottom of the slide and catch me this time?"

Maybe this is why Cole and Colby get along so great. Their personalities are as similar as their names.

When Rhonda finally emerged from the restroom, she proclaimed, "Dawgs, I know this is crazy since we just ate, but I gotta get my snack on! It's that time of the month, you know. Bryant, you got any change for the vending machine?"

My dad patted his pockets, then marched to fish some change out of the Durango's never-used-for-smoking ashtray. To keep myself from saying something rude to Rhonda, I listened to the weather report, which was broadcast in a tinny, scratchy female voice over a speaker right above the map. "Chance of rain in Dodge City today," I said to Cole in a low voice. "Some cowboys might get wet."

"It's only a 20 percent chance," he noted, tilting his head toward the speaker.

Dad returned, jingling a fistful of coins. "Anyone else need refreshments?" he asked cheerfully.

I studied the choices and quickly deemed most of them unworthy. However, I was tempted by the Milk Duds. How great that in today's overhyped society, someone actually names a food Duds. Defective-Looking Milk-esque Globules would have been even better, but that probably wouldn't fit on the box. Also, I checked out the ingredients once, and milk ranks fifth. And get this: The list includes nonfat milk, followed immediately by milk fat. Why not just use 2 or 1 percent milk in the first place and save yourself one ingredient? Besides, the way it stands, the two ingredients cancel each other out—kind of like my mom's and dad's presidential votes always did.

All in all, though, I hold no malice for the fine confectioners who make Milk Duds. The humility of bearing the "Duds" moniker more than compensates for the dubious practice of playing fast and loose with dairy-related ingredients.

"Dude!" Rhonda's piercing voice tore me from my analysis. "You gonna stand there all day, bogarting the snack machine, or you gonna give a sista a chance?"

I stepped back and gestured at the vending machine as if I were introducing Rhonda to the king of France: "Mademoiselle Eccles-Someday-to-Be-Smith, I present to you His Highness, Monsieur Jacques de Vend-O-Matic."

Rhonda began wagging her head vigorously. "I'm trippin' yo; there's nothing healthy in there. It's all nasty junk food."

Then came my retort: "Rhonda, *sista*, it's a freakin' vending machine. At a highway rest stop. Between two lavatories. You want a lean salmon steak, some sautéed fresh vegetables, a fresh-baked baguette? You're kinda out of luck. You want hydrogenated oils, sugar, and enough preservatives to embalm a rhino? Then you're gonna be okay. So there's your reality check, dude. And, in the future, no more complaints about vending machines being devoid of health food, got it? That's like complaining that Japan doesn't have enough giants."

Actually, I muttered my Rhonda rant under my breath as I walked briskly away from her and her nutritionally bankrupt machine. But I kinda wish she could have heard me. I think it was a pretty good speech.

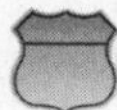

Rhonda finally settled on a small bag of beef jerky, which was so tough and chewy that it kept her quiet until she fell asleep on my dad's shoulder again.

It was almost 5 p.m. when we hit the outskirts of Oakley, Kansas, which is one of my favorite places in the universe. You know you're getting close to Oakley when you start to see the wooden signs, beacons of commerce on the west Kansas highways:

Skunks
Peacock
Fox
Live! Six-Legged Steer
Rattlesnakes
Russian Wild Boar

And my favorite . . .

See the World's Largest Prairie Dog!

For our first summer after the divorce, Dad drove Colby and me to Estes Park, Colorado, for a week in a mountain cabin. On the way, I was joking with Dad about the World's Largest Prairie Dog and how big it might be. Since a typical prairie dog is only about as big as a rat, Dad guessed that a bulldog-sized specimen could easily be a record holder.

I disagreed. "They wouldn't put up all of these World Record signs for something like that," I said. "People would totally feel ripped off."

"I don't know about that," Dad countered. "Imagine a prairie dog that is three or four times its normal size. That's a rather large rodent."

"But Dad, you said they charge you a lot of money to see this thing, right? Well, if you pay money, you want to see something spectacular, not just a prairie dog who grew up somewhat bigger than his brothers and sisters. I'm thinking it's gotta be the result of some failed science experiment. You know, radiation or steroids. I'm thinking this critter's gotta be the Andre the Giant of prairie dogs."

"I wanna see Andre the Giant's prairie dog," Colby cried. He had been asleep in his big-boy car seat. "Andre the Giant was in *Princess Bride*!"

I winked at Dad. "You can't ignore that kind of logic. You gotta exit when we get to Oakley."

It turned out that both my dad and I were wrong about the World's Largest Prairie Dog. He was bigger than any breed of canine. And he was bigger than Andre the Giant, may God rest his gi-normous soul.

The World's Largest Prairie Dog towers about twenty feet high, sitting on his haunches. He weighs in at eight thousand pounds. That's 571.4 stone for our British friends. There's only one problem: He's made of concrete. That's right—you gotta read the fine print, even in Oakley, Kansas.

I don't know who was more disappointed, me or Colby. "I wanted him to be a real prairie dog," my brother whined. "I wanted to pet him. I wanted to watch him eat."

"Well," I pointed out, "you can still pet him."

"Yeah, right! Who cares? He's fake!"

Dad, however, was impressed. "Think of the size and complexity of the mold they must have used," he marveled, staring up at the prairie dog's concrete belly. "And imagine transporting this behemoth, then getting it to stand erect on his haunches like this."

You're probably wondering, so yes, I *did* start snickering when my dad uttered the word "erect." Colby asked, "What funny, Griff?" and my dad shot me a stern look and said, "Nothing, Colby. Your brother's just being childish. He needs to grow up."

I agreed with my dad then, and I agree with him now. Still, I continue to snicker every time I hear that particular word used in a nonsexual context. It's something I yearn to grow out of—I hope by the time I'm thirty.

A final note on Prairie Dog Town: The six-legged bovine was lying down in such a manner that its extra limbs were hidden from view. And most of the rattlesnakes were sleeping or lethargic. Even when our tour guide shined a bright light over their chicken-wire covered home, only a few of them stirred and rattled. It sounded like bacon frying. And it reminded me of how Mom used to cook big Saturday-morning breakfasts for the whole family. Leave it to Griffin Smith to follow the pathway of caged rattlesnakes to depression and gloom.

We did love the Russian wild boar, however, even though there was no way of verifying he was indeed Russian. I asked a sloe-eyed girl in the gift shop, "You got any papers on that Russian wild boar?" She just rolled those sloe eyes at me and then tried to pressure me into buying a lacquered wall clock featuring the countenance of Dale Earnhardt Sr.

There would be no Oakley stop on this particular trip, though. No checking in to see if the Russians had been able to reclaim their boar. I didn't even mutter any cynical comments, for fear of waking Rhonda and hearing her exclaim, "Hey, don't be hatin' on the six-legged steer, homeboy. And don't dis the giant prairie dog, either. I think they're both dope!"

We were only a half hour or so from the Colorado state line when we saw the forlorn skinny guy standing on the edge of I-70, waving his arms like a third-base coach. On crack. Most people, decent people, would have seen this as an opportunity to be a Good Samaritan, to reach out to a fellow human who appeared to be in need. I saw it as one more barrier to my quest to at least cross the state line before Day 1 of our journey ended. And accordingly, I fixed my eyes on the road ahead. I'm not responsible for aiding him whom I pretend not to see. That's my motto—one of 'em anyway.

I was contemplating what penalty I would need to impose on myself for my impending sin of omission when Cole rapped his knuckles on the side window. "Griff, pull over—quick. That dude looks like he needs help."

"Huh?" I said as I accelerated and sped by the guy.

"Stop!" Cole said in a voice not loud but emphatic all the same.

I took my time decelerating and veering onto the shoulder. It's the people who slam on their brakes who cause accidents, you know. "Hmmm," I observed, peeking in my side-view mirror, "he's a long way back there. Too risky to back up all that way. I'm sure somebody else will stop."

Cole frowned. "I don't know, Griff. He probably wouldn't be gesturing like that unless he was feeling desperate; it is getting kind of dark and cloudy. It could start pouring down rain soon. Who knows, maybe a lot of people have passed him by, thinking the same thing you are."

I yawned. "Could be, but we can't really back up now. I think there's a traffic law against it. Plus, I'm not a very good backer-upper."

"Well, let me at least run back there and see what the problem is, if you really don't want to back your way there, which if you did, I could guide you."

I knew then that it was hopeless. If I launched any more excuses, Cole would shoot them down like clay pigeons. And I knew it was only a matter of time before he reminded me of the Good Samaritan parable, which he must have heard a half-dozen times during the two years he went to Grace Fellowship with me, back in grade school. He still remembers quite a bit—a few biblical parables, a handful of principles. He sometimes reminds me of the latter—usually when I am about to violate one. I hate it when people use my own religion against me.

The skinny kid quit doing his free-form aerobics when he saw us backing toward him. He knew help was on the way, or perhaps he was just tired.

"Thank *goodness*!" the guy said. He was staring right at Cole as he spoke, almost like he thought Cole's name was Goodness.

He was maybe five-ten, slightly built. A near-exact replica of me. *He must be on the same ineffective workout program as I am*, I thought. *Or maybe he hasn't touched a weight in his life. Same difference.* "My name is Chris," he said. "I can't tell you how many cars have just whizzed by me. I was beginning to think there was no such thing as a Good Samaritan anymore. It's kinda embarrassing." He gestured to a dark blue Corolla sitting on a dirt frontage road down from the highway. "My car's down there. It's got a flat tire, and, well, I've never fixed one before."

"There's a first time for everything," Cole observed, smiling at Chris. Cole doesn't smile very often.

Cole and I followed Chris down to his car. Dad started to clamber out of the backseat, but I waved him off. "We got this, Dad," I called to him. It's a five-minute job, tops. No need to get any more people out here than necessary."

Chris knelt by the driver's-side rear tire. "You think you could give me a hand here?" he said, picking up a tire iron from the dirt. I noticed he was holding the iron like a club. "I think the lug nuts might be stripped. You wanna take a closer look?"

Cole's arms hung at his sides, but they didn't seem to be completely relaxed. He reminded me of a Wild West gunfighter, ready to slap leather. "You wanna set that tire iron down," he said. It was more a command than a request.

Chris cocked his head. "Huh?" he said.

"The tire iron, Chris. If you want our help, you need to put it back on the ground right now."

"Relax, buddy," Chris said. "I don't want any trouble. I just want some help here. What's your name, anyway? I told you mine."

Cole waited for a truck to pass by. "Last time, Chris. Put it on the ground, or we're gone."

I was about ready to tell Cole to chill when Chris's much-larger accomplice lurched out of the backseat and looped around the front of the car, stalking Cole from his blind side.

"Wolf!" I screamed. I wish I could say I barked or bellowed the word. Even hollered wouldn't be as bad as screamed. But I don't holler. It's against my religion.

Why "Wolf!"? you might be wondering. It's basketball terminology. It's what you yell to a teammate who's dribbling upcourt, with a defender charging from behind to steal the ball. I called out the warning to Cole a lot during two years of high school basketball. The guy charging Cole had something in his right hand. I couldn't tell what it was, but it sounded heavy when it tumbled from his hand and hit the ground—just a second or two before the guy did.

Cole had whipped around, his body low. His attacker didn't even have a chance to swing at him before Cole's right arm struck out like a rattlesnake. Fist met nose. Chubby Accomplice Guy met ground.

The guy was out. He was even snoring. I was thinking how odd the whole snoring thing was when I realized Chris was on me, ready to club me with his trusty tire iron.

My instincts screamed at me. Unfortunately, they were sending mixed messages. I was getting a strong "Duck" vibe, but an urgent "Run, Coyote Boy, run!" directive was coming through as well. Ultimately, I'm shamed to say, it was the internal "Cover your head with your arms and curl into a fetal position" command that I obeyed. That's the problem with "instincts," plural. It's like your immediate and extended family trying to tell you which college to attend. Everyone feels the need to opine, and no one agrees.

Fortunately, Cole's instincts are more finely honed. He tackled Chris before he could smite me. While Cole wrestled Chris for control of the tire iron, I unfolded myself from my defensive posture. I saw Chris's accomplice struggle to his feet, then list to his left and almost tumble to the ground again. He appeared to be out of the action. If there had been a referee present, he no doubt would have stepped in and ruled Cole the winner by TKO.

Thus, I probably shouldn't have loaded up a roundhouse right and popped the big guy across his left ear. He staggered slightly to his right, but he seemed more surprised than hurt.

I turned toward Cole as I heard him grunt. Across the milky sky, I saw the tire iron helicopter in a parabolic arc, landing about 140 feet into a field. Cole threw the discus 167 feet at the state track meet, but a tire iron isn't as aerodynamic.

Cole brushed past me and grabbed the big guy in a head-and-arm. For those of you not well versed in the science of high school wrestling, a head-and-arm is like a headlock, only you have your opponent's arm locked up too. Hence the name. With a quick shifting of his hips, Cole flipped the big guy to the ground. Then he stood over him. "Stay down, please," he said, panting only slightly.

"Let's go, Scott," he said to me.

I was halfway to saying, "My name's not Scott," when I realized that Cole was helping to cover our tracks.

Dad was out of the car now, looking timid and groggy, but evidently feeling responsible for taking charge of the situation. Cole held up his palm like a crossing guard and wagged his head slowly.

"We need to go, sir," he said flatly. "I can drive for a while."

"Gosh, I don't know," my dad countered. "I think we should call the police."

Cole was still wagging his head. "That would be very time-consuming, sir, and it could get quite complicated. We're already behind schedule. I have their license number. We'll phone in an anonymous tip later if you want."

Now Rhonda was out of the car too.

"Get back in the car, Rhonda," Cole commanded. His tone

wasn't annoyingly hyper-respectful like it was when he spoke to my dad. Rhonda looked to her fiancé, who nodded in support of Cole. After the two back doors had closed, nearly in unison, Cole looked at me as we walked briskly back to the Durango. "You need to put your weight behind your punches," he advised. "A mere arm punch is not going to do you much good. You gotta step into it; use your hips, use your shoulder. And you need to punch *through* your target, not just make contact."

I shrugged. "Sorry, Ninja Master."

Cole shrugged back. "I'm just offering constructive criticism, like when you tell me not to use so many short, choppy sentences on my essay tests."

"Fair enough," I conceded. "Next rumble we get in, I'll pop my hips just like Griffey Junior."

We rode for a while in silence. Then Rhonda spoke up. "I don't feel right about this. Those guys are gonna be long gone before the police show up."

Cole fished in his front pocket and produced a bottle-opener key ring. "They're not going to get far without these," he said. "And they've got a flat tire and no lug wrench. Besides, I don't think they'll try to do that kind of thing anymore. They're not very good at it."

At a truck stop outside of Colby, Kansas, Cole called the police from a pay phone. We debated on staying the night there, in honor of my little brother, but I insisted we press on to Colorado. "Can't we at least cross the state line tonight?" I pleaded, annoyed at the nasal whine of my voice.

"But dude," Rhonda countered, "I am so worked."

Worked. An odd word choice for someone who had done little more than slump across my dad the whole trip. "How about Burlington?" I said. Let's just please, for the love of all that is good and true in this world, make it to Burlington."

"Um, okay," Rhonda said after a while. "As long as we can stay at a place with a swimming pool. I could use a swim."

"Me, too," Cole said, sliding next to Rhonda in the backseat.

"You sure you need to swim? You already got your workout on, busting up those two would-be carjackers back there."

"I'm not sure they were carjackers," Cole said philosophically. "I think they were, maybe, mentally unbalanced or something. They weren't true thugs. Kinda soft, really. Maybe their car broke down, in addition to getting a flat, and they just got desperate to find another vehicle."

"If that's the case," my dad said, "we shouldn't have left them back there. What if they try something on the next well-intentioned motorist who stops?"

"I don't think they will, sir. They are banged up pretty bad." Cole's voice sounded almost bored, as if he pummels criminals as a matter of daily routine. "That guy Chris—I'm pretty sure I broke his eye socket. And the other one—I threw him down pretty hard. He's gonna be moving slow for a while. Like that guy from Basehor I suplexed at state this past year. He had to default his next match."

"I'm not surprised," Rhonda was gushing now. "Dude, you can sure handle your business! I didn't know you had those kinda skills. Do your knuckles hurt or what?"

"They're okay." Cole sounded a bit embarrassed. Or maybe what I was picking up on was my embarrassment for him.

"Well, anyway, I bet a cool swimming pool will feel great after what you've been through."

"I guess so," he said. "What about you, Griff? You up for a swim if we find a place with a pool?"

I heard Cole's question but didn't respond. I was still pouting that my cheap shot on the big carjacker hadn't even been mentioned. I wondered if this was how Robin felt, always playing second banana to Batman. The car, the copter, the boat, and the motorcycle are named after Batman. All the gadgets are named after Batman. Even the freakin' cave is named after the Caped Crusader. What, was it completely out of the question to have a Robin-rope, or perhaps a stun gun called the Robinator?

The more I thought about it, the more I realized what a pathetic hand the super-hero dealer had laid on Robin. It all started with his moniker. What kind of wimp lets himself be called Robin? Not Hawk, Falcon, or Condor. *Robin.* What criminal is going to cower in the presence of someone named after a red-breasted birdie? "Oooh, watch out, Mr. Freeze. It's Robin! Better be careful, or he'll chirp real loud in the morning and wake you up too early. Or maybe he'll steal all of the night crawlers from your yard. Then you'll have to go to 7-Eleven and *buy* your bait instead of get it for free! Nooooo!"

I understood Robin. He was a skinny guy too, living in the shadow of a physically superior being. The only difference was that in his case, the shadow was shaped like a bat, while mine is shaped like that of an Abercrombie and Fitch model.

No question, Robin and I could be friends. While Batman and Cole were out pummeling ne'er-do-wells, the Boy Wonder and I could sit in a bar, drink a beer, and compare ignominies:

Robin: Dude, you should see Batman do push-ups. He's a machine.

Griffin: Tell me about it. Cole can do one-handed push-ups. And his teeth are perfect and white and straight, too. Look at mine; I still look like I have my baby teeth. And they're kinda gray, like an old sidewalk.

Robin: I always get pimples between my eyebrows. It's this stupid Halloween-party mask Batman makes me wear. I think he ordered it from a Frederick's catalog or something. It itches, man. Meanwhile, that cowl of his? It's lined with pure imported silk, baby. And he's got like a dozen of 'em. By the way—and you didn't hear this from me—he stuffs his codpiece.

Griffin: Figures. I bet it was his idea to make you wear those green Speedos with the tights, too, right?

Robin: Don't even get me started! Holy bat humiliation! Can you even imagine trying to pick up a girl wearing this crap? It's all a woman can do to keep from giggling out loud when she talks to me. The only time . . . aww, forget it!

Griffin: No, what were you going to say?

Robin: Well, it's pretty embarrassing, but once, we chased the Penguin and his henchmen into a gay bar, called the Hide & Seek. I was hit on so much I came out of that bar needing a hot shower.

Griffin: Sounds rough. Hey, I just thought of something, though: Why would the Penguin seek refuge in a gay bar? I mean, is he . . . ?

Robin: Are you kiddin' me? The Penguin? Hello! Let me give you a little clue here, buddy. When you see a guy carrying an umbrella around all the time but it's not raining, well, then, *you* connect the dots.

Griffin: Oh. Good point.

Cole was shaking my shoulder so hard that I thought he might dislocate it. "Griff," he said. I could hear the concern in his voice. "Where are you at in your head, man? Are you okay to drive?"

"I'm fine," I snapped.

"You sure? Because Rhonda and I have been trying to talk to you, and you've just been staring a hole through the windshield."

"Like I said, I'm fine."

"Okay. I just wish I knew where you went, you know?"

It took everything I had not to answer, "The Batcave, if you must know." But Cole wouldn't have understood. Neither would Dad or Rhonda. Only Robin, the Boy Wonder, would understand, and there are no words to describe how depressing this was to me.

Presently, though, my depression gave way to that familiar unsettling feeling that sits in my stomach like a brick whenever I face the prospect of sharing a swimming pool with Rhonda and her Victoria's Secret Does Swimwear attire. It's a big problem now, and it will become even bigger if God ignores my prayers and Rhonda and my dad actually follow through on their ill-conceived marriage plans.

Here's why: Teens are supposed to be embarrassed over how *bad* their moms look in swimwear, not how good they look. I and my peers can handle pasty-white thighs and droopy triceps and a few pooched-out stomachs. We'd prefer not to, of course. We'd prefer that our moms—and their sisters, cousins, and coffee-shop friends—abide by this sacred rule: When your thighs, buttocks, stomachs, and upper arms get so large and/or saggy that you start giving them names (for example, the Lower Continent, the Lumpy-Bumpies, the Aunties, the Jelly Roll, the Hanging

Gardens of Buttocksylonia), it's time to keep them covered when in the presence of anyone other than your spouse or personal physician.

But we know this rule will be flouted, and we've come to accept it. We aren't happy about the fact that every summer, our moms choose to display flesh that should, by most standards of decency, be covered by the grace of Target clothing. But for 2.5 months out of every year, we can nod knowingly at each other, roll our eyes, grit our teeth, and get through it.

Rhonda is another story. If she possesses any body fat at all, it must be confined to her head. Her legs are too long and her abs are too flat and her arms are too toned for her to be a mom—especially *my* mom.

The first time Dad brought Rhonda over to swim, I remember hoping she would have some glaring flaw—thighs like a fullback, perhaps, or maybe some unsightly scars as a result of a knife fight or acid spill.

But no. She pulled off her T-shirt and wriggled out of her board shorts, and I was horrified to see nothing but way too many square feet of perfect skin and a minute amount of fabric. I knew my life was ruined. Well, actually, just more ruined than before.

You see, before Rhonda and her minimalist pool attire first paraded into my life, I had always wished the summers would never end, that they'd just keeping playing out on a continuous loop. Run. Play pickup basketball at the park. Swim. Lounge. Eat. Take Colby for ice cream. Think of an excuse to call Amanda. Repeat. But that all changed after Dad met Rhonda and she eventually became a fixture at the Cheyenne Vista pool. The summer between my sophomore and junior years was when I first anxiously counted down the days between Memorial Day and Labor Day, which is when the pool is open. And now I know the "___ Days Till I Don't Have to See Rhonda Almost Naked" countdown will become an annual ritual—like the New Year's Eve ball drop in Times Square or the Muscular Dystrophy Telethon.

I believe it was an answer to an unspoken prayer that during the summer between my junior and senior years, the pool was closed for two weeks in July because, as Colby so eloquently put it, "Somebody pooped-ed in our pool!" So I was spared fourteen days of Rhonda parading around our apartment in her white or electric-blue bikinis, both options faithfully true to her form.

Cole has been the only one I can talk to about how I feel. No other guy in the high school would understand. They would start referencing the *American Pie* cinematic oeuvre or singing a permutation of "Stacey's Mom," and someone would get hurt. Probably me.

"If I didn't *know* her, it would be fine," I said to Cole one day as we tossed a football in the Cheyenne Vista parking lot. "She'd just be some kinda-hot older chick I stole a glance at once in a while at the pool. But it's different when it's your dad's, uh, woman. It changes the whole dynamics."

"I think I know what you mean. I don't like to see my mom in a swimsuit, even though hers is this big onesie kind of thing."

"Rhonda's not my mom," I snapped.

I half-expected Cole to say something like, "Not yet." But he didn't. He just gave me this look, somewhere between pity and compassion on the continuum of consoling looks.

During Dad and Rhonda's first fall as a semi-serious couple, my life improved greatly because the weather grew cold and the Rhonda debacle moved indoors. No more poolside leers or whispered exchanges from our Cheyenne Vista neighbors. Best of all, Rhonda began to wear actual clothing, and in a directly inverse relationship, the more layers she put on, the easier I found it to shuck my layers of embarrassment, unease, and bizarre-o sexual tension.

Still, I was a mess. I imagined that even Freud, if he were still alive, wouldn't be able to help me. "I know this kind of thing is supposed to be in my wheelhouse," he'd tell me, "but, dude, your situation is, what we like to call in my profession, royally messed up. I wouldn't touch your problem with a ten-foot pole. And don't read any symbolism into my 'pole' reference. If I had an *actual* ten-foot pole—made of maple, perhaps—I wouldn't deign to bring it into the proximity of you and your problems. All I can say to you is whoo-ee-boy-howdee, am I ever glad I am not you!"

Imaginary Freud would have been justified in being so blunt. Who could fault him for simply being frank about my grim prospects for peace—of mind, heart, and hormones? Sure, with the arrival of the fall chill, one well of my anxiety had been temporarily capped, but another one was soon gushing. Rhonda's near-constant presence at Chez Smith forced me to realize how small a two-bedroom, one-bathroom apartment really is. Before Rhonda, I'd never been self-conscious about using the bathroom or releasing any pent-up personal gases.

But over dinner one night, I allowed myself a satisfying yet nuanced root beer belch, and Rhonda shot me this glare, then mumbled something to my dad about "bad manners."

I wanted to stand up and scream at her, "It's not about manners, woman. It's about chemistry. Carbon dioxide is our unforgiving taskmaster, and we must do his bidding, or suffer the cruel consequences." Instead, I retired to the bathroom. But I found no sanctuary there. Instead, despite the fact that I had chugged enough root beer to float a dinghy, I found myself "unable to perform."

Great, I thought. *I already have Test Anxiety, Public Speaking Anxiety, and Anxiety About Having So Much Anxiety. Now I get to add Urination Anxiety to the list.*

I found myself tumbling into the habit of wandering down to use the facilities in the Cheyenne Vista workout room, which smells like . . . Well, if you've been in any truck-stop bathroom from Rhode Island to Redondo Beach, you know what it smells like.

Here's something I have discovered about male human nature: If it's not a bathroom that you—or your significant other—must clean, urination accuracy ceases to matter. And why even bother flushing? Who can endure that tedious one-second task? Besides, it's only disgusting human waste. Why are we so eager to usher it out of our lives?

And one more thing: The Cheyenne Vista workout-room john is always out of paper towels. It's annoying, and it makes me wonder if the cleaning people ever wash their hands. If they did, they'd know about the paper towels, right? Still, enduring the stench and drying your hands on your T-shirt is better than dealing with a quasi-adult woman knowing too much about your digestive cycle.

I don't know what it is about me: I'd rather let Rhonda read one of my journals than hear me pee.

For a long time, I have wanted to ask Cole about this, but I'm afraid he'll nod and give me The Look. The Look tells me, "It's all right, Griff; I'm still your best friend. But better not mention this to anybody else, okay?"

So I often leave the comfort of my home and hold my breath in the vile Cheyenne Vista facilities. And on those occasions when I just can't bring myself to venture out, or I get caught by surprise using MY OWN BATHROOM, I run the water, turn on the fan, and sometimes even hum a Dylan song. But I know I'm not fooling anybody. Rhonda can hear me. I know she can. Our apartment is so small that I could drop a Q-tip on the bathroom floor and she'd probably yell through the door, "Hey, you okay in there, homeboy? Anything break?"

I look forward to college for many reasons: establishing my independence, gaining the knowledge and skills needed to find a job and be a productive member of society, competing in college athletics, and, please, God, posting faster times than that punk Nicholas "The Frosh Phenom" White. But what tops the list right now is the opportunity, finally (finally!), to attend to basic bodily functions free from the scrutiny of the fascist Rhonda Regime.

We stopped for dinner in Goodland, near the Kansas/Colorado border. Rhonda and Dad reiterated their argument to find a hotel there as well, but I told them, "I am going to make it across the state line tonight, even if I have to walk. In fact, you could cut off one of my legs, and I'd hop to Colorado, using my bloody stump as an improvised crutch. Are you both understanding my feelings about this?"

Rhonda nodded, and for the first time, I saw something enticing in her eyes when she looked at me: fear. I tried not to smile; I knew it would be the annoying, self-satisfied smile of a vegan or hybrid-car owner. But it was hard to harness my glee. Fear is not something I elicit every day, or, more accurately, any day. No one fears me. When I'm running, even the squirrels don't get out of my way until I almost trip over them. So to see someone looking at me as if I were one of Hannibal Lecter's scary nephews was a rush. I made a mental note to threaten self-dismemberment more often.

Cole took over the driving duties as we headed out of Goodland. I sat in the front passenger seat, growing more impatient with the unyielding straight sameness of I-70. *My kingdom for a bend in the road*, I pleaded silently. *Give me a dip, a hill, a pothole, something. For the love of all things good and pure, somebody plant a tree or at least put up a radio station!*

We crossed the state line just as "Cinnamon Girl" ended. The song made me think of Amanda Mac. It's not that her eyes or hair are the color of cinnamon—she just really likes cinnamon toast. I like it, too. I started thinking about how much I preferred cinnamon to carrots and wondered if this was supposed to be a sign unto me. This is the kind of thing I wish I could speak to God about, just to make sure I wasn't getting my signals crossed. But, then again, I wonder just how much of my confused sign seeking he would indulge:

Griffin: So, sir, about this Cinnamon Vs. Carrots Sign thing?

God: Ah, yes, the Cinnamon Vs. Carrots Sign thing. I'm with you so far.

Griffin: Um, uh, yes. Well, as you know, I view cinnamon as a symbol for Amanda. Meanwhile, I guess that carrots would represent, uh, the girl called The Carrot.

God: Point of clarification: You say Amanda, yet there are two Amandas in your life, to varying degrees.

Griffin: Oh, yes, forgive me. The Amanda in this case is Amanda Mackenzie. As you know, we've been friends since fourth grade, and I began to have, uh, romantic feelings toward her, uh, I guess in the summer before my freshman year.

God: So you have had these romantic feelings for Amanda Mackenzie for more than four years now?

Griffin: Whoa. Yeah, I guess so.

God: And you're looking for some kind of sign about her, relative to a girl you have never met in person, based on the spice called cinnamon?

Griffin: I guess I never thought of it like that. Dumb question on my part. My bad, sir.

The first time you cross from Kansas to Colorado, you feel a little ripped off. You expect to instantly be in the shadow of towering, snowcapped mountain peaks and awed by the beauty of stately evergreen and aspen trees. In reality, however, eastern Colorado is just more Kansas—flat farm country—and that's not a bad thing. As my dad is quick to tell anyone who will listen, "One farmer can feed 188 people like you; you can see the signs noting this fact all along I-70. Farming is the backbone of this country." I know Dad is right. Even if those signs used to say something like, "One farmer can feed 226 people . . . ," I'm sure the farmers are working just as hard as they ever were, so I guess People Like Me are eating more than their fair share these days.

For a while, Bryant T. Smith talked about buying a farm and taking care of his couple-hundred people, but, thankfully, he lost so much money and credibility on his other post-divorce ventures that I was never truly scared that I would be awakened at five thirty every morning with the gentle but firm command, "Griffin, buddy, time to tend to the swine and so forth. And make sure you get right home after school. We have hay to stack—a veritable plethora of hay."

Instead, Dad is now fielding customer-service calls for a telecom company like the one he and Mom worked at when there was a "he and Mom." (He quit his job after the divorce because, as he so dad-fully put it, "So many of my coworkers were friends of both mine and your mother's, and I can't bear the ignominy of facing them, in light of recent events.")

I think he pretty much hates his job now, but what he's

sacrificed in adventure, he's gained in stability. It's pretty hard to bankrupt yourself sitting in a cubicle with a keyboard and a headset and a five-by-seven of your two sons. And he has sick days and two weeks of vacation every year, one of which he is wasting to drive halfway across the country and back, all for the sake of family bonding. And bonding, obviously, has never been our family's strong suit.

"Oooh, peep that!" Rhonda squealed as we took the first exit into Burlington. "Heated indoor pool at that motel on the right! I can feel that soothing water already."

I could feel my dinner rising in my throat already, but then I had an epiphany (another word that never failed to bring glee to Mr. Ross). I didn't have to swim. I didn't have to stand next to Cole in my swimming trunks, looking like a living Before and After Bowflex commercial. (He's no taller than I am, but it's amazing the difference that thirty pounds of well-sculpted muscle can make.) I didn't have to expose my troubled eyes to Rhonda strutting around like a waterlogged Victoria's Secret model. Let everyone else have the pool. I was going for a run. A long, long run.

"Are you sure you should run, son? It's already unsettlingly dark?"

"Dad," I said as I stood in the hotel lobby, stretching my quads, "I gotta keep my mileage up, or I'll never make the traveling squad at Lewis. Look, I can run down the frontage road parallel to the interstate. There are plenty of lights. Plus, the moon is full. Plus, I run in the dark all the time. It's no big deal."

"But it would be a shame to hurt yourself so close to your inaugural season as a collegiate runner."

"Dad, I've been folded up like a giant work of origami in the stupid SUV all day. I need to run. And I won't get hurt, really."

For the first half mile, I felt as if I was running on borrowed legs—specifically my Grandma Smith's. She's seventy-one and has arthritis. But ten minutes into the run, I began to loosen up and find a rhythm, or at least as close as I get to finding a rhythm. I was heading back east. I'm not sure why. Maybe I was already missing running in Kansas.

People can say what they want about my state, but few can deny that it boasts legendary runners. My favorites are what I call the Jayhawk Trinity: Billy Mills, Wes Santee, and Jim Ryun. Mills might be the only American runner in the next bazillion years to win an Olympic gold medal in the 10,000 meters. The Kenyans and Ethiopians own us now. Santee, back in the 1950s, dueled with Roger Bannister to become the first person to break the legendary four-minute mile. It was only via timing and luck, not talent, that allowed Bannister to smash the barrier first.

Then there's Jim Ryun. For distance runners like me, Ryun is our Michael Jordan, our Muhammad Ali. He not only ran sub-four, he did it as a high school student. Three minutes and fifty-five seconds. On a dirt track. With cruddy shoes that would get you laughed off of your junior high track team today. Let me put this in perspective for you. If you fancy yourself a pretty fair athlete, trot over to your local high school track and sprint just one lap as hard as you can. Chances are, you won't be able to run it in under sixty seconds. It's a lot harder than it sounds.

So, if you take me up on this challenge and stand there gasping after grinding your way to a 70-second quarter, think about this: As a teenager, years away from a runner's prime age, Ryun ran four 59-second quarters in a freakin' row. And the first one was just to open his pores.

For years, the United States' best high school milers attacked Ryun's record. They ran on state-of-the-art tracks, in state-of-the-art shoes. Race organizers handpicked the runners, including guys to set the proper pace, all in an effort to chase down Ryun's record.

Ten years passed, then twenty. Then thirty . . . and thirty-five. A few guys got close, but nobody could break even four minutes, much less equal Ryun's time.

Finally, after thirty-six years, Alan Webb finally did it. But, no disrespect to Mr. Webb, if Jim Ryun had access to the nutrition, sports medicine, fast tracks, energy-return shoes, and all the rest of the benefits today's runners enjoy, everyone else would still be chasing him.

After becoming the fastest high school miler in history, running for Wichita East, Ryun went to KU in Lawrence and became the fastest miler in the world—at age nineteen. Just about the age I am now. I wasn't even the fastest miler in my own little four-hundred-student high school. (And one of the two superior Talbot milers was only a freshman. That freak of nature White.)

Anyway, whenever I'm in Lawrence or Wichita, I never miss the chance to run. I imagine I'm covering the same ground as Ryun, albeit much more slowly and clumsily. I note the red-tailed hawks gliding above me and wonder if they are the great-grandchildren of the hawks that accompanied Ryun during his long treks.

On my favorite cross-country course, one portion is called the Jim Ryun Skyline. Every time I hit that part, I imagined him running beside me. It always made me go faster. Not fast enough to ever win a race, or even be the first Talbot High runner, but faster than I would have run without the inspiration.

So fifteen minutes into my run from Burlington, I imagined

Ryun beside me, pacing me. I realized that he would have to be wearing lead deep-sea divers boots and suffering from shin splints in order for me to keep up with him, but remember, I did use the word *imagined.*

I shifted from my normal short, choppy strides to Ryun's long, graceful, ground-gobbling strides. I even started to roll my head from side to side, just as he did when he was really getting his speed on.

At the eighteen-minute mark, I felt a hot needle of pain in my left ankle and wished Imaginary Ryun would have said, "Watch out for that rock in the road, Griff."

"Stupid! Stupid! Stupid!" I heard myself muttering.

"You're not talking to me, are you?" Imaginary Ryun asked. His voice rang with concern.

"No," I assured Imaginary Ryun. "I'm the stupid one. I've rolled this same ankle about a dozen times. You'd think I would have learned to be more careful by now. It's not your fault. I shouldn't have been trying to emulate your style. You're outta my league."

"It's okay," he consoled me. "I'm honored that you tried to emulate me. It means a lot to me that Kansas distance runners like you haven't forgotten me. You take care on that ankle, now, okay?"

"Will do, Imaginary Ryun. Thanks for running with me. I wish I could have hung with you longer."

Soon Imaginary Ryun pulled away from me. He disappeared around a bend in the road, and I wondered if I would ever be able to conjure him again. I hoped so. He seemed like a really cool guy.

I tried to shorten my stride and see if I could run through the pain and stiffness, but this was, as Cole would say, a Big Hurt. And you don't run your way through a Big Hurt. I started limping back to Burlington, hoping that a carload of Burlington cheerleaders would stop, pick me up, and pool all of the crushed ice from their Super Big Gulps to fashion me a cold compress.

And if a couple of them wanted to make out with me, to help take my mind off the pain, that would be okay too, as long as it was done respectfully and therapeutically, in the true Hippocratic spirit. I have my moral standards, after all.

In the end, no Good Samaritans or Good Hot Cheerleaders stopped to aid me as I limped along like Long John Silver. However, a van-load of punk baseball players did slow down long enough to ask, "Hey, what's wrong—you got a load in your pants?"

I thought about giving them my best one-finger salute, but then I remembered the Cole/WWJD incident of my junior year.

To place the incident in its proper historical perspective, I must tell you this: One night, our youth director, Ted Marcy, offered to hand out those infamous WWJD wristbands to anyone who wanted one. Normally, I would have used that opportunity to dash to the restroom, but on this particular night, I was sitting next to Amanda Mac, whose hand shot up like a bottle rocket. Then she looked at me and raised one of her perfect dark eyebrows just a bit, and I would have volunteered to wear a kilt made of live scorpions to gain her approval.

The problem came later that night, at home in my room, looking at the most intimidating four-letter combination in the history of our alphabet. The problem was this: Half the time, I had no clue as to WWJD. The other half, I knew exactly what he would do, and in those cases, it was the polar opposite of my inclination. And I didn't need to sport a constant reminder on my wrist of just how short I measured up on the old "You Must Be at Least This Righteous to Ride This Religion" chart.

I tried to concoct a plan in which I would keep the wristband in my pocket and don it only at church and in the two classes I shared with Amanda Mac. But I knew myself well enough to know that even if the concocting phase of this mission was successful, the execution would crumble to the same sad rubble as all of my other plans that require constant vigilance and consistent performance. It would go something like this:

Griffin walks down the science hall toward chemistry class. Knowing he shares chemistry with the esteemed Ms. Amanda Mackenzie, he dips his hand into his pocket to retrieve his trusty WWJD wristband. But, wait! What's this? There's something shiny on the floor! And we all know that Griffin is basically a chimp who is oh-so-easily distracted by shiny objects. Could it be a quarter? Perhaps it's a doubloon that Mr. Coker meant to show to his history class. Oh, alas, someone has kicked the shiny object under the lockers. Griffin does not have time to wait for the hall traffic to clear so he can find it. Woe to Griffin—he could be doomed to forever ponder the nature of that alluring shiny circle.

Fast-forward fifteen seconds. "Hi, Griff. Good to see you. Hey, where's your WWJD band? You *promised* me."

"Uh, gosh, Amanda. Did that darn thing fall off again? You know what Jesus would do? He would choose a wristband that wasn't too big for him! Heh-heh-heh. That was a good one, huh? Amanda . . . Amanda, where are you going? Aren't you gonna sit by me anymore?"

To avoid this inevitable scenario, I wore my WWJD, loud and proud, for a whole nine days. Then came the homecoming dance. I failed to ask Amanda, for the third year in a row. (I'd make it a perfect four eventually.) I went to the dance anyway, just to see if Amanda would show up and, if so, whom she might choose to dance with. That way, I could go home later, jealous and miserable, and castigate myself until dawn. (Just to clue you in a little bit, for me "castigating" involves privacy and disposable lighters or, perhaps, a gi-normous hair dryer.)

At one point, I was out on the floor with Nina Majors, trying not to step on anyone, when Carlton Tucker and Amanda "The Other Amanda" Carlisle dance-dance-revolutioned their way up to me. Carlton was behind Amanda, grinding on her like someone had sewn their pants together.

"Hey, Griff," he shouted over some crappy remix of a song that was also crappy in its original form, "get over here. Get in front of Amanda. Make an Amanda sandwich with me!" This was a big thing for Carlton, the making of the Amanda Sandwich. He did it at every dance. I had succumbed to the pressure a time or two, I confess. But this night was different.

I studied Amanda, and even though she was obviously drunk, she clearly was not enjoying the old game in which Carlton treats her heart like his personal hacky-sack.

I shook my head at Carlton. "You'll just have to settle for an open-faced Amanda sandwich," I said.

He cocked his head like a puppy. "What?"

The music swelled as the lead singer intoned, "It's yo duty, shake yo booty!"

I raised my voice. "Carlton, I'm not going to help you treat your girlfriend like a piece of meat. And if you can't learn to respect her, you should set her free and go back to your old girlfriend—you know, the inflatable one!"

Amanda Carlisle leaned toward me and looked up at me with

those dark-chocolate eyes of hers, and I was 58 percent sure the expression on her face was saying, "Thank you for sticking up for me. I wish *you* were my boyfriend, Griffin Smith." Of course, there was also that 42 percent chance she was merely indicating, "I had one too many Jagermeisters before coming to the dance, and I'm quite certain that I will projectile-vomit within the next thirty seconds. So, you might wanna watch your step."

Then Carlton stepped between Amanda and me, just as the song mercifully ended. "You better watch that mouth, Smith," he said, breathing Jagermeister and corn chips in my face. "Just 'cause my woman's with me, that doesn't mean I won't scrap. Remember that."

Then he wheeled around, and I searched my mind for a parting shot that could stop him cold. But, as is so often the case, I had nothing. The open-faced sandwich line had bankrupted me. But Carlton wasn't getting away without some closure. I felt my middle finger rising, and I thrusted it toward his back. A few nearby underclassmen looked at me, their jaws dropping. I could tell they were impressed. I just hoped they didn't realize I was praying fervently that Carlton would not turn around and see my middle finger floating in the air, a beacon to my stupidity and lack of self-control and class. (And yes, you are right to ponder the irony of someone praying to God in heaven that an obscene gesture, rendered with an appendage sporting a religious accessory, won't be seen by the gesture's intended target. Welcome to the sad paradox that is my life.)

Anyway, before Carlton turned around, I felt a hand on my shoulder. It was Cole's hand. He looked troubled. As a slow song began, he leaned toward me. "Griff," he said, "when you flip somebody off, don't you think you should avoid doing it with the hand that's got a WWJD band on it? I'm just sayin'."

I wanted to tell him, "Who are you to judge me, Mr. Cole 'My Life Is One Big Skankfest' Sharp? In fact, I did tell my best friend that. But he just gave me one of his trademark one-shouldered shrugs and went to go find a cheerleader to make out with. He knew I was busted. So did I.

That was the last time I wore the wristband. I took it home and gave it to Colby. "Thanks, bro!" he said. "It's pretty-kinda big, but I'll grow into it."

I walked away from him, thinking, *Yeah, you'll grow into it before* I *do. That's for sure*. Then I went to my room and closed my door before my little brother could ask me why I was giving the band away in the first place.

Amanda Mac was another story, of course. I knew she would ask, so I decided to employ a preemptive strike. I called her about an hour after I got home from the dance, which she did not attend.

"Amanda," I said, "I need to tell you something. I'm sorry, but I'm just not ready to wear the WWJD band, like you do. It's just not my style. And it puts too much pressure on me. And I don't want to damage the cause, you know? I guess I'm just not ready to wear it."

"I know," she said softly. Someday two words might hurt me more, but I doubt it.

So that's why I didn't salute the van o' Burlington punks. In fact, I don't do that particular salute to anyone anymore. I get mad and I start to make the gesture, but then I begin to feel like I'm still wearing that stupid wristband.

As I limped into the motel parking lot, I tried to lighten my mental load with a less-taxing burden. Namely, which hotel room were Cole and I checked into? I knew it was similar to the title of an old-school album, but was it Rush's *2112*, Elton John's *21 at 32*, or Van Halen's *OU812*?

Since the hotel had only three floors, the Sammy Hagar-era Van Halen option was out. I hobbled up the concrete stairs to the second floor and shuffled down the exterior walkway that paralleled the frontage road.

Room 212 seemed familiar, so I slipped my key card into the reader, and with a green signal, I stepped inside. I was immediately confronted by a question: *Who in the wide world of sports is Cole kissing? We've been in Burlington less than sixty minutes, so this is a quick hookup, even by Cole standards. And if it's a Burlington cheerleader, I'm simply going to start crying right here on this badly stained taupe carpet!*

Cole's hookup woman had her back to me. They were standing near the bed. The only light was one of the two lamps that flanked the bed closest to the door.

Cole slid his head to one side. "Hey, Griff," he said, his voice flat. "I thought you were going for a ten-mile run."

"I rolled my stupid ankle less than three miles out. I was gonna soak it in the tub, if it's okay with you and, uh, . . ."

Rhonda looked at me over her left shoulder. "Oh, crap," she said.

Key Life Lesson #2: Those John Hughes movies of the late eighties are really cool, but they are wholly unreliable in their portrayal of that little thing called Real Life—especially the crisis aspects of real life. It's compelling on screen when the music swells at just the right time and Eric Stoltz or Lea Thompson or even Emilio Freakin' Estevez—eyes burning with intensity—drops the perfect one-liner. But in real life, you stand there like an actor who's forgotten his lines, or maybe neglected to learn them in the first place. You aren't sure what to say, how to breathe, how to stand. Even your own head, containing your own addled brain, feels like something you rented for forty-eight hours from Home Depot, and you forgot to get the operating instructions for it. *Boy-howdy, this big lumpy thing on my shoulders sure feels heavy,* you marvel. *I hope it's attached securely. But I bet if I move it too much, it'll fall right off and break. And if that happens, good luck getting the damage deposit back!*

Lesson 2 clubbed me atop my tingling head as I stared at Rhonda and Cole, who had broken their embrace and stood side by side. If this were a John Hughes movie, I thought, I would tilt my head at a thoughtful angle and toss off a line like, "I'm sorry . . . did I come at a bad time?" Then I'd pivot and jock-walk to the door. I'd pluck the Do Not Disturb sign from its little plastic sleeve and hang it outside the door as I left. Then I'd stroll down the walkway, smoking a Merit, while a Simple Minds song echoed in the background. I'd go find a smart science buddy and fashion myself a perfect robot girlfriend. Only mine wouldn't look like Kelly LeBrock—she'd look like Amanda Mac.

Instead, I just stood there, playing out my movie scenarios. Cole was silent. Occasionally, he'd nod toward Rhonda as if to say, "You're the adult here. We're waiting on you."

But Rhonda was a statue, or maybe a pillar of salt. I wondered if she was mentally flogging herself: "Girlfriend, you are so busted. You been caught creepin' with the best friend of your stepson-to-be!"

I told myself to be brave—that even Anthony Michael Hall would strive to be brave—but I couldn't shake the fear that my feigned composure was about to melt like butter on a hot skillet in front of Rhonda "The Cliché" Eccles. *Come on, Griff,* I mustered. *You stand upon the moral high ground on this one. The view should be breathtaking. You get to look down at the mess and shake your head sadly and sigh that world-weary sigh and make that clucking noise with your tongue, if you choose. And you know what? You can even pray to God and ask him to forgive the iniquities of your best friend and your dad's cliché. Because that is just the kind of John Hughesian, forgiving person you are.*

I was just about ready to pray to God on behalf of my moral inferiors when I noticed that I wasn't breathing. I dashed from room 212 and gulped Burlington night air like it was Gatorade. I got this image of Dad pacing his hotel room, his face sandwiched in his hands. He was muttering something I couldn't decipher.

"This is gonna kill him," I heard myself whisper as I leaned on a wobbly steel railing and looked at the collection of minivans and SUVs slumbering in the parking lot.

"Griff?" Cole said. I turned and studied him for a moment. He moved next to me and trained his eyes on something beyond the parking lot.

I waited awhile, even though I knew it was pointless. *He* was waiting on *me*. To explode. To start firing questions like dodgeballs. To turn my back on him and storm away. I scrolled through these options and a few more, including Punch Cole in the Throat and Make Him Gag, Then Crumple to the Ground.

None of the choices had any pull to them, so I waited on

Cole. I resolved to outlast him. And I had the advantage: For once I wasn't the one who had stepped in an ethical gopher hole. Plus, I got to wait up on my moral high ground, where, legend has it, the waiting is good.

I started counting to one hundred in my head. I completed the task twice, and it became boring. So I counted backward once, then changed things up by doing a high-low count: 1, 100, 2, 99, 3, 98 . . .

I was bearing down on 50 from both ends when Cole spoke again. "I am sorry, you know."

"I know." My voice was a little raspy. I liked that. It sounded raw and ragged, and it would enhance Cole's guilt.

"You're probably wondering why?" he offered.

"I suppose it might have something to do with your being an amoral horndog. What, you couldn't delay your annual Summer Skankfest till you got to Boulder? You know what? You're no different from Carlton Tucker."

"Do you really think that?"

His voice carried worry, not anger.

"I don't know, Cole. I mean, I know that most guys would consider her hot. 'Most guys' being straight males with at least one functioning eye and/or testicle."

"It wasn't like that, Griff. She just said she wanted to talk to me. Then we end up sitting near each other on the bed. We talk for a while, then I say I'm going to the workout room. She goes to hug me good-night, and the good-night hug turns into another kind of hug . . . you know what I mean?"

"I don't have much personal experience with such hugs. But I've read articles. Seen a documentary or two on that Oxygen channel."

"Well, anyway, it's kind of, uh, interesting for a little while. We kiss a little bit, and I start thinking how I've never hooked up with anyone but high school girls. I start wondering, *What about an adult woman? Do I have that kind of game?* I can't say the thought hasn't crossed my mind before. I mean, those bikinis she wears? But then I start thinking of you and your dad, so I stand up. I tell her, 'I really need to work out.' But then she stands up too. And you know, I start to think, *Hey the workout room is open twenty-four hours. What's my hurry?* Then, thank God, you come in."

I pushed myself back from the railing and crossed my arms. "What would have happened if I hadn't come in? Huh? I really want to know." It occurred to me that I sounded like a TV prosecuting attorney. It felt good.

Even though I couldn't see him very well, I could tell Cole was agonizing over the question. After I counted to nineteen in my head, he said, "I honestly don't know what would have happened. I'd like to think one of us would have put the brakes on."

"What for? I mean, she's not officially married, so she's fair game, right? I mean, what's a lousy puny-diamond engagement ring count for, anyway? That's not like a red stoplight. It's yellow: Go on ahead. Everybody does it. Drive right through. Hurry, though, while you still have the chance."

"Whatever," Cole said wearily.

"Am I boring you here, Sharp? Please forgive me if I am, because that would be real insensitive of me. Insensitive, just like—I don't know—macking on an engaged wom—"

I heard a door creak open. Rhonda was slinking toward us. "I need to talk to you," she said. I began formulating scathing comebacks, and I had two pretty good ones, when I realized she wasn't talking to me. Cole moved to her side, and she grabbed his elbow, but it wasn't a romantic grab. It was like my sixth-grade teacher Mrs. Strothers' "Let's go visit the principal's office" grab. Cole looked at me over his shoulder, and he reminded me of a prisoner being led away to his execution.

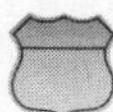

The hotel's "state of the art" fitness center looked like a converted storage room, with mirrors along one wall to make it seem bigger.

The off-brand weight machine that sat in the center was ancient and creaky. The lat-pull setup whined with every rep. I let the stack of weights smack down after each rep. Normally, it tweaks my nerves when some newb does this kind of thing in the school weight room, but on this night it felt good. I imagined the 120 pounds' worth of weight plates slamming down on Rhonda's twiggy fingers. "Gonna be tough to fondle my best friend's six-pack with both those mitts in a cast," I muttered.

I had just positioned myself under the bench press when I heard the door open and close. *Don't be Rhonda, don't be Rhonda, don't be Rhonda*, I chanted in my head as I lifted.

On my eleventh repetition, my left arm began to wobble as if my radius and ulna had suddenly turned to rubber. I squirmed and coaxed the weight stack halfway up, then took my hands off the handles and let the whole apparatus crash down. The resulting noise was pleasing to my soul.

"You, okay, dude?" Rhonda said.

"No strain, no gain," I observed.

"That can't be good for the weights."

I managed an indignant cough. "You're worried about

damaging the cheap weights at a cheap motel, are you? Guess I should expect that from a cheap woman."

"I can't believe you're saying that!" Her voice was almost a whisper.

"Oh, you've gotta be kidding me! You're getting the 'edited for TV' version of what I feel like saying! And how dare you even try to make yourself a victim! What about my dad? What about what *you* have done to *him*?" I didn't know where this double-rhetorical question came from, but I thought it was effective. I sized up Rhonda. She looked lost, kinda like me in physics class.

"Here's the thing," she began. "I love your dad—and don't give me that drop-jawed look, okay? Please let me finish. I have thought a lot about my getting married to someone quite a bit older than I am, and I believe I am coming to a place of peace about that. But I'm not going to lie to you, dude. Up till your dad, I've dated mostly guys my age or even younger. And as I've contemplated becoming Mrs. Bryant Thomas Smith, I've wondered if I'm totally down with leaving the days of the young hottie-katotties behind.

"Over the past few months, I've found myself asking, 'Rhonda, are you really and truly over all that?' I've wondered if the only way to be sure, was to . . . well . . . I even considered cooling things out with your dad for a while so we could both have some time apart to sort everything out, but then he asked me to marry him. I said yes. And once that happened, it really wasn't a good time to say, 'You know, Bry, perhaps we should consider seeing other people for a while.' Griffin, are you feelin' any of this?"

"Maybe. But let me get this straight: You've been thinking about hooking up with some young guy for a while now, in your spare time from wedding planning? And Cole just happened to be around when the moon was full or something? I mean, I know that pretty much all he has to do is stand there and women start jumping on him, but— "

"You've got it so wrong, dude! These thoughts and doubts and desires, they're not something I take out and play with once in a while. They haunt me. They torment me. I want them to go away, but they just won't. Then tonight, Cole and I are talking, and what he did with those carjacker dudes . . . that was so street, you know? So brave. Then there's always been this weird chemistry between him and me, and— "

I stood up. "Pardon me while I go throw up in the hallway. I'll only be a minute."

"Please let me finish, Griff. *Please*. Tonight, things start going down this road with Cole, and I decide to just let 'em go. I feel like it's safe. I had no intention of ever letting things get too far. But I had to know. I had to know if I could put the allure of the younger man behind me and commit to a wonderful, mature man for a lifetime. And you want to know the verdict?"

"Do you really think I care?"

She looked up at me, and her eyes were glistening with tears. "Yeah, I believe you do."

"For Dad's sake, not yours," I whispered so softly that I doubted Rhonda could hear.

She took a step toward me. I took two steps back, wincing as I backed into the bar-dip apparatus. "Okay, okay," she said, "I'll keep my distance. But I can see you're hurting, and I just want to hug you."

"Don't you think you've done enough teen-boy hugging for one night?"

"Okay, I probably deserve that. But please set aside your anger at me for just a moment and listen: There was no spark between Cole and me, and he's probably the hottest young dude in the country."

I closed my eyes and swallowed hard. "Okay, back to my need to vomit."

"Stop!" It was more plea than command. "Griff, I am just keepin' it real with you. I was letting things play out with Cole, just to make sure. And I can honestly say now that that part of my life is behind me. I know what I want—uh, I mean, *who* I want."

"It's just too doggone bad that you had to cheat on my dad—with my best friend in this whole stupid world—to find that out, Rhonda. But at least *you* got things all sorted out for yourself. So it's all good in the 'hood, right?"

I positioned myself for some bar-dips but kept eyeing Rhonda, her face fallen like a soufflé, her bottom lip quivering. I searched for a comment that would shove her out the door sobbing, but the 'hood rhyme had done it. She trudged out of the room, sniffling.

I pumped out eighteen dips, one for every year of my impossible life. I had no idea I could do that many. I was fueled on the last few reps by a thought that snuck up on me like a mugger: *Why didn't Rhonda have wildly inappropriate feelings toward* me? *Why does it always have to be Cole?*

I finished my post-infidelity-crisis workout with thirty minutes of cardio on a squeaky exercise bike. The pain in my ankle flared up on every downstroke, but after a while, I ceased to care.

I decided that I would shower, find Rhonda, and relay to her an ultimatum: Confess to Dad, or take a bus back to KC and go play with someone her own age. Neither choice would leave everyone unscathed. In fact, both would crush Dad's heart, and that sucked like one of those vacuums that's so strong it can pick up a bowling ball. But at least I controlled the choices.

I left the weight room and walked through a hallway and out to the parking lot. The night air was heavy. I felt my T-shirt clinging tightly to my back. Then I saw my father, pacing at the far end of the lot, head hanging. I wondered who got to him before me, Cole or Rhonda.

In any case, I knew that the news I was prepared to break to him was already broken—along with, most likely, his heart.

"You okay, Dad?" I asked, uttering one of the stupidest questions in the all-time history of stupid questions.

"I think I'll be okay, Griff." His hands were buried deep in the pockets of his off-brand department-store jeans. "I hope *you* are all right. I fear that this situation has placed you in a very untenable position."

Was this guy kidding? My fiancée hadn't just cheated on me—with my son's best friend. I had to stifle a sad chuckle. "I'm fine, Dad. I'm worried about you. Look, I think that Cole and Rhonda . . . they both just kinda lost their senses for the moment. I mean, they really broke the code, broke the rules, you know, but—"

Dad's head, which had been drooping like it was going to fall off, snapped to the full upright and locked position. "It's not about breaking a code, son. It's about hurting someone. They hurt me. This is *personal.*" Then his voice became a whisper. "This hurts, Griffin. It really, really hurts."

I became aware of my arms dangling at my sides like bendy straws, all unwieldy and awkward. I thought about placing one of them across my dad's shoulders. But I felt like I was in one of those big earthmovers, and I couldn't figure out which levers to pull, which buttons to push, to make anything work. So I just stood there.

"Anyway," Dad said finally, "we have a lot of driving to do tomorrow. We should try to get some rest."

I nodded. *Come on,* I scolded myself. *So what if you can't show any physical sign of support; at leas*t say *something!*

"Hey, Dad?"

"Yes."

"Well, I just want to tell you that what Cole and Rhonda did was really low. Believe me, Cole's gonna hear about it. In fact, he kinda already has. And Rhonda . . ."

"Yes, son?"

"Well, I agree with you that she's an adult and should know better. What she did—that was a real ho-baggity thing to do."

Dad's right hand was jammed so far into his pocket that it took him two violent yanks to free it. I saw the hand ball into a fist, and somehow I knew a punch was coming. I had plenty of time to duck or back away, but life sometimes presents situations so surreal that you just have to let them play out.

The punch caught me high on the left shoulder. It was a decent punch, and I wondered if it would leave a bruise. I hoped like crazy it would.

"You will not use that kind of language about my fiancée, understand?"

There was an element of Clint Eastwood in Dad's voice. I had never heard it before. He's much more Clint Howard than Clint Eastwood. "I understand, Dad," I said. "I really didn't mean to insult Rhonda, though. I was referring to the kind of thing she did, not her as a person."

I wondered if he would sniff out such a bald-faced lie.

"That's a bald-faced lie, Griffin."

"Whatever," I said, trying to sound sulky and hurt. "I was just trying to defend you. What Rhonda did to you isn't right. That's all I am trying to say."

He placed a hand on my sore shoulder. "I appreciate that. But no more with that kind of language about her."

I nodded.

"How's the shoulder?"

I started to say that the pain was almost gone but then reeled those words back in. "Well, Dad, I think that's gonna leave a mark."

He squeezed his face, vise-like, between his hands. "Son, I am so sorry. I have never done that before. I never even spanked you."

I shrugged. "It's okay, Dad, really. I kinda had it coming" (for roughly the past sixteen-plus years).

"I just can't believe I lost it like that. You know, your mom always pressured me to spank you, but I always resisted. You see, my own father used corporal punishment on me, for everything from losing a library book to spilling Kool-Aid on the carpet. I remember how that felt, and I promised myself I would find other forms of discipline with my own children. And then look what I go and do!"

"Like I said, Dad, it's cool. Really. But, hey, why did Mom put pressure on you to spank me? I can remember her saying stuff like, 'Are you going to discipline your son or not?'"

Dad forced a smile. "She didn't want to be the only one who spanked you. She was afraid that you would look at her as the Bad Parent. She didn't want that."

Then he went quiet. I sensed that he needed some time alone, and I knew *I* needed some time alone, so I awkwardly roped my arm around his shoulder. Then we tried to hug, but it was like two people learning judo for the first time. What made the whole thing all the more awkward was that I realized I was now a good inch taller than my dad. And I'm only five foot ten. He had always seemed like a giant to me. "I'll give you some time, some space," I whispered.

He nodded, and I began to limp toward the pool. I hoped the water would be cold enough to soothe my ankle. "Lynnette Smith: The Bad Parent," I heard myself chuckle. I thought of all the Mom spankings, with the yardstick, the wooden spoon (which, as a toddler, I had dubbed the Spankin' Spoon), and the hairbrush—bristle side right on top of the head.

I wondered how many spankings I endured from ages two to twelve, which, thankfully, some parenting expert on TV said should mark the end of physical punishment. I was so thankful Mom trusted TV experts so much. Some spankings made me angry; others made me scared. None made me truly sorry for what I'd done—only regretful and critical toward myself for getting caught. But no spanking made me think of my mom as the Bad Parent. The Overreactive Parent and the Irrational Parent, perhaps, but never, never the Bad Parent. Only stuff like adultery and abandonment could grant someone that title.

Mom usually apologized to me after spanking me, sometimes digging deep into the Parenting Manual for the "That hurt me more than it hurt you" spin. But she never had apologized for abandoning her family in favor of Maxwell the Mediocre. Adults stupefy me sometimes.

I sat on the edge of the pool and lowered my ankle into the tepid water. I needed a drink, ideally from a caring cabana girl who would fetch me some vodka and soothe me with tender words (and perhaps a mentholated rubdown). I looked at my shoulder, wondering if Dad's punch would eventually raise a bruise. I was pretty sure it would. He sure put a lot into it. Sure, I knew I tweaked a nerve with "ho-baggity," but I've said lots worse and elicited little more than an eye roll and a heavy Dad-sigh. This punch wasn't really about my language; this was fueled by the betrayal of your wife of fifteen years ditching you for a hack writer, by the betrayal of your new love hooking up with a teenager. And maybe he was also lashing out at the injustice of toiling away in Business America for twenty-four years and finding himself to be just another cubicle monkey.

As I thought about it, I figured it was good to get all of that out. Besides, packing a bruise-worthy punch is something that should be in every man's repertoire. Sure, bruising one's own son would make the bruise power bittersweet, but you've gotta demonstrate your prowess on someone—why not your own flesh and blood? Keep it all in the family. After all, other people's kids are likely to sue and/or talk to the media and/or start a blog about it.

But to be honest, I needed the bruise as much as Dad did.

The pain was already fading, so I needed to make sure the mark wouldn't fade too. I needed the reminder of how I had hurt my dad's feelings. And if Dad couldn't leave a mark, I'd have to do it myself. However, after almost three years, I was getting tired of the ritual.

I got the idea about six months after Mom left, while watching a TV special depicting people who re-created aspects of the Crucifixion to ostensibly show their devotion to the Lord. Some had themselves affixed to crosses with skinny aluminum nails. Others walked down a dirt road, being scourged by helpful accomplices. I guessed they were friends, relatives, or fellow members of a small-group Bible study or Core Group. One guy was whipping *himself* with something that looked like a pom-pom from hell. His back resembled a raw steak.

I wondered about these people's true motivation. Was their masochism truly a sign of devotion to Jesus? Were they ashamed of their sins and desperate to demonstrate their penance? Or were they seeking punishment only so that they could get over the guilt—the guilt that even their most earnest prayers for forgiveness couldn't seem to erase?

I thought about some people from my school. Francis Croft drove drunk and smashed his nose against the windshield of his Sunfire. His parents took his car away. Plus, he had the whole smashed-nose thing to deal with—and he wasn't all that good-looking before the accident.

Robin Richards got pregnant and got kicked out of her house. She ended up in a state-run refuge center.

And me? Nothing. My dad was so guilty about the divorce that all of the boundaries he had set and monitored so diligently eventually faded away. The many bottles of airline-portion hard liquor rested undiscovered in my sock and T-shirt drawers. My dad has always respected my privacy, but he soon neglected the weekly interrogation that always began, "Are you using alcohol or drugs, or have you felt tempted to do so?"

One Saturday afternoon, I spent two debauched hours in my room with Ally Long, culminating with my giving her a remarkably symmetrical hickey just above her belly ring. Dad was home the whole time, slumped across the living room couch, watching a PBA bowling tournament. He never even knocked on the door to ask, "How are things going in there? You two kids need a refreshing beverage? You wanna come out and catch the tenth frame with me?"

And he began to take at face value assurances such as, "I'm going to hang out with Cole and some of the other guys from the track team tonight." He ceased furrowing his brow and asking me to "elaborate on who 'the guys' will be and where the 'hanging out' will occur." He didn't even ask for a disclaimer, which I could have told him really fast, like one of those radio-ad guys: "'Hanging out' might include an unsupervised party at the home of Amanda Carlisle, aka Amanda Sandwich, which may feature one or more of the following: binge-drinking, public displays of extreme affection, clothing-free hot-tubbing, drunken fistfights, freak-dancing, and voiding where normally prohibited. Your actual level of debauchery may vary. No purchase necessary. Not available in Alaska and Hawaii and the maritime provinces of Canada. Batteries not included."

In short, I was getting away with everything. And, believe it or not, I was miserable. Miserable *and* paranoid. Because my being allowed to run buck-wild with impunity meant one of two things: (1) This was a giant scheme in which my family, school counselors, and church friends and a team of law enforcement officials were complicit. I was being set up, and soon I would get busted big-time in the most publicly humiliating fashion. There would be much head-wagging and hand-wringing and sermonizing—and then I would be sent away to military school to room with someone named Butch. My suicide would follow within ten days.

Or (2) No one cared. God didn't care. Dad didn't care. Youth Pastor Ted didn't care. I wasn't even *worth* punishing. Or perhaps I was so far gone that all rehabilitative efforts had been deemed hopeless. I was like one of those Pharisees whose hearts had been hardened, and I'd been handed over, like a slave, to the mastery of my most base desires. The time of death had been called for my morality. The white sheet had been pulled over my troubled head. And God, my dad, my pastors, and even Amanda Mac had sighed sadly, pulled off their surgical gloves, and gone out for a beer.

After much thought, I'd decided that #2 was the more-likely scenario. And I just couldn't lie there and let it happen. *Griffin Smith is not even worth rehabilitating through loving corporal punishment? We'll see about that.*

Then I started to obsess about the TV special and all of those pious, devoted self-mutilators who had gone before me. I couldn't see myself reenacting any aspects of the Crucifixion. I wasn't worthy of that. And it seemed disrespectful. Jesus and I weren't particularly close at the time, but while I lacked fondness and devotion, I sincerely respected him, as I always will. I wasn't going to be so presumptuous as to be a wannabe Crucifixion victim. That was poser territory. And I was content to leave the posing to the Carlton Tuckers of the world. So I bought a multipack of brightly colored lighters and let the tough love begin, my way.

The first time you hold your open, virgin palm over the tip

of a flame, you jerk it away in about two seconds because, hello, it hurts. But then you learn discipline. If you get past the initial moment of fear and panic, you can give yourself a painful welt, suitable punishment for stealing a ten-dollar bill out of your father's wallet, or calling your innocent younger brother an "ugly little freak" and then raising your fist like you're going to hit him. You cover the burn with a bandage, publicly deem it a blister or a rope burn from PE class, and no one is the wiser.

In the winter, when long sleeves are a must, your upper arms are fertile ground for reproaching via roasting. But it's best to shave your arms first, if needed. The stench of singed hair is a real turnoff to the ladies. And it can tip off The Man, aka your dad. You can't let your father know that you're doing part of his job for him, for Pete's sake, because then you'd feel guilty because you made *him* feel guilty, and you'd have to do something about *that* transgression too. It's ironic and complicated, no? Rest assured, I didn't want to ride that vicious cycle. Dad couldn't know I was covering for him. I knew, and that was enough.

I had a great system. When I sinned—omission or commission variety—retribution was swift. And when I knew I was *about* to sin, I could save myself time and trouble later by pre-punishing. You don't know how freeing it is to head over to Ally Long's parentless house on a Friday night knowing that any debt you're likely to incur has been prepaid and you've got the burn behind your left knee to prove it. All you have to do is make sure Ally Long doesn't somehow grab that left knee while in the throes of passion.

But then I got careless. I used the Blister Excuse twice in a row. And I quit opening my bedroom window whenever it was time to make like the Human Torch.

One night, I noticed Dad sniffing my bedroom air like a

bloodhound and frowning. "Did you blow a fuse in here, or did something burn?" he asked me. "Something smells vaguely like a fire."

"Uh, I made toast a while ago," I offered. *Good one, Griff. Real smooth. Lots of people cook their toast over an open flame. In their bedrooms.*

About a week later, I looked up from my microwavable ravioli to see him studying something on the kitchen counter. It was a sky-blue lighter I had carelessly left out after grilling my left triceps like a campfire hot dog. That's what has to happen when you break four of the Ten Commandments in one night. (Technically, it was only three of 'em, but I broke them on the Sabbath; hence, the revised total.) And if you're curious about which Commandments, let me give you a few hints. I did not covet my neighbor's livestock. None of them even has any livestock, although the Jacksons do own a Great Dane that is about as big as a cow. And I made no graven images. I'm lousy with arts and crafts. It's amazing I didn't flunk out of Vacation Bible School every summer. So, you can probably figure things out from there.

Anyway, I knew then that the lighter had to go. Dad would think I was smoking pot, or maybe even cooking up a little meth or practicing to burn down the school.

Quick sidebar here: Lest you paint my dad as reactionary for suspecting his Kansas schoolboy of being involved with meth, let me explain something. Some people say we're behind the times here in the Kansas 'burbs, but we can cook up meth with the best of 'em. Tanya DuPree, who was one year ahead of me at Talbot, had amassed a five-figure meth-built empire before they raided the lab she had tucked away in a corner of her family's partially finished basement. She had told her parents it was a darkroom.

That cracked me up, because she wasn't taking photography and wasn't on the yearbook or school newspaper staffs. I don't think she even owned a camera, except the one on her cell phone.

But she could cook the meth. She was the Rachael Ray of meth.

The Tonya DuPree scandal had been, as *The Talbot Times* put it, "a wake-up call for suburban parents—and the entire community!" Just like Tyler Isaacson's suicide my freshman year was a wake-up call, and the fatal drunk-driving rollover accident my sophomore year was a wake-up call. I wonder why parents—and the entire community!—keep needing wake-up calls. They must be in the habit of falling asleep on the job.

At any rate, Tonya DuPree's saga, combined with my suspicious and careless behavior, was now turning my docile dad *back* into DEA Dad. I knew that if things didn't change, a confrontation was imminent. And somehow I could not see him being comforted by my explanation. I could imagine the scene:

Dad (waving government brochure titled, "Get High on Life, Not Meth," or maybe "Don't Let Your Life Go to Pot"): Griffin, is there something you want to tell me?

Griffin (arms held out, palms up in a supplicatory pose): Gosh, no, Dad. Is there a problem? Have I upset you in some way?

Dad (brow furrowed with concern): I guess I'll be blunt. Are you burning blunts, son? Have you gone the way of the Marley? Are you dancing with Mary Jane, as your friend Mr. Petty notes in one of his songs? Or, heaven forbid, are you mething with meth—excuse me, *messing* with meth? Goodness me, I'm so rattled that I can't even converse properly!

Griffin (with a dismissive wave of his hand): Let me set your mind at ease; I don't smoke pot at all. I hear it's bad for you. Not interested in it, really. And I will never, ever "meth" with meth.

I much prefer getting privately stupid-drunk in my bedroom, on at least a weekly basis. But that's not really germane to this conversation.

Dad (brow still yet to unfurrow): Point taken. But are you being truthful and candid with me about the smoking? Because I have detected the odor of smoke emanating from your room. And this particular odor . . . I know it's not cigarettes. I must confess that I don't know what cannabis smells like, per se, but . . .

Griffin (with a hearty chuckle): Oh, good golly gumdrops! *That's* what has you so concerned? Please, Dad, relax. You're going to laugh when I explain. That smell isn't me smoking—or cooking—an illegal substance; it's me burning my own flesh out of the crippling guilt for the awful things I have done and/or am about to do. You see, I'm unsure that you love me—unsure that even God loves me. I mean, why else could I get by with the heinous stuff I do on almost a daily basis? So *that's* why I need the pain and the marks on my skin. They're my assurance that I am not alone and abandoned in this big, cold world. I really didn't want you to catch on to my system, though. At least I *think* I didn't. That's why I used lighters, not matches; I felt the former would be less likely to arouse suspicion. But I guess I got careless. Anyway, I hope that all of this explains why you've noticed an aroma that was unfamiliar to you, silly. You've just never been around someone playing Grill Master with his own skin. So that's the scoop. I'm virtually drug free, unless you count all of the painkillers. But I don't *smoke* anything, not even cigarettes. Don't you feel a whole lot better now?

Dad (mopping his finally smooth brow): Son, I can't tell you what a relief this is. Thank you for reassuring me. You are such a good, good boy. And to think I was afraid you were dabbling with marijuana and so forth!

No, indeed, I could not risk my private system of Crime and Punishment crumbling right before Dad's narrow nose. I began to panic. The balance of my universe would be toppled unless I could think of a less telltale method. Soon.

Then I remembered the hair dryer, which I had affectionately dubbed the Hair Tornado 3000. I recalled the time I was drying Colby's hair before church and got distracted trying to recall which state contained Mesa Verde. Don't ask me why.

Suddenly, Colby yelped, "Griffin, what are you doing? You're gonna burn a hole in my head with that thing, dude. You gotta move it around, like Dad does. You can't just hold it in one place."

I mumbled some sort of apology, then ushered Colby out of the bathroom. I had time to give myself a nice sunburn-esque square on both upper thighs—shame on me for hurting my little brother—and still get to Sunday school five minutes early.

Thus, the Hair Tornado 3000 became my heat-spewing little friend. Snapping at Colby for interrupting a phone call with Amanda Mac? A light braising near a hip bone. Pre-punishment for an impending lie to dad about where I was going on a Saturday night? A blister-burn near the right armpit.

Sometimes fortune smiled on me and I didn't even need my punitive appliance. Like the time I went to Sonrise Books & Music to pick up the new Relient K CD and found myself lusting after the cover model on one of those "girl abstinence" books. Ironic or pathetic? You be the judge. But, man, you should *see* her. Leaving the store, I was deliberating whether this was a "bake" or "broil" offense when a gust of wind blew the car door shut on my hand. My pinky finger swelled to the size of a Jimmy Dean breakfast sausage, so I decided to call things even.

The combination of a more high-tech punitive method and

happy accidents, like the one at Sonrise, ensured that the wobbly scales of my moral self-worth stayed pretty much balanced. My thirst for validation through painful discipline was quenched. Don't do the crime if you can't do the time—under the Hair Tornado 3000. Pick a metaphor, any metaphor. As a bonus, I was saving God, my dad, and all other authority figures in my life the trouble of disciplining me. It was enough for me just knowing that they *wanted* to discipline me but trusted me to take care of the pesky details myself. It was proactive delegation, and all good leaders know how to proactively delegate.

I didn't need day-to-day authority, I decided—I just needed some privacy and a working electrical outlet. And one of the best things about the HT 3000 was that it left marks less suspicious than those of a flame—wounds that, if revealed by accident, could easily be passed off as a rash, a sunburn, or gnarly bug bite. Just before spring break of my senior year, Dad noticed a welt on the inside of my elbow and remarked, "That red mark looks painful, Griff. What happened?"

"Dodgeball," I said without thinking. "Cole nailed me real good."

"Would you like an ice pack for that?"

"Nah, Dad. It looks a lot worse than it feels."

He nodded and looked relieved. I walked away wondering how I got to be such an effortlessly good liar. I hadn't played dodgeball since junior high.

I drew my foot out of the pool. It didn't feel less swollen or less sore than it did before. But it was wetter, and that was something. I started to think about college and how I was going to manage to keep myself good and punished with the burden of a roommate. I had heard stories about The Weird Roommate. The roommate who sang show tunes in his sleep. The roommate who obsessively pulled out all of his body hair — and I do mean *all* of his body hair — by hand. I did not want to be that roommate.

Panic came over me like a fever. *What was I going to do?* It seemed that I would need to either stop sinning or stop punishing myself, and both prospects seemed equally dubious.

I looked at my upper left arm. It wasn't even red anymore. I swung my right arm out and then back toward my body, like a wrecking ball, smashing the palm side of my fist into the exact spot where Dad had struck his fateful blow. Have you ever tried to punch yourself in the arm? It's much harder than you might think. I swung again and again and again, all the while looking around nervously. This would be tough to explain: "Oh, hi there, Mr. Pool Maintenance Man. Boy, the mosquitoes around your indoor pool are certainly hearty; this one on my arm simply will not succumb! He's got an iron constitution."

After a while, my left shoulder was as red as a stop sign. Soon it would be deep purple, followed by the ever-attractive purple-turning-to-yellowish-green-under-ripe-banana-esque stage. Too bad I would already be alone in California before the metamorphosis was complete. Dad would miss out on the progress of his handiwork — or at least what he would *believe* was his handiwork. "Well," I whispered, rubbing my arm, "now, at last, I have a decent bruise. I guess if I want punishment that leaves a mark, I'm always going to have to do it myself. Nice try, though, Authority Figure. I know you did your best."

I stood up and shook my head. *Who was I talking to? Dad? God? My mother? Ted the Youth Pastor, perhaps? And was anybody really listening?*

It was close to midnight when Dad decided that he "must convene our quartet" in the room he had planned to share with Rhonda — in two separate double beds, of course. "Engagement does not give one license to fornicate," he had noted to me when explaining the "parameters and regulations relative to the trip" the night before we left.

Cole and I sat on the bed nearest the window. I was perched near the headboard, and he sat at the foot of the bed. Dad faced us in a hard-backed wooden chair near a desk, and Rhonda had just backed her way, like a punch-drunk boxer, onto a fake leather chair that Dad had pulled next to his.

It was quiet for a while, and I was thinking how much I was going to enjoy the proceedings. This was the kind of confrontation/intervention I liked: the kind where I wasn't the focus. I was wishing I had some popcorn to munch while I watched Dad rip into Cole and the Cliché — until I saw a tear slide down his face.

"I don't even know where to begin," my father said, his voice little more than a rasp, "but we all need to talk this out. We in this room have a long way to travel, figuratively and literally."

"Bryant," Rhonda said earnestly, "like I told you earlier, I am truly, truly sorry, and I ask you to forgive me. I know that I broke the code, and — "

My dad's head snapped to attention. I had to stop myself from whistling through my front teeth, because I knew what was coming: "It's not about a code, Rhonda. It's not about breaking rules and regulations. You *hurt* someone. You hurt me." He nodded in my direction. "And you hurt my son."

Rhonda bowed her head. "I'm sorry," she said again. I didn't want to, but I found myself tempted to believe her. She was clearly torn up—so torn that she hadn't spoken hip-hop for a full five minutes.

"I forgive you," my dad said. But he said it like he was reciting the Pledge of Allegiance. And how many people really think about, much less truly believe in, those words? To me it's more like The Pledge of Trying to Convince Everyone Around Me That I'm Patriotic. That was the vibe I was getting from B.T. Smith. He *wanted* to believe what he was saying, but it sounded like he was having a hard time convincing even himself. He sure wasn't convincing me. I wasn't sure what Rhonda was thinking. Further, I could put my hand on my heart and swear that I didn't know what I *wanted* her to think. And on TV they make this family drama stuff so solvable.

I heard Cole clear his throat. "May I say something, sir?"

Dad nodded.

"I want to say that I'm sorry too. I was a part of this whole mess, and I should have acted more maturely. I treated the whole thing like Rhonda was just another teenager, but in the back of my mind somewhere, I must have known that isn't true. I didn't think about you, sir. I didn't think about Griffin, either. I was selfish—too, uh, impulsive, I guess. I need to grow up."

Dad nodded again. I wanted to savor the expression that had crossed Rhonda's face when Cole compared her to just another one of his teenage hookups, but the atmosphere wasn't right for savoring.

Dad waited awhile, glancing at me a couple of times. But there was no way I was jumping into this pool. I'd rather jump into the kiddie pool at the Talbot rec center, and that thing has about a 23:77 urine to water ratio. It freaks me out every time Colby steps into it.

Seconds chugged by, and finally Dad stood and slid behind his chair, steadying his hands on it. "Well," he said, "perhaps we should call it a night, then."

"Wait," Rhonda said. "I don't want to call it a night when you're obviously still angry, Bryant."

Dad wagged his head slowly. "I am not angry."

"Well, you sure don't look happy." Rhonda's voice was quivery.

"I am hurt; I'll acknowledge that. But I am not mad at you." He looked at Cole. "I am not mad at anyone."

"But, Bry," Rhonda protested, "I'd rather have you mad than hurt! You can't just say you're not mad, then walk away and deem the problem solved. You and I have a *lot* to talk about. In private."

"When and how do you propose we do that?" I could sense irritation creeping into my dad's voice. I recognized that irritation, because usually I was the one causing it. "I am too spent to discuss this further tonight, and tomorrow the four of us will be in close quarters in the Durango again. So there you go."

Rhonda stared at the ceiling. If she was calling on God for wisdom, I hoped she was getting a busy signal—or maybe a recorded message from a nasal-voiced angel: "We're sorry, but due to a high volume of sin and resultant repentance, all heavenly circuits are busy. Please hang up and try your prayer again later."

"Well, hmmm," Rhonda began after a good solid minute of uneasy silence. "We were all planning to spend a day of fun in Denver, right? Hit Six Flags or something. Maybe Cole and Griff can still do that, and you and I can find someplace to have a nice long heart-to-heart. Decide what we're going to do about . . . about us. Is there even going to be an 'us' anymore?"

"That's not just for me to say."

"Well, crap, then, Bryant! We need to spend some time together tomorrow."

"So you expect Cole and Griff to just go off and do their own thing while we sort through this mess? I mean, I was looking forward to spending the day with my son. I can't just toss him aside, can I?"

I had to fight to keep myself from snorting and saying, "Are you *kidding* me, Dad?" I mean, the mere thought of having to see my father on rides like The Mind Eraser and the Vomit Comet had almost brought me to my knees in shame and dread. And I feared that every time a pack of girls in bikini tops and Daisy Dukes strolled by, he'd start quoting the Epistles to the Romans to me.

I began, for the first time in a month, to look forward to a day of diversion in Denver. Then, approximately eighteen seconds later, I realized that the roller coasters would have to roll and coast without me. Someone else would have to ogle the sun-baked Denver honeys. Someone else would have to cheer on the Rockies, for all the good it would probably do — unless that one good right-hander was on the mound.

I was going to Wheatland, Wyoming, instead. Mom had invited me as soon as she heard we would be heading in her general direction. She didn't invite Dad, citing the "inherent awkwardness and relational dynamics of the current and ex-loves all in the same place." At least she had gleaned something from my dad: a power vocabulary. Too bad she'd missed the lessons on How to Be a Good Parent/Spouse/Human Being.

My mom: Who else in the whole world could make me want to shake her, laugh in her face, and hug her—all at the same time?

I had to play her words five or six times in my head, just to make sure my brain had registered them correctly. *Inherent awkwardness and relational dynamics?* What about the relational dynamics between a sixteen-pound Brunswick meeting a vehicle door? What about the inherent awkwardness of smashing the family vehicle and running off with a hack writer, right in front of your kids, your soon-to-be ex-husband, God, the neighbors, and many of the neighbors' pets?

These were the kind of playful rhetorical questions I could ask my mom in person if I took a quick side-trip to Wyoming. And I could press her about where she got phrases like "inherent awkwardness" and "relational dynamics." "Surely not from any of Maxwell the Mediocre's novels," I would scoff. "As far as I can tell, the biggest words he knows are 'heaving' and 'bosom,' which usually appear together in his fine books."

I announced my intention to Cole when we left Dad and Rhonda, at about 12:30 a.m. "You don't mind, *do* you, Sharp?" I asked, accusingly. "I just really need some drive time—time to myself to think through all of this. And I really should go see my mom. It's been two years since she and Maxwell came through town on that book tour. And given that he's the worst writer in the history of the printed word, soon his publisher and the American reading public will catch on, and there will be no more Maxwell books—and, thus, no more book tours."

"I understand," Cole said, nodding. "Some of the other walk-ons called me about getting together in Broomfield, maybe working out or something. We might even head over to Boulder and tour the campus. Anyway, I can find plenty to do. So go."

We walked in silence back to our room. By the time I finished brushing and flossing, Cole was already in bed, his head like a hamburger patty between two pillows.

I clicked off the light and slid into my bed, the one nearest the door. I waited for that soft, wheezy snore that would mean Cole had fallen asleep. The guy can sleep anywhere, anytime. Once, he drove me to a doctor's appointment when Dad couldn't get away from work. I came back to the waiting room after the doc was done with me, and there was Cole—in a room full of coughing, sniffling people—sleeping peacefully with his open mouth tilted toward the ceiling, like he was trying to catch snowflakes on his tongue.

But I knew Cole wouldn't be dozing off so easily on this night. I could feel something in the silence. My dad would call it a pregnant silence, but I hate that term. When you're an almost-nineteen-year-old guy, *pregnant* is a scary word, in any context.

I thought about trying to fake-snore, so that Cole would think I had fallen asleep, and thereby absolve myself from any further discussion about our Fateful Night in Burlington (which sounded to me like a good title for a Maxwell the Mediocre novel). But I knew I'd be a lousy fake-snorer. I had done okay, so far, as a fake smart person, a fake athlete, and a fake Christian, but I knew I was pushing my luck on all counts.

"Griff?" Cole said finally, mercifully. I dreaded the impending conversation, but at least it had started; therefore, it could end.

"Yeah, what's up? You need a bedtime story?"

"C'mon, man, we really didn't get to finish *our* talk about what happened tonight. Rhonda kinda pulled me away. I know we all four had that really good talk your dad led, but I'm still wondering about me and you. I don't feel like the air is clear yet."

I sighed loudly. "Well, dude, this whole thing is a dead horse to me, but why not give it one more good beating."

"It's not dead to me. I don't feel like things are okay."

"Well, that's on you, then. You apologized. Apology noted. Now let's move on, okay?"

The room grew quiet again. I began to entertain the hope that now Cole *would* doze off.

Then it came. "Griff, you just said, 'Apology noted.' But does that mean you, like, forgive me?"

"Forgive you? Who am I—God?"

"Well, God says we are supposed to forgive each other. I remember that from when I used to go to your church. And your dad forgave Rhonda and me earlier tonight, before we all met in his room. He said that he was trying to forgive us, and that meant everything between us would be just as it had been before. It sounds too good to be true, though. But I hope it will be true."

"Well, my dad never says anything he doesn't mean."

"Yeah. Well, it was trippy to hear. I've heard a lot of people talk about forgiveness, but I never thought of it the way he put it. I didn't know if I'd ever be comfortable around him again. I'm still not sure. But he made me feel like I *can* be. Maybe."

"Well, you could try sucking up to him again—calling him 'sir' every five seconds like you've been doing the whole trip."

"I'm just trying to show respect."

"Here's a hint, Sharp: Next time you want to show respect for the man, try *not* macking on his fiancée."

"Griff, you're right. Look, I am sorry. I really am. And I know I'm lucky your dad has such . . . I don't know . . . such an easy way about him. But there was nothing easy about what he did. I could tell he was hurt. Angry, too. If my fiancée cheated on me, I would ground and pound the guy. It would be a bloodbath, no matter who it was. And the girl, she'd be kicked outta my life forever. No apologies. No second chances. I'm just saying it took a lot of strength for your dad to handle his business the way he did."

I yawned. "I guess I never thought about it that way. But thanks for saying that about my dad. Now can we please get some sleep?"

I heard him mutter something under his breath, and Cole is not a mutterer.

"Okay, what is it *now*? You wanna hold hands and sing 'Kum Ba Yah' or something? You picked the wrong guy to be your best friend."

"That's the thing that's still in the air, Griff. The best-friend thing. Am I still your best friend? That's the question."

"Yeah, sure, you're still my best friend. It's been almost nine years. One night's not gonna change all that. I gotta factor in how many times you've saved my butt. Remember Carlton Tucker's big brother when we were freshmen? Plus, you're the one who told Ally Long she should go out with me. I owe you big-time for that. I wouldn't be able to manage that kind of league-skimming without your endorsement."

"I guess so. But that's only half of what I am talking about. See, when I asked if I'm still your best friend, I think that was a question for *both* of us. So *you* might be sure, but *I'm* not sure, and that's what's killing me."

I had thought Cole's hooking up with Rhonda was going to be his biggest surprise of the night, but that comment came close.

"Huh?!" I said. Griffin the Articulate. William F. Buckley, bow down and worship at my Chuck Taylor–shod feet.

"It's like this, Griff." (I was so glad Cole was talking again, because other than saying "Huh?!" a few more times, I was tapped out.) "For a long time, I've held the title of your best friend, and that means a lot to me. But after tonight, I'm questioning myself. What kind of friend am I?"

I had never heard this kind of pain in Cole's voice — not even when he talked about his parents' split-up, which went down about a year before mine. I knew *that* hurt him, but there was always as much relief in his voice as there was pain. So I figured it was time to recapture my linguistic skills and prove what kind of a friend I was.

"Look, Sharp, we all make mistakes. Look at me: I'm a mess, and you know just how bad of a mess better than anyone but God himself. Yet you're still my friend, right?"

"I'm not saying you're perfect, Griff. But even with all of your problems, you'd never do dirt to me or my family like I did to you tonight. Tell me I'm wrong."

I wanted to say, "But what about my moodiness, my disrespect for adult authority, my private binge-drinking, and my cavalier misuse of prescription painkillers?" which Cole knew about (the whats but not the whys). "And what of my self-mutilation and constant fear over the imminent damnation of my soul?" which would have been revelations, even to my best friend. But I knew all of that would be off-point. I *wouldn't* betray Cole. Not for love, money, or even a game of naked racquetball with Janine Fasson. Un-be-freaking-lievable. I had finally stumbled upon one area in which I was stronger than Cole.

This revelation should have been good for me, made at least a small deposit in my paltry ego bank. Instead, it was terrifying. It was like being a weenie-armed pop star and learning that your massive bodyguard is soft and weak and slow—an even bigger wuss than you are. And that big gun he carries? It's made of Styrofoam.

I had just formed a good mental image of myself as a pathetic white-boy pop star—and it was not a pleasant image—when I was interrupted by the sound of Cole sniffling.

Oh, please, God in heaven, let it be allergies. Let it be these lumpy down-filled pillows. Cole Sharp cannot be crying in my room. No more emoting tonight, from anyone. I will have to rend my garments and fling myself off the balcony.

"I can tell by your silence, Griff, that you know I'm right—about our mutual loyalty and how maybe it's not so mutual."

"Hey, there are a lot of ways to be a good friend."

"Not in my book. There's only one way, and that's the kind of friend you've been to me. That's the kind of friend I want to be to you. That's what I'm shooting for from now on."

"Well, there's a lot we both can learn from each other. Can we please just let this go now? Everything's cool. Really."

"So you forgive me, then? The way your dad said?"

"Aw, crap . . ."

"I need to know. I need to hear it from you."

"I just can't give you that right now, Sharp. Because I just don't get you."

"What do you mean?"

"Ugh! I mean, why Rhonda? Why her? For that matter, why, oh, let's say 48 percent of the girls in the whole freakin' high school, not to mention those from rival schools? What exactly are you trying to prove? Listen to me: Women find you attractive, okay? You just stand in a room and it's like you're a glob of honey and females are ants. You've made your point. Now why don't you chill for a while? Give the girls a rest—unless you're in some kinda contest you haven't told me about. . . ."

"There's no contest, Griff."

"Then what is your major malfunction? What exactly are you looking for?"

A half minute of silence passed before Cole spoke again. "You really want to know what I'm looking for?"

"Yeah. Color me curious, my horndog friend."

"I'm looking for just one girl who looks at me the way Amanda Mac looks at you."

This was cheating on my best friend's part. Not the kind of cheating he just did with my dad's cliché but the kind of cheating that makes you feel even a little sorry for the last person in the world in need of pity.

"I've seen lots of girls look at you. And I've heard what they say, too. Good thing I have a strong stomach."

"You know it's not the same thing as you and Amanda."

"Correction: There *is* no me and Amanda."

"I'd like to ask *her* that. But anyway, dude, I am worked. I can barely stay awake. So, if you can't forgive me, can we at least have a truce?"

"Okay, all right. Truce. What-ever! I might even be able to forgive you, unless you keep talking to me like we're on Doctor Freaking Phil."

Cole laughed politely and was asleep within five minutes.

I, of course, was doomed to limp about Burlington in the early morning hours, contemplating the significance of all that had transpired, and make myself even more baffled about life than usual. What, exactly, had I just witnessed? The messy, awkward beginnings of forgiveness—forgiveness in the larvae stage? Or the obligatory, useless placing of the defibrillator paddles on the chest of a corpse? Was the Smith Family, Volume II, circling the drain—and taking my best friend with it?

At about 2 a.m., I decided to check the glove compartment of the Durango to see if any snacks might be lurking there. I found my dad, asleep in the front seat, which was reclined at a forty-five-degree angle. I tapped lightly on the side window. I saw his eyes flutter open. Then he lowered the window. "You okay, son?" he asked.

I had to laugh. "Well, Dad, I'm not the one sleeping in the parking lot, so all things considered, I'm pretty good. But what about you? Did you and Rhonda get into another fight or something?"

"No. Nothing like that. I hold no malice toward her—at least I don't think I do. I just couldn't get to sleep. I was tossing and turning, and my breathing was forced and too loud. I was driving myself crazy, so I can only imagine what I was doing to poor Rhonda. I told her I was taking a little walk, and I sort of wound up here."

"Dad, you can't sleep here. You've got a bad back."

"Actually, I was indeed sleeping, until you happened along."

"Well, I think it would be better for your back if you were to lie awake in a real bed rather than snooze in an SUV. Look, if you're afraid of keeping Rhonda up, you can go sleep in my room.

Cole's out cold, and believe me, you won't wake him. You could even do a little welding or maybe blacksmith yourself a set of Clydesdale horseshoes and he'd still be in dreamland."

"What about you, Griffin? Where will *you* sleep?"

I reached in and put my hand on his shoulder. "Dad, I'm not sleeping tonight. It's just been too trippy. I have way too much on my mind."

"Such as?"

"Such as, is this *really* all going to work out? Are things really going to be cool between you and Rhonda? Even between you and Cole?"

He smiled at me. "Son, forgiveness is a powerful thing." Uttered like lines from a play.

"No offense, but so is betrayal. So is infidelity."

He sat up. "And you're telling *me* this?!"

I thought of my mom and the bowling ball and how my dad must remember every time he walked through the living room and saw her reading one of Maxwell's crappy novels. I wondered if she ever read them in bed, while he was reading Lewis or Buechner or the Bible. Then I lowered my head. I was a worse son than Charles Manson. I bet even *he* wasn't this insensitive to his old man. Sure, there was the whole mass murder factor with the Chuckster and being crazy as a rabid warthog, but I bet Teen Chuckie never said anything as stupid and hurtful as what had just spilled out of my stupid mouth. I bet that when Teen Chuckie felt the urge to spew out some garbage to his father, he channeled that urge into something more productive, like marching up to his room, finding a rusty nail, and carving swastikas into his flesh.

Dad was pounding the heel of his left hand on the SUV door. "Griffin, my son, you've abandoned me *again*?"

I didn't bother to raise my head. "I'm sorry, Dad."

"Where *do* you go inside that head of yours?"

"It's complicated, Dad. Anyway, the thing is, I'm sorry for saying something so stupid, so insensitive."

"It's okay. Apology accepted. Now, if you're really serious about that bed next to Cole, I'm thinking I will take you up on that offer. My lumbar region is starting to tighten."

"Get on up there, Dad."

"But what about you? Is your insomnia truly that severe? You're going to be a wreck tomorrow. And you're our ace driver. Our road warrior."

I forced a smile. "That's why God created coffee. Keeps a guy going strong, you know."

"He created forgiveness first. And I hope that's what's going to keep me going strong. But Griffin . . ."

"Yeah, Dad?"

"Right now, I'd settle for just surviving. I need to tell you: I believe that I will get past the anger, but I don't know how I'll get over the hurt. It's strange: If I had cancer, I'd believe that God could cure me if he wanted to. I can picture myself sick, then cured. But right now, I can't picture myself not hurting."

I shook my head and felt myself smiling. I hoped Dad could tell it was a sad, sad smile. "Believe it or not, I can relate to that."

My dad nodded. "Well, maybe we can help each other, then. Maybe that's one reason God has placed us in each other's lives."

"Maybe. But he's also placed a whole bed up the stairs there. You need to get in it."

My dad gave me an unconvincing chuckle and spilled out of the Durango. I watched him Frankenstein his way up the stairs. A man in need of a chiropractor if ever there was one.

I felt myself shudder as a wall of unusually cold wind hit me. But the wind carried with it the smell of donuts in the making. Somewhere—I hoped in a small mom-and-pop shop, not some corporate entity like Donut World, Ltd. (a subsidiary of Fried Pastries International)—donut dough was frying.

Finding the source of the donuts, I decided, would be my quest in the couple of remaining predawn hours. The quest to understand what had happened to my family and my most important friendship, and the quest to understand the concept of forgiveness—those would have to wait. I was too tired and too immature for them. But I could find me some donuts. And just to prove that I had cracked at least the first few digits of the Forgiveness Code, I would buy donuts for everyone. Even Rhonda. She seemed like a sprinkles kind of woman to me.

"Okay, these are the Best. Donuts. Ever!" Rhonda announced. "Where in the world did you find them?"

"Don and Dawn's Donuts, just about half a mile or so up the road from the hotel," I said, my mouth half-full of my third or fourth yeast-raised glazed. "You should taste 'em when they're still hot. I never believed all that 'melt in your mouth' hype, but these things really do."

I turned to Cole, who was sharing the backseat with me. "You want another one?"

"Nah," he said. "Four is my limit."

When Rhonda finished her donut (white icing with pink sprinkles – told ya), I saw her slide her left arm over and place it on Dad's knee. He startled, then turned to her and flashed her a forced smile before fixing his eyes on I-70 again.

The scene took me back to another ride in the Durango, after the opening cross-country meet of my senior-year season. I had finished 38th in a field of 162, with a 5K time of 18:02. I was third among Talbot High runners. Chuck Francis, a senior like me, beat me by more than a minute. But he beat everybody else, too. No one was within ten seconds of him. Nicholas White beat me as well. He took third overall. And, as we have established, he was only a freshman. If I were to grab a thesaurus and really apply myself, I might be able to describe how bad it feels to get waxed by a freshman, but I'm not up to it right now. Maybe later. When I'm eighty-six and the shame has subsided. Somewhat.

Dad was driving home from the meet. I had wanted to ride the bus with the rest of the team, especially because Janine Fasson (remember her?) was out for cross-country for the first time. But Dad had said, "Rhonda and I have a few things we'd like to share with you, and the ride home will give us ample opportunity to do so."

Once we were on the road, Rhonda had twisted around in the passenger seat and handed a large Styrofoam cup to me. Vanilla shake comin' at ya, dawg," she said. "That was a fierce race today. I think you ran pretty well. How the wheels feelin'?"

My kingdom for a snappy retort, I thought sadly.

"Uh, you know, pretty good," I said.

"Dude, that little freshman on your team is smokin'! I can't believe he's only fourteen!"

I felt my head swinging like a pendulum. "I can't believe it either."

I saw Rhonda turn around and nudge my dad with her elbow.

"Ahem," Dad said. (In case you're wondering, he actually says "ahem" when he clears his throat. And in case you're still wondering, yes, this troubles me deeply.) "Griffin, today you embarked on the beginning of what we all hope will be a rewarding cross-country season."

I sat in the backseat wondering if I had ever heard anyone else's dad use the word "embark." I was drawing a blank.

"Griffin?" my dad said.

"Yeah?" I mumbled.

"You with us?"

"I'm right back here, Dad. Not going anywhere." *Just waiting on the fatherly analogy that I know will be forthcoming.*

"Oh. I wasn't sure you were paying attention."

I put my shake in the cup holder, sat up straight, and folded my hands in my lap like a kindergartner. I doubted Dad could see that, but I wasn't doing it for him—I was doing it for me.

"Any-hoo," he began again, slowly, "we were talking about beginnings."

I nodded. "Yes. We were."

He sighed the Dad-sigh, which is okay when you're in your mid forties and a dad. "You will experience many exciting beginnings this year. In fact, you have already begun to experience some, like today. Rhonda and I have been talking about beginnings as well, after establishing something of an identity as a serious, committed couple over the past several months. You see, Griffin, life can bring new things, even to someone as old as I."

I stared at the roof of the Durango. Colby had poked a hole in the upholstery, probably with one of his supposedly blunt-tipped arrows. "Dad, are you and Rhonda engaged or what?"

Rhonda giggled and squeezed my dad's knee. He glanced in the rearview mirror, no doubt trying to gauge my facial expression. "You have always been perceptive, Griffin."

Rhonda twisted herself around in the seat again and smiled at me. I tried to force a response smile. I think all I could muster was a grimace. *If you think I'm gonna congratulate you, you annoying rebound chick,* I thought, *you are crazy—oh, excuse me—I mean wack! I'm not endorsing this debacle.*

Five seconds later, the words tumbled out: "Congratulations, Rhonda," I said. "You too, Dad. Way to go. I hope and pray that you'll both be truly happy."

I held my straw like a cigarette and vacuumed the last bit of milk shake into my mouth. I wanted to finish my tasty beverage before God flung the lightning bolt down from the heavens to french-fry my lying carcass. I wondered what kind of mess I would make on the seat cover.

Hope and pray that my dad and his cliché will be truly happy? That's a lie on par with Cain, another traitor to his own kin:

God: "Cain, where is your brother Abel?"

Cain: "I don't know. Am I my brother's keeper?"

I'd like to think I'd have done better if God, not my dad, cornered Griffin the Self-Centered somewhere in the Garden of Kansas. But I know I wouldn't do *much* better.

God: Your heartbroken father has found love again. Are you truly happy for him?

Griffin: No.

God: At least you're honest, for a change. Selfish, but honest. What *would* make you truly happy?

Griffin: Hmmm. Let's see. First of all, how about Cheyenne Vista turns the swimming pool into a skate park so Rhonda has to wear clothes during the summer? And I would love it if *Entertainment Weekly* and *USA Today* gave Maxwell the Mediocre an F-minus review of his next book, resulting in his banishment from ever writing anything more extensive than a grocery list. Then all his books would be remaindered. Then *he himself* would be remaindered. Additionally, it wouldn't be the worst thing in the world if Ex-Mom could send me birthday greetings at least in the correct month. And no cards with ducks or fishing equipment or deer on them, please. Who does she think I am — Davy Crockett? Finally, I hope that when Colby starts school, he won't get teased too badly for being named after a type of cheese. *Way to go, Lynnette Smith. Why didn't you just name your little boy Wisconsin Sharp Cheddar?*

Okay, I know I already said, "Finally," but I just thought of one more thing. Cole and I do the same ab workouts: captain's chair, leg raises, reverse sit-ups, the whole regimen. And we both do old-school sit-ups like crazy—sometimes together. In our living room, we lie side by side, toes stuffed under our big ugly copper-colored couch, hands interlaced behind our heads. We rip off a hundred reps at a time. Three sets of full range-of-motion, gut-busting sit-ups; none of that barely-lift-your-head-off-the-ground celebrity personal trainer crunch garbage. So how come he has an Abercrombie & Fitch-model six-pack you could play the xylophone on, while I remain a skinny guy who sure can do a lot of sit-ups? The only ripples in my lower-torso region are my ribs.

God: Are you sure that completes your list, my son?

Griffin (after several moments of deep thought): Well, I suppose I would like to see an end to war and world hunger. AIDS and poverty and child abuse, too. Guess I should have led off with this one.

About an hour from Denver, Rhonda asked Dad if she could drive. I sat in the backseat sending him a telepathic message: *No. No. No. No. No. No way. Rhonda no drive. Rhonda bad driver. Rhonda get distracted by squirrels and billboards for Stuckey's. She loves those double entendres, like "Comfort. Food." and "Rest. Stop."* Dad eased the Durango onto the shoulder. "Okay, copilot," he announced, "time for you to take over."

Way to go Obi-Wan, I scolded myself. *The old Jedi mind tricks are working as well as ever.*

I thought about offering to drive again, but I was in that hazy world between consciousness and unconsciousness, and I decided we all would be safer—albeit only marginally safer—with Rhonda behind the wheel.

Then I saw Rhonda stabbing her forefinger at the Eject button on the CD player. "Wait till you all hear this new artist, Ian Lawson Pope," she gushed. "Or ILP, as we Ian-ites like to call him. He's got the voice of Placido Domingo, yet with a youthful, hip-hop vibe."

The whole concept sounded to me like the aural equivalent of some freaky mythological character that Hercules might have been forced to battle: MC Placido Doggy-Dogg-Killah, with the head of a Viking, the body of an ostrich, and the tail of a crocodile.

I closed my eyes and pictured Amanda Mac and willed myself to fall asleep quickly and dream about her. Most all of my dreams are about being chased through quicksand by a pack of cannibalistic children or falling to a crushing death—lately from French monuments such as the Eiffel Tower and the L'arc de Triomphe. But a guy can dream about having better dreams, can't he?

The last thing I heard before I tumbled into sleep was someone singing Italian, over someone else doing that beatbox thing with his mouth. I hoped that if Rhonda crossed the median and crashed head-on with a truck, I would awaken before impact so that my own pre-death screams, not ILP, would be the last thing echoing in my ears.

I woke up when I noticed that the Durango was crawling along at funeral-procession pace. I blinked, then stared at my watch. Only thirty minutes of rest. It wasn't nearly enough. "What's up, Rhonda?" I yawned. "We hit some construction?"

"I don't know, dude, but this is some kinda fierce traffic jam. I hope it's not too long."

I studied the road ahead. I couldn't see any flashing lights or traffic cones—just a long line of vehicles snaking along at about ten to fifteen miles an hour.

I saw Dad shrug to life in the passenger seat. He rubbed his temples with his middle fingers—he calls it his brain massage—and craned his neck forward. "I can't tell what's causing this delay, but I hope we're past it soon. It could severely truncate our downtime in Denver."

"Truncate?" Rhonda said.

What's wrong, Rhonda? You no speaka PBS? You better get your thesaurus on, girlfriend!

"Well, I suppose that *truncate* is a rather arcane word," Dad began, and I was begging for Rhonda to query, "Arcane?" when Dad ruined the whole thing by saying, "Uh-oh. Uh-uh-ohhhh. I see what the problem is."

I mashed my head against the side window, but I couldn't see anything except the back of a yellow Hummer. "What is it, Dad? Is it a wreck?"

"No," he said slowly, "it looks like a family up ahead is having some sort of trouble. Possibly broken down. Odd that no one is pulling over to help them. I see a young boy, and he appears to be quite upset."

"Dad," I pleaded, "I don't want to sound unchristian or anything, but couldn't we please, please let another carload of

Pretty-Good Samaritans come to the rescue this time?"

"You are right, Griffin. You do sound unchristian."

I slung myself against the seat back, just the way Colby does. "Okay, then, Dad, by all means, let's stop. After all, it worked out *so* well yesterday. Cole and I are lucky we didn't end up in the hospital."

"Not really," Cole helpfully pointed out. "Those guys were pretty weak."

I glared at him. He shrugged at me.

"Pull over," Dad instructed Rhonda, turning around and shooting a disappointed look at me. "This does not look good."

Rhonda coaxed the Durango onto the shoulder. We pulled behind a blue Accord. I rolled down my window and poked my head out to assess the situation. A kid about Colby's age was standing behind the car crying and trying to pull away from a bear-sized bald man in a Pittsburgh Steelers jersey. Number 75, old-school—Mean Joe Green's number. I liked the guy instantly.

"You can't go out there," Steeler Dad said. "It's too dangerous. Too many cars rolling by."

"But Daddy," the kid wailed, "I want Discus back!"

"We'll get him back, I'm sure," Steeler Dad answered. "We just need to be patient."

I slid out of my seat and scanned the highway. A butterscotch pup about the size of a bread loaf stood whimpering on the far shoulder of eastbound I-70, four lanes of traffic and a large grassy median away.

Cole was by my side now. "Your dad's right," he whispered. "I don't like the looks of this. A lot of traffic between that kid and his pup."

Dad was out now too. "Anything we can do to help?" he asked, raising his voice to compete with the rumble of a passing semi.

Steeler Dad rubbed his unshaven cheeks with the pads of his fingers. "I dunno. My kid, Casey here, his little dog—we stopped to let him take care of his business, ya know, and before I could get a leash on him, he bolts off after a butterfly or something. We been sittin' here for ten minutes, waiting for a break in traffic so I can go fetch the dumb mutt."

"He's not dumb!" Casey protested. "He's a good dog, and I don't want him to get hurt!"

"That's why we gotta be patient," Steeler Dad said impatiently. "You just can't be sure all these people are gonna stop, Casey. And I don't wanna get hit by a car, even if it's not going that fast.

I studied the westbound lanes. A pack of cars was creeping toward us, doing about twenty-five miles an hour, but behind them there was a quarter-mile gap.

When the pack had drifted by, I caught my dad's eye. "Median," I shouted, letting him know that I was going to sprint to the divide between the west- and east-bound lanes, then wait for a chance to get the rest of the way to the dog.

But Dad was already moving. He scuttled to the median, using short, choppy strides. I hadn't seen him move that fast since he dodged a clock radio Mom hurled at him during one of the last battle royals before they called in the heavy artillery: the lawyers.

Standing in the middle of the median, Dad turned around and bent over, propping his hands on his knees. I watched him panting, and all I could think was, *Without the regular challenge of dodging Mom's projectiles, the old boy has lost a step*. Another inappropriate thought at an inappropriate time. If I had a dollar for every one of them, I'd be richer than Oprah.

"Halfway there!" I heard Dad gasp. He seemed to be talking

to Casey more than anyone else. "The traffic is starting to thin now. After this next group of cars passes by, I'll be over to Discus. Just a little bit longer."

One of the cars honked at Dad as it passed by. He waved as if the honk were to say "Good luck in whatever endeavor has brought you to the median of a busy interstate." But this was a long, annoyed honk that was more along the lines of, "You are a stupid, stupid man. Probably a drug addict. I hope whatever folly has brought you to this dangerous place gets you mangled by a speeding automobile. Just not mine. I can do without the gore on my car and the insurance hassles."

"Heckuva nice old man you got there," Steeler Dad observed. "Gutsy, too. Not many guys would do a thing like this for a total stranger's pooch."

I nodded and watched a Peterbilt semi roar by. Then eastbound I-70 was clear.

"Oh, Discus!" Casey cried. "Please don't get hurt!"

In the momentary calm, Discus apparently heard Casey's voice. The fat little dog began trotting across the highway.

"That's it, Discus," my dad called out. "Keep comin' this way. C'mon, boy."

I could see a dot of a car in the distance coming toward us from the west. "It's okay," I heard myself assuring Casey. "Discus has plenty of time to get to my dad."

Dad must have seen the approaching car too, because his calls to the dog grew more frantic. And he started slapping his thin thighs like they were bongo drums. As the dog approached, Dad lowered himself into a baseball catcher's crouch and held his hands toward Discus. The vehicle was bearing down on them now, a Montero maybe or some other kind of suburban assault vehicle, like ours.

Discus was maybe a yard from my dad when he slowed to a tentative walk. "Discus!" I heard Steeler Dad boom. "For the love-a Franco Harris, get movin'!"

The dog's head snapped to attention. Then he darted past Dad's outstretched hands, loped across the median, and headed toward us.

The westbound car that hit Discus was moving so fast that I didn't get a clear look at it. It was one of those low-to-the-ground, wedge-shaped numbers. A Firebird, Cole would guess later.

Whatever it was, one of its tires cut the puppy in half. In the middle of the near westbound lane, I could see a glistening string of pink intestines between the front and back ends of the dog. Casey started screaming. His dad covered his son's eyes with one of his oven-mitt hands and guided him toward the backseat of their car. "Keep your head down, son," Casey's father said. "Don't you look at the road for nothin'." The voice was shaky.

I looked to the median. Dad was muttering to himself, which worried me. Like Cole, he isn't much of a mutterer. Then he started walking back across the highway. Walking. He made it across the far westbound lane, waited for a honking van to shoot by in the near lane, and then resumed walking.

I felt panic inflating like a balloon in my stomach. A string of cars was bearing toward him. My panic balloon popped when my dad stopped and knelt by the dog.

"Dad!" I heard terror in my voice. "Cars!" Then, like an idiot, I pointed.

He stood up, and I tried to calculate the ever-shrinking distance between my father and involuntary vehicular manslaughter. If he started moving again — now! — he would be okay.

"Whoa," I heard Cole say as Dad turned to face the oncoming

cars and raised his arms, palms out, toward them like he was Yoda or something.

The lead car began clicking its headlights on and off. Another driver mashed his horn. Neither vehicle appeared to be slowing down much.

And still my apparently shell-shocked father stood there, doing the Yoda. I looked to Cole. "Let's go grab him!" I shouted. "Something's wrong with him!"

"No," my dad commanded. "Stay put, boys!"

The lead car slowed and angled toward the median. The woman in the passenger seat lowered her window and started screaming something at my dad. I wasn't catching all of it, but if you've ever heard a George Carlin routine, you'd be familiar with the vernacular. She could scream all she wanted, as far as I was concerned. Her car was on the shoulder between the median and the far westbound lane, and my dad was no longer in her kill path.

It was the next car that was going to get him—in about eight seconds, I guessed.

Dad must have sensed that the Force was not with him, because he lunged toward me and Cole just before impact. The car lurched to its left and hit its brakes. The squeal of rubber on pavement made me cringe.

Once the driver was past us, he slowed down and pulled over to the right shoulder, about a football field ahead of us. Two guys, smaller than Steeler Dad but bigger than my dad, popped out of the car and started toward us, shouting. They must have heard a Carlin routine or two as well.

Cole started walking toward them. I saw him slide off his sports watch and tuck it into his front pocket. I heard him call out something to them. I heard the words "puppy" and "killed."

The two guys looked at each other, nodded, and headed back to their vehicle.

Dad, meanwhile, was tapping on the rear window of Steeler Dad's car. I saw the window come down, and my Dad handed something to Casey, who was tucked into a tight, sobbing ball on his father's lap.

Then Dad came back to the Durango and slapped the hood with the flat of his hand. "Everybody inside. Now. I'm driving."

"Shotgun," Cole said.

Squaring himself behind the steering wheel, Dad bowed his head. "A moment of silent prayer for that poor family," he said softly. "I hope it's at least a small consolation to Casey that I was able to retrieve Discus's collar for him. This way, the boy will have something to remember his dog by. A boy needs that."

Before I closed my eyes to pray, I turned to Rhonda, then nodded in Dad's direction.

"That street enough for you? That brave enough for you?" I whispered accusingly.

We ate lunch once we were inside Denver's city limits, then discussed strategy for the remainder of the day. I would drop Dad and Rhonda off near the 16th Street Mall, where they could eat, talk, shop, kiss, and generally do whatever adults do to mend injured relationships. It's so much easier for us teenagers. We just break up and move on to the next person.

Cole had already used his cell to arrange for a pack of fellow Buff football hopefuls to hang with him. I was going to drop him off at the Omni, a conference center in nearby Broomfield, where an assistant coach and a few alums would speak before an informal workout and probably an even more informal party. Meanwhile, I would take the Durango to Wheatland, spend a few uncomfortable yet important hours with Mom, then return by mid-evening. I also promised Dad that I would do my best not to be disrespectful to Maxwell the Mediocre by doing such things as referring to him as Maxwell the Mediocre.

When I returned, we would put in a few more hours of driving before stopping for the night. And if everyone was simply emotionally and/or physically exhausted, we would stay in Denver and get an early start the following morning.

I deposited Dad and Rhonda at a smoothie place, and before I drove away, Rhonda leaned into the SUV and gave me this look that said, "I'm about to have a brief Very Special Episode of Your Favorite Sitcom chat with you."

"Griff?" she said somberly.

"Yes?" I answered, mimicking exactly the tone of her voice.

She closed her eyes for a moment, probably begging God for the self-restraint to resist strangling me, then continued. "I want to tell you again that I am sorry about last night. I will make this right, to you and your dad. I promise."

"Uh, okay?" I said, narrowing my eyes at her. I hoped I looked like a cop from any of the twenty-eight versions of *Law & Order*. (Mine would be called "Law & Order: Amoral Hoochies Face Justice.") I could almost feel Rhonda's insides squirming. She took a step back from the Durango.

"Look, I know this must be hell for you. The divorce. Your dad and me. The current problem between your dad and me. You and Cole. I can't even begin to understand what all of this is doing to you. It breaks my heart. And now you're going to visit your mom, her new husband, and their son. He's about your age, right?"

"Right." *And I bet Mom gets him* his *birthday cards on time. Just a hunch.*

"Well, like I said, it's gotta be hell. And I want you to know I'm keeping you in prayer."

"Thanks." I didn't mean for my "Thanks" to sound sincere, but it did.

Usually, you see, this kind of offer doesn't evoke warm feelings in me, because, as I learned during our little family drama, "keep you in prayer" means "keep you at a safe distance from me, in hopes that whatever bad juju is plaguing your life won't rub off on me."

That's how it was after the big old Smith affair/divorce scandal flew into the proverbial fan. Many of my fellow students at Talbot told me they'd keep me in prayer. So did a couple of the faculty members, including Mr. Ross. And I know he's pious, because the back bumper of his Taurus depicts a Jesus fish swallowing that little Darwin critter.

It was the same at youth group. Lots of my peers told me they'd keep me in prayer and even go through the effort of "lifting me up in prayer." That can't be easy. I'm a solid buck-fifty, and some of them don't look very strong. But while I seemed to have lots of prayer partners, not many people wanted to sit by me—not during snack time, wacky youth group game time, nor even segregated watching of the abstinence DVD series time. I felt like I had a disease: Bird Flu on a bed of Leprosy with a side of SARS. Yes, there's nothing like being a child of divorce in an institution whose nickname is The Family-Friendly Church.

Amanda Mac was different, of course. The sound of bowling ball against SUV door was practically still ringing in my ears when she appeared on our porch crying.

She came in and hugged me fiercely and asked me to tell her how I was doing, how I was feeling. I spent about an hour telling her that I basically had no clue. I think I said something about playing a football game and taking a linebacker's helmet-first hit to the gut, so hard that you can't speak, can't see straight, can't even breathe. Then the linebacker takes off the old helmet, and you realize that the linebacker is your mom.

Then I realized what a bad analogy this was, given that Amanda Mac doesn't like football. (That's about her only fault, by the way. That, and simply being such a good person that I shouldn't even be breathing the same air she does. It makes me feel guilty, unworthy.)

Eventually, her cell phone went off—who else but Amanda would have "Love Broke Thru" as a ring tone?—and she excused herself with much apologizing. Before she left, she hugged me again and said, "I wish I could have done something besides sit here and cry for you for over an hour."

And I wanted so bad to tell her that what she had done was enough. Way, way past enough. But I know I would have crumbled like Jericho's walls about two words in. So instead, I waited till she was gone, then e-mailed her what I lacked the courage to tell her in person. Before I hit SEND, I sat there staring at my words, thinking they were the most honest words I had ever communicated to a girl.

Amanda wrote me back and said, "Thank you for being real with me. And know I will always be here for you."

The next half-dozen times we talked, Amanda made a point of saying that she would keep praying for me. She would wedge that into a conversation, whether it fit or not:

Griffin: You should have seen the game Sal Ernst had against the Shawnee Mission West jayvees last Friday. He's gotta be one of the hardest-hitting defensive linemen in the state. Too bad he's such a thug. But I bet he'll be the MVP of the Leavenworth Prison football team someday. I just hope he doesn't fashion his trophy into a shiv.

Amanda Mac: Griff, you know I'm still praying for you, right?

Griffin: Um . . . okay. Thanks. Cool.

There was one post-family-disintegration week that was particularly tough: Thanksgiving week, the week of Colby's birthday. At youth group the preceding Sunday night, I tried to ask for prayer for Colby, and I almost lost it.

The next day, I saw Zeke, Amanda's ten-year-old brother, hanging out at the high school, waiting on his sister. "Hey, Griffin," he said, "my sister prayed for your brother last night—and you, too."

I nodded at him. "That's cool. Tell her thanks for me, okay?"

He kind of cocked his head at me. "Um, I don't think you get it. She prayed for you guys last night—all night. She looked like a zombie this morning, and she kinda got in trouble from my parents. She never gets in trouble, so I thought she would freak. But she didn't seem to mind too much."

I stood there staring at Zeke. I couldn't tell if he was proud of his sister, or incredulous that she had spent a whole night on me. Colby was worth it, for sure. But me?

"Your sister," I told him, "is something else."

He nodded, then leaned toward me. "Know what else?"

I widened my eyes, trying to spur the boy along.

"Sometimes she steals those little paper cutout things from your locker—the ones that say stuff like Run Down the Rebels or Smoke 'em, Griffin. She tapes them on her bedroom walls and stuff. But don't tell her I told you this, okay? It would embarrass her."

I nodded at Zeke. *Well,* I thought, *now* that's *an interesting development.* Occasionally, I wondered what happened to those little construction-paper works of art fashioned by the Pep Club and taped to lockers before a big meet. Chuck Francis let them gather like moss on his locker. Cole sometimes lined his into rows, with military precision. I figured Carlton was pulling them off my locker, as revenge for being the victim of my occasional rapier wit.

I left Zeke waiting for his sister alone. It would be weird for me to hang around now. I didn't trust my restraint to keep from grinning like a butcher's dog when I saw her.

I was halfway to my car when my internal Jerk Alarm started to go off. *What?* I asked myself defensively. *What did I do* this *time? Is there something wrong with enjoying the fact that Ms. Mac is intrigued enough by me to commit petty theft and place little reminders of me around her bedroom—perhaps even upon her headboard?*

Oh, I know what you're thinking, I accused myself. *Amanda stays up all night praying to God, praying for him to comfort you and your little bro because you're hurting. She becomes so caught up in pleading with the Almighty on your behalf that she loses track of time. She even evokes the wrath of her parents. Some people say they'll keep you in prayer just to keep you away, but Amanda keeps you in prayer, close to her heart—all night long. But that's not what makes an impression on you, is it? It's the teen-crush, MTV-reality-show stuff. You, Griffin Smith, are shallower than your little brother's old inflatable wading pool.*

As I zoomed the Durango across the Colorado/Wyoming border—at a brisk eighty-eight miles per hour—Amanda occupied every thought, every emotion. I recalled how she stuck to me like gum on my shoe after the Great Smith Split. And gum on your shoe is not always a good thing. It's dependable, oddly comforting, but it gets annoying after a while. I needed to be alone a lot of the time, but it was hard to tell her that. She was worried about me. I think she was afraid I was a suicide risk. Silly girl. No need to go to that extreme, not as long as there was alcohol and narcotic painkillers. (It's crazy—write a couple of school-newspaper features about the athletic prowess of Sal Ernst and the guy will procure practically anything for you.)

It was a good thing Sal loved my writing so much—or at least my writing when it was about him—because once the divorce became final, I dramatically increased my RDA of brain-anesthetizing substances. There were times I couldn't even walk from my bedroom desk to my bed. Not without falling and worrying Colby or my dad, anyway. It wasn't uncommon for me to be emoting drunkenly in one of my journals late at night, then wake up with my head on my desk and a cramp in my neck.

My dad even came in and saw me like that once. "Goodness, son," he said, his voice as warm as a summer breeze, "did you fall asleep studying? You need to give yourself a break sometimes, you know? Have a little fun. Cut loose, at least a bit. You can't have your nose in a book all the time. I mean, I do admire your academic passion, but—"

"Okay, Dad," I said, relieved that I wasn't slurring my words. "I'll try to cut loose. Just a little."

Sometimes Amanda would call me late at night. If I was level, we would talk almost all night. If I was wasted, however, I would have to feign being overcome by the emotion of it all and thereby unable to speak.

I wasn't sure which transgression made me feel guiltier—duping Amanda or duping my dad. But I made sure I paid for what I did to both of them.

Early in my senior year, though, the Hair Tornado 3000 started making a funny noise, as if something were caught in its motor. I panicked. Given the improved technology and stricter safety regulations, I doubted that any device as absurdly dangerous as the HT 3000 was still in production. But I tinkered with it one night, shaking it and poking a toothpick into the screen-covered vent opposite the business end. I turned it on, and voila, the noise was gone. The HT 3000 was as good as new. I couldn't recall any sins from that particular day, and much to my surprise, my foreseeable social calendar didn't call for any burnable offenses. Ally Long was grounded for two weeks. Let this be a lesson to you budding young substance abusers out there: Don't leave your pot where the family Pekingese can find it. And with cross-country meets and practice, the school newspaper, and slightly-better-than-sporadic church and youth group attendance, how was a guy supposed to fit in any quality sin time?

Still, it seemed a shame to have fixed the HT 3000 for nothing, so I aimed its shotgun-like barrel at my left wrist. I had been feeling a familiar melancholy—the one that came with it being late September, eight days after my birthday to be exact, and hearing nothing from my mom.

But soon the melancholy had been firmly ushered out by the pain across my wrist. It was a Eureka Moment: When I wanted to feel something other than sadness, regret, guilt, or any of the other of my frequent companions, the solution was as close as my own bathroom. Yes, burning via the HT 3000—it wasn't just for punishment anymore.

You see, sometimes feeling physical pain is better than feeling depressed or hopeless. And even when it wasn't better, at least it was different. And sometimes that's enough—feeling something different from the stuff that has become as familiar and confining as a lifer's prison cell.

Naturally, there was a big problem with this new development: If one inflicts physical pain on oneself to escape from the emotional pain, is the self-inflicted physical pain a sin? And if it is, is it appropriate to punish oneself by inflicting even *more* physical harm? By the time Christmas break rolled around, this hamster wheel became so tiring and dizzying and confusing that I almost retired the Hair Tornado 3000 forever. I thought about ceasing with the lying and covert transgressions, too. The whole thing had simply become inconvenient, painful, and exhausting.

My dad sometimes calls lying "the easy way out." He is right most of the time, but he's wrong on this one. There's nothing easy about lying. If you tell the truth, you don't have to possess a good memory. But if you lie, you must remember the lie—and the lie you had to tell to cover your butt when someone called you on the first lie. And so it goes. My façade was threadbare.

I was so desperate that I resolved to at least start being honest in conversations with people I cared about.

After we finished our first-quarter exams, Amanda and I met for coffee at the Big Bear. I had taken only a couple sips of my double-shot café mocha when she tried to get me to participate in this game she invented. It's called Five Minutes of Truth. Three hundred seconds of conversation, and you must answer every question honestly. You must feign neither emotion nor reaction. I looked into her earnest eyes and thought about the welt on my wrist, the chemicals in my sock drawer, the amorous mayhem that was likely to be wrought when Ally Long was freed from her destructive-lifestyle-cramping bonds. Then I let myself feel the burning resentment in my heart for my mom, Rhonda the cliché, Maxwell the Mediocre, and the punk who had cut in front of me on the way to school that morning. I wondered what kind of combustible materials I was storing inside.

Start being honest in conversations with people you care about? I chided myself. *My dear boy, what* were *you thinking when you made that resolution?* Then I told Amanda that I thought it was strange that she wanted to turn the vital concept of Truth into a game. She studied me for a moment. "Fair point," she said. "I'll give what you've just said some thought."

The words "Don't bother; it's all a bunch of smoke" lunged against their chains, desperate to break free. But I yanked them back. *Down, boys,* I commanded. *We can't have the love of my life discovering that my intriguing little speech about Truth was a complete lie. That would be one too many ironies in the fire.*

Cheyenne comes up pretty quickly once you nudge your way into Wyoming. I thought about stopping there, as the need to recaffeinate my system was growing stronger. What I needed even more than coffee, though, was something to erase the regret of not sharing Five Minutes of Truth with Amanda—not at quarter break, not during Christmas vacation, not after finals, not ever. After a while, she quit asking. And lately, I hadn't even shared many minutes of Superficial Banter with Amanda. (To be fair, the Superficial Banter was always mine. The pleas to "Please stop it already with the Superficial Banter" were hers.) I estimated that over the past few weeks, I'd conversed more with Rhonda than with Amanda. "That figures, I guess," I muttered. "Rhonda is a complete poser, just like you."

Then something hit me. When Rhonda had told me earlier that day she was praying for me, she sounded a lot like how Amanda had sounded after my mom and dad's marriage went into cardiac arrest. I didn't want to admit this haunting similarity, but I like to keep my daily self-delusions in the high- to mid-teens, and I was already well over quota.

I stopped at one of those convenience marts just north of

Cheyenne, finally succumbing to the orange "Empty" light that had been lit up for the past fifteen minutes. I filled up the tank, then went inside in quest of coffee, as I was so tired that I was tempted to play one of Rhonda's freak-of-musical-nature artists just to disturb me so much that I would stay awake.

I stood staring at a row of spigots, each topped with a homemade flavor tag. Mocha Java. Sweet Turtle. Midnight Frost. African Queen. Grasshopper Mint. *Mega* Mocha Java. Sweet Turtle Lite. Turbo Midnight Frost. African Queen Decaf. Grasshopper Mint Lo-Fat. "Ah, for the love of Juan Valdez," I muttered. "I'm too tired to make any decisions."

Dad speaks wistfully of bygone days when there was only one hot beverage for people on the go: coffee. And only one flavor: coffee. But here I was, at this pitiful roadside Gas & Sip or Pump & Go or whatever it was called, facing no less than a dozen different coffee-related variations.

Disgusted, I pivoted and went to the cooler. There was more than one way to give myself the heart palpitations, ringing in the ears, and beer-coaster-wide eyes that I would need to get me to my destination: *Just give me some stinkin' Red Bull, and I'll be on my way. But wait—what was this? Yes, there is Mr. Red Bull, in all of his liquid-lollipop glory. But he's not alone. He's not the only refrigerated legal neurostimulant in town anymore. Now we also have a plethora (that's for you, Mr. Ross) of oversized cans: Blue Oxen, Orange Yak, Has-Been Rock Star, Liquid Lava. (Isn't lava, by definition, liquid? Okay,* that *energy drink is out of the running.)*

Ultimately, I picked the smallest can, noting the calculation first completed by Galileo—or maybe it was Einstein or perhaps Nina Majors' big brother when he was really drunk at his nineteenth birthday party: The sum of the amount of stimulant beverage one can consume on a given journey must be divided by the coefficient of the extra urination stops rendered necessary by said beverage. If not careful, one can actually tip the delicate bladder balance and render the stay-awake factor useless. In other words, if you end up having to stop and pee every twelve minutes, you're better off just pulling behind a Denny's and taking a nap.

I placed my beverage on the counter, being careful not to cover the laminated three-by-five handwritten card that noted NO PERSONAL CHECKS. NO EXCEPTIONS. This sign was rendered in the same script as a larger one that hung above the behind-the-counter rack featuring cigarettes, dirty mags (and videos and DVDs), Trojans, and, believe it or not, Bufferin and Midol. This sign gently informed, DON'T ASK US TO BORROW OUR TOOLS, AND WE WON'T ASK TO BORROW YOUR WIFE.

I smiled at the sign. It made me wish Rhonda were with me. "Hi, I was wondering if I could use your spark-plug wrench for just a sec—oh, and have you met my new bride?"

"Will that be all, darlin'?" The woman behind the counter was as tall as I was. I guessed she was about fifty-five, or maybe forty-five but had led a very hard life. It's not often that you look at a woman and think, *Yep, this person could whup me in a Wyoming minute. She could take me apart every day of the week and thrice on Sunday—once for each of her teeth.* It's not often that someone calls me "darlin'" and I want to run away and hide in a bomb shelter.

"I also got gas," I said, trying to smooth the tremolo out of my voice. "Pump four."

She rang me up and handed me a receipt. "Be careful out there, young man," she said. Urging, not scolding. "You look tired."

"Thanks," I said, raising my energy drink as a toast to her. "This will help."

"Vaya con Dios," she said.

I started to say "Chili con carne," which is my go-to smart-aleck comeback on such occasions, but I held my chili for once. And not because I was afraid Sip & Go Sally would hammer me like a dulcimer.

There was something about her. I guessed that she had crawled inside a bottle or six back in the day. But somehow she'd found her way back out—alive and with enough goodness in her heart to call a punk Kansas kid "darlin'" and sound like she meant it. I made a mental note to stop at her place again on the way back to Colorado.

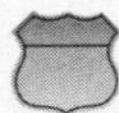

I guessed I was about a half hour from Chez Maxwell when I heard myself singing, "Hell for you, hell for you. This must be hehhh-ellllll for you." I was singing in a Bob Dylan voice, but this wasn't a Dylan song. (Dylan would swallow his harmonica—sideways—if he ever even thought about writing this little ditty.)

I realized I had song-ified some of Rhonda's parting words to me. Then I started to think about all the stuff that people compare to hell. Divorce is hell. War is hell. Calculus is hell. Lots of jobs are hell. Ironically, unemployment is hell. Substance addiction is hell, and, you guessed it, recovery from substance abuse? Also hell.

I wondered if the people in the real hell get offended at all the comparisons: "You think a root canal is hell, little Timmy? What do you know from hell? We'll show you hell! Give us five minutes, and you'll be begging for a mouthful of root canals—hold the novocaine, baby!"

Then again, maybe I was wrong. Maybe hell actually is custom-designed for each person:

"Welcome, Frank, to Your Own Private Hell."

"Uh, thanks?"

"This unabridged dictionary-sized book here is full of crossword puzzles. You will need to complete them before dinnertime, or we'll have to let a jackal in to eat some of your toes."

"Crossword puzzles? But I'm dyslexic—that should be in my files, Mr. Fallen Angel, sir. Plus, I'm stupid. The only book I ever read was *Heidi*, and that's only because I promised my dying grandmother I would! And I really didn't understand it. How pathetic is that? So I hope you can see that there has been some administrative mistake here."

"Sorry, the rules are the rules, big fella. Now get on with it; you're scheduled to play Wheel of Fortune after dinner."

"Noooo! Didn't you just hear me? Dys. Lex. Ic!"

"But your mother-in-law and former boss will be so disappointed!"

"My mother-in-law? And Evil Mr. Schneider—The Schneid? Oh, have mercy. I mean, I'm not surprised that they're *here*, but for the love of Vanna White . . . !"

"Again, sorry, Frank. Now chop-chop—which, by the way, is what your mother-in-law and ex-boss get to do to your private parts if you lose in WOF!"

"AIEEEEE! Please, no-no-no-no!"

"Aw, poor Frankie. Look, pal, I don't usually do this, but I'll give you a little tip: Buy a vowel."

Yes, the more I pondered it, the more it made sense. If we can have personal pan pizzas, why not personal, customized hells?

And, for people like me, Cole, and, yes, Janine Fasson (whose dad had an affair with, and then married, the weekend TV meteorologist), it wasn't hard to equate divorce with hell. Lawyers, family "counseling sessions" that start calm but heat up like a microwave frankfurter, a judge asking you, in essence, "Which of your two parents do you love more?" Yep, sounds like hell to me.

But I was introduced to the concept of hell way, way before my parents took their arguments out from behind closed doors to the living room, the kitchen, and even, as God is my witness, the breezeway. Nope, I can't thank my parents for Intro to Hell 101; I must thank Brother Bo.

Brother Bo, the shepherd of our little flock at Church of the Holy God, the first church I ever attended, was big anywhere you put him. Like a soda machine with a head and limbs. But he looked particularly large in our living room one Saturday afternoon with me and about a dozen of my fellow Church of the Holy God second graders half-circled on the floor around him.

"Hell," he said, letting the word hang in the air like smoke. "Hell is an awful, miserable place. There is weeping and gnashing of teeth."

I didn't really know what gnashing of teeth was, but I imagined that some cruel demon would start yanking teeth out with a pair of pliers, then put them together in a pot and mash them together while all of the terrified and toothless hell-dwellers looked on in horror. That, to me, was gnashing.

Brother Bo was smiling, somehow lifting his sagging cheeks toward his eyes. "And do you have any idea what Hell smells like?" he asked. "Can you even fathom the stench of Hell?"

Then, with magician-like flair, Brother Bo produced a rectangular box of matches from his pocket. He plucked a wooden match from the box. He stared for a moment at the tiny blood-red match head, then struck it against the side of the box, admiring its quivering flame. Then, with one short burst of his breath, he blew out the flame, bent over, and held the smoking match under my nostrils.

The smoke burned the inside of my nose like acid. I jerked my head back, but Brother Bo moved the match to follow me. It was as if the match was attached to my nose by a short strand of fishing line. It felt like the smoke had invaded my brain, via my nostrils, and now it would leave everything in my head raw and covered with soot.

Then Brother Bo stood straight. I looked up at him through eyes that felt impossibly moist, like I was viewing him from underwater. He glared down at me; he seemed pleased with himself. Then he fired up another match and proceeded to repeat his experiment on Roger Daily, who was sitting next to me.

Soon our living room was full of sniffling, watery-eyed grade-schoolers. Claudia Koltenbacher was the last person to be subjected to Brother Bo's object lesson. She began crying before he even struck her match.

Four years later, early in sixth grade, morning announcements would begin on a somber note. Principal Ford began with his typical monotone, and I wasn't really paying attention. I was drawing Spider-Man crawling up the margin of my notebook. But I stopped when I heard the phrase "terrible tragedy."

Claudia Koltenbacher, whom I knew had grown quite sick, was dead. "Cystic fibrosis has taken her from us," Principal Ford said. The girls in my class started sobbing and hugging each other. I stared down at my half-finished Spider-Man and ordered myself to breathe.

I started to think about Claudia, who hadn't been in school for a long while. Her parents were homeschooling her and, I heard, pounding on her back for an hour a day so she could breathe better. The first image that came to me was of her shrinking back from Brother Bo's smoking match. I hoped that as she lay dying, she wasn't terrorized about waking up in hell with the stench of sulfur burning in her nostrils. I kept looking at Spider-Man while I prayed to God that Claudia went peacefully and woke up in heaven to the smell of flowers and fresh-baked chocolate chip cookies and cocoa butter sunscreen.

I still pray this for Claudia, by the way. Nearly every week. Sometimes for days and days in a row. I know it's probably illogical to pray about something that happened so long ago, but I can't stop myself.

I also can't stop myself from flinching sometimes when I hear the scratch of a match on a matchbook. (Maybe this is another reason why I used a lighter, then the Hair Tornado 3000, for all of my personal self-disciplining needs.) Anyway, I hear a match and immediately I can feel my nose twitch like I am going to sneeze, and I hope there's a tissue nearby because sometimes my eyes start to water too and I can't see anything clearly. Thanks, Brother Bo.

Brother Bo's hellacious presentation that Saturday afternoon didn't end with the terrorization of Claudia Koltenbacher. The object lesson was only the beginning.

After the sniffling and eye-dabbing subsided, Brother Bo addressed us. "Now," he said, "you've all had just a little taste—or should I say sniff?—of what hell will be like. And I promise you that what you've experienced is mild compared to the real thing."

He stopped to smile humorlessly. "So how many of you want to be saved from going to hell?"

About a dozen hands shot up. Mine was the only one that didn't. I don't know why. I wish to God I did. Maybe I was angry at Brother Bo for what he'd done to us. Maybe I just didn't like him. Maybe I was too scared or thought that the whole thing was a trap and Brother Bo was going to do something *else* to all who raised their hands—something to test the sincerity with which they thrust their little hands toward the Smith living room ceiling.

Whatever the case, Brother Bo wagged his bison-like head sadly. "Well, look at this, boys and girls," he said. "Isn't this sad? There is one among us who, I guess, wants to go to hell and burn. Forever. Indeed, this is one of the saddest things I have ever seen."

That brought my dad in from the kitchen, where he was pouring milk into paper cups.

I sat there, blinking in disbelief as my skinny dad got in Brother Bo's face—or, more accurately, his chest. I don't remember all of what he said, but I remember my mouth dropping open when he called Brother Bo a jackass.

I had never heard my dad swear before, and even though jackass isn't high on the totem pole of obscenities, when you're in second grade, hearing such a word from a dad like mine is like being stun-gunned.

"M-M-Mister, Smith," Brother Bo stammered. "Such language! And in front of the children! How dare you!"

I remember my dad's voice being eerily calm. "I'm just talking to you like a man," he said. "Do you want to talk to *me* like a man?"

"I have nothing to say to you, Mister Smith. But rest assured, the elders will hear about this incident."

"Indeed they will," Dad said. "I will contact them straightaway. But now I must ask you to leave my home."

"But what about these children?"

"I will take care of these children. Now, goodbye, sir."

I was sure Brother Bo was going to beat up my dad, right there in our living room. And it still shames me to admit that I was more concerned about how such a beating would humiliate me than I was with my dad's impending abrasions, contusions, and broken bones.

But Brother Bo just stood there awhile before smiling sadly and moving toward the door. He paused in the doorway and looked like he was going to offer us kids one final admonition, but Dad took two steps toward him and ensured that the exit would be without comment.

Then we all sat and drank milk silently and waited for parents to arrive and retrieve their no-longer-hellbound kids.

Later that night, I was struggling to get to sleep, the smell of sulfur still haunting my nose, when Dad appeared and knelt at my bedside. "Griff?" he whispered. "I have something important to tell you. I'll make it short, okay? I know you must be tired."

"Sure, Dad."

"It's okay that you didn't raise your hand today. Do you know that?"

"Uh, I guess so. But is it really, Dad? You're not disappointed in me?"

"I'm not disappointed. You see, Griff, when you decide to ask Jesus to come into your life, I want it to be because of how much you love him and because you understand how much he loves you, not because of how scared you are of a place called hell. Does that make sense?"

"I guess so. But I *am* scared of hell, Dad. Maybe I made a big mistake today."

I felt his warm hand on my forehead. "Griff," he said, "you didn't make a mistake. Maybe think of it this way: Do you like it that I'm your dad?"

I reached up and put one hand on his. "I love it that you're my dad. You're the nicest dad there is."

"I'm so thankful that you feel that way. I'm thankful that you like having me as a dad because I'm nice and that you know I love you. It wouldn't be the same if you liked having me as a dad only because all of the other dads were mean or cruel. And it's kind of the same thing with Jesus. Does that make sense?"

I remember so bad wanting to say yes. I had already told my dad so many lies—and have continued to do so—but this time I couldn't."

"Um," I said.

"It's okay, son," he assured me. "This is difficult stuff. Here's the thing: What makes our relationship special is that I love you and you love me. We care about each other, and we like being close. We *want* to be together. I don't go around thinking, *I love Griff because if I didn't have him, I might have some rotten kid.*

"Like Carlton Tucker?"

"No comment," Dad chuckled. "And you don't go around saying, 'I like my dad because if I didn't have him I might get adopted by some Monster-Dad.' Right?"

"Right."

"Well, it's the same thing with you and Jesus. The right reason to want him in your life is that you love him and he loves you. Being close to Jesus is about love, not fear or terror. Does that make sense?"

I nodded, but it was a small nod, and Dad wouldn't have even known about it if his hand weren't still on my forehead, smoothing my hair out of my eyes. I think I was beginning to understand the concept, but it was like seeing a sign through a haze of smoke, and the thought of smoke wasn't something I wanted to entertain.

Dad kissed my forehead and whispered, "I love you," as he left the room. I tried to respond in kind, but I was so tired that I'm not sure the words ever made it.

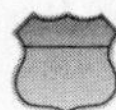

We never went back to Church of the Holy God. I prayed regularly that Brother Bo would move away and pastor another church—in another state—because nervousness and fear would drape over me like an X-ray apron whenever I saw him around town.

If we saw him at Food Supply, I'd tug Mom or Dad toward another checkout line. If I spotted his dirt-brown Capri in front of McDonald's, I'd blurt, "You know, I'm sick of burgers. Let's go get Mexican."

Still, in a Kansas suburb of fifty thousand, you can't avoid bumping into someone forever—especially someone Brother Bo's size. Sometimes we'd be seated at Grandma Brooks, my dad's favorite restaurant, and Brother Bo and his tiny wife would be led toward the table next to ours.

I remember trying to will the hostess to change her mind and decide to place Brother and Mrs. Bo at a booth, instead. My will never did a bit of good. So I would pretend not to notice the giant pastor. I'd study the dessert menu or work on my food with the diligence of a surgeon, cutting my chopped sirloin steak into perfect squares the size of postage stamps, or separating my mixed vegetables until they weren't mixed anymore. They became tiny, segregated collections of yellow, orange, white, and green, sitting on my plate like prairie dog mounds.

Dad, though, never failed to say hello to Brother Bo, or at least nod deferentially in his direction. And sometimes Mom would engage in a brief conversation with Brother Bo's wife across the backs of their wooden chairs.

I sometimes wonder if that's part of the reason I chose a Southern California college: to get far away from Brother Bo. There's little chance he would ever take a job that far west. He's just not a So-Cal kind of guy.

I was picturing Brother Bo in board shorts, playing beach volleyball, when I heard the whining of my tires on those grooves they cut into highway shoulders to warn drowsy drivers who veer off the road.

I shook my head violently, then nervously checked my rearview mirrors. Fortunately, no one—and most significantly, no highway patrol officer—had witnessed my lapse of consciousness.

"Okay," I said, hoping the sound of my own panicky voice would help plant me firmly back into the land of the conscious, "that was trippy. Was I *dreaming* about Brother Bo? Why couldn't I dream about Amanda Mac—or at least The Carrot?" I glared at my empty can of energy drink in the cup holder. "A lot of good you did," I scolded the can. "Stupid lightweight slop."

Up ahead I saw a boarded-up gas station, just past an exit that proclaimed, NO SERVICES. *No problem. I don't need any services,* I thought. *I just need a place to grab a twenty-minute power nap.*

I awoke to the the tuba-like call of a semi's horn. I gazed out the front window and began pounding the steering wheel with the heels of both hands. "Ah, for the love-a Rip Van Stinking Winkle," I moaned. It was dark out. I willed my eyes to focus on the Durango's LED clock. It read 8:19, but that couldn't be right. Then I remembered that we were in the Mountain time zone now, and Dad probably forgot to adjust the clock. I looked at my watch, which informed me that it was indeed 8:19—and of course my dad had remembered to set the clock because he's Mr. Responsibility, and my proposed schedule for the evening was shattered. And to make things even worse, my mom was probably freaking out because I hadn't arrived at the nonworking farm, and she tends to throw things when she freaks out.

I slid in Clapton's *Timepieces* and headed for the on-ramp. "Twenty-minute power nap," I muttered. "Good call, Griff. Lucky you heard that truck, or it woulda been a twenty-*hour* power nap."

I was formulating excuses for being late when I hit the coyote and we had our falling out. And that little encounter freaked me out so much that, as I watched my former brother-animal bound away, I honestly began looking forward to Mom opening the door and inviting me into the House of the Nonworking Farm. At least I would be dealing with bipeds now. I had experienced a gut-full of canine.

"Griffin!" my mom said when she answered the door. "It is so good to see you. It's been too long! Are you okay? We were worried about you. We expected you a couple of hours ago, but I have been keeping dinner warm for you!"

All the feigned enthusiasm of a game show host, I noted as I began my mental evaluation of the evening. *Nice job, Mom.*

She held out her arms, looking like one of those cartoon sleepwalkers who get lured out of their beds by the smell of pie. I dutifully stepped inside the hug, and she patted me between the shoulder blades like she was trying to burp me.

Well, that was fun. I've had physicals less awkward. I should have turned my head and coughed. Would have been totally apropos.

"I made your favorite dinner," Mom said too loudly. "Just like

I told you on the phone. Lasagna."

My favorite food is pizza. The best meal I've ever had, however, was half an organic peanut butter and fruit-only-jam sandwich on nine-grain bread, which Amanda Mac shared with me during the last week of senior year. My lunch account was more in the red than usual, and when you get into those double-digit deficits, the lunch ladies will cut you off cold no matter how much you smile at them.

"Good sandwich?" Amanda had asked me after my first bite.

I nodded. "I'm spoiled for life. I don't think generic peanut butter is gonna do it for me anymore."

Generic peanut butter never "did it" for me. Unless you mean ensure my regularity. Really, really ensure it, if you know what I mean. But I still eat generic at home. It's what Dad buys, and I'd feel guilty asking him to buy organic stuff, without all of those cost-cutting hydrogenated oils and sugars in it. I don't see even Peter Pan or Jif in our immediate future.

We did get Peter Pan when Bryant and Lynnette Smith were a couple, and I preferred Peter Pan over lasagna, hands down. Lasagna? My *favorite* food? I was wondering how my mother conjured up that notion, when it hit me: Lasagna is *her* favorite food. Maybe she likes all the layers. It's a good thing she gets layers in her food, because she sure as Chef Boyardee isn't going to get them in her spouse's novels.

I dutifully ate my *favorite* lasagna, nodding deferentially to Mom and even asking her what brand of ricotta she favors. And I asked Maxwell what he was working on.

I want to point out, for the record, that I did not scoff, sneer, or even smirk when he told me, "Vampires, my boy. Lots and lots of vampires. But one of them is a private detective—tragically, she is in love with the leader of a rival vampire coven."

These words were slamming against my tightly closed lips: "Coven of vampires, eh, Max? Are you sure that is the correct term? Isn't it gaggle of vampires? Wait . . . no—flock of vampires? Shucky-darn! Could it be passel? Yeah, I'm feelin' that. 'Come away with me, Vladimir. Denounce this vile passel of vampires, and let us escape under cover of night to Arizona!'"

But I said not a word in response. I was as silent as a coven of vampires at noon—as in asleep in their coffins and so forth.

"A lot of people are already interested in the film rights for *Love at Stake*," Mom noted, spearing a black olive with her fork.

"Yes," Maxwell chimed in, wiping his mediocre mouth with a napkin. "But I hope this one doesn't suffer the same fate as *Naked Raven*." He fixed his eyes on me. "I'll tell you, Griffin, what a circus. They had Ed Begley Jr. all but signed for a key role, and then the whole project went belly-up. I was going to have script input and everything. Talk about Curse of the Naked Raven. That curse transcended the literary realm, that's for sure."

"It sure did," I concurred. And yes, I meant it in a snide, shallow way, but come on, you gotta give me that one.

As we finished the remnants of our dinner, I saw Mom drumming her fingers on the table and occasionally looking quizzically at Maxwell.

"Okay, okay," he grumbled finally, "I'll go get him."

Maxwell pushed back from the table and left the dining room. Mom leaned across the table and whispered conspiratorially, even though there was no one in the room to conspire against: "Be extra, extra kind to Dalton, please, Griffin. None of your sarcasm. This whole thing has been as hard on him as it has been on you."

Interesting observation there, Mrs. Smith-Maxwell-Mediocre—

given that you have no clue how hard this has been on me, largely because you never really took the time to ask.

Dalton followed his father into the room, lurking behind him like one of a boxer's seconds. He deposited himself in a chair at the foot of the table and fixed his eyes on a crumb of French bread.

"Hey, Dalton," I said.

"Hey," he said without looking up. He had a low voice. It reminded me of one of the deejays on our local alternative-music station.

I studied him out of the corner of my left eye as Maxwell began to yammer on about "really taking vampires to a new place, literarily speaking."

Dalton had one shock of black hair that hung like an old sock in front of his left eye. Something inside me wanted to brush the hair aside. Watching him eat, I found myself pushing my own hair up off my forehead. I had to stifle a laugh. Even tugging on it, my hair wouldn't reach my eyebrows.

As she rose to "fetch the apple pie," my mother stopped beside Dalton and reached toward his forehead. He recoiled and glared at her from the one eye I could see. Then he slumped in his chair and muttered something. Mom exhaled heavily and marched to the kitchen. I wondered how many times this scene had played out since she started playing surrogate mother to MTM's son.

We picked at our pie in silence. I broke off the fluted edge piece of my crust and began nibbling. That's usually my favorite part of a pie, but my mouth was so dry from nervous tension that the crust turned to dust in my mouth, and I wondered if I would choke.

Finally, Mom turned to Dalton. "Would you like to show Griffin your room?"

Dalton's jaw went slack. His visible eye widened. He looked as if she had asked, "Would you like to show Griffin your testicles?"

He pushed his chair away from the table. I saw Mom wince as the chair legs squeaked and stuttered across the hardwood floor. "C'mon, Griffin," he recited the words like lines in a play. "We can listen to music while I show you my model-airplane collection."

Dalton's room smelled like expensive cologne, something musky and wood-like. His room wasn't like mine, decorated with varsity letters, medals, and a bulletin board full of award certificates, press clippings, and honor roll listings. Instead, there were five posters, all of the same woman sporting four different bikinis. Actually, in one pose, she wasn't modeling the bikini—in the sense of wearing it, that is. She appeared to be whirling her top like David's sling while looking seductively over one shoulder. I recognized her from one of those reality shows but couldn't name her. Above the bikini-top-as-sling poster was a hand-lettered sign that proclaimed, BAN THE OBJECTIFICATION OF WOMEN.

"You can sit on the bed if you want," Dalton said, gesturing to his bed before plopping to the floor and crossing his legs.

"Thanks," I said, lowering myself onto the carefully made bed.

I nodded toward one of the posters. Reality Girl had her hands on her hips as if she had put on a barely existent bikini and teased up her hair just to scold someone. "I've been seeing a lot of her on TV," I noted. "What's her name again?"

Dalton didn't raise his head. He kept studying the same patch of carpet that had held his attention since he sat down. "Does it matter?" he said.

I wanted to turn to Cole and give him a look that said, "Can you *believe* this guy?" But Cole was a state away. I started to miss him big-time. Cole is never sarcastic. He'll always give you what is the rarest commodity in today's world: a straight answer.

Okay, Dalton, I thought, *I'm not going to let you bait me. Let's see how deep this well of sarcasm goes. I spent four years as a reporter on the high school newspaper; I'm in Quill & Scroll, dude. I have enough questions to last us the night.*

"So," I said, "where did you get the posters?"

Still no eye contact from Dalton. "It's kind of funny," he said humorlessly.

"Yeah?"

He shook his head slowly. I thought I saw the beginning of a smile. "Actually, they're my dad's."

Have you ever asked a question, and the answer is better than anything you dreamed it could be? This was better than, "I have these pictures of Reality Girl because God revealed to me, when he appeared to us one night in the pot roast, that one day she will be the mother of my thirteen children," or, "I have placed these provocative photos on my walls so that I can confront my lust head-on, just as Gandhi used to invite beautiful women into his bed to test his self-control."

But the fact that Maxwell the Mediocre had somehow obtained near-nudie shots of a girl less than half his age was just too good. So good, in fact, that how the images had ended up in Dalton's room was a mildly intriguing backstory, at best. (Still, I was hoping that Dalton had won them in an arm-wrestling contest with his weenie-armed, pervy old man.)

"Uh," I said, trying to sound prickly yet sympathetic, like one of those TV reporters during an up-close-and-personal interview, "if the posters are your dad's, what are they doing in your room?"

This time Dalton did smile. For almost a whole second. "They were in this magazine Dad subscribes to. And I'm not talking about the one from AARP. You know the kind of magazine I mean; it's really just soft-core porn, but they toss in an article about a car or some piece of high-tech entertainment equipment to throw the wives and girlfriends off the scent. My dad usually picks up the mail every day, so I don't even know if your . . .uh, Lynnette, knew he subscribed. But this one day, he drove somewhere to sign books, and when he gets back, she's retrieved the mail, rifled through the magazine, and pulled out this photo spread and plastered pics everywhere. On the living room walls, the refrigerator. She even used three of them for place mats at dinner that night."

I stifled a laugh. Mom's mean streak always troubled me when we were under the same roof, but it was pretty amusing now that someone else was the victim.

I studied Dalton for a while. He was a tough read. "So when your dad got home . . ." I prompted.

"He starts talking really fast, telling Lynnette how she doesn't understand the 'nuances of a men's magazine.'"

Dalton was now doing a near-perfect imitation of my mom in her shrill-scream mode. "I would expect to find such images in Dalton's room," Dalton shrieked, "but not in the possession of a supposedly mature fifty-six-year-old adult!"

I nodded at Dalton, giving him, as Rhonda would say, "props" for the spot-on imitation. "So, you're just sitting there watching all this? Or are you part of the argument?"

Dalton pointed at my chest, like he was picking me for his playground basketball team. "I wasn't going to get involved, until Lynnette mentioned me. Then I decided to break in. I was on the couch, but I stood up and said to my dad, 'You know what? She's right. One *would* expect to find this kinda stuff in my room, so

I'm hereby claiming what's rightfully mine.' Then I start plucking Brandi off the walls and stuff and carrying her away to . . . here."

I nodded. "But what about the sign?" I said, pointing.

"Well, part of Lynnette's tirade was about the 'objectification of women.' That phrase kind of stuck in my head. So I got my girlfriend—well, she's my ex-girlfriend now—to letter the sign for me. She's pretty good with calligraphy."

"Yeah," I said, standing. "Hey, that was a great story. But, Mom . . . er, Lynnette isn't pissed about you having these up in your room?"

Dalton smiled at me dismissively. "She's not allowed in here, Griffin. He's not either. But I don't think either of them would care, really. Like the woman said, I'm the right age for this kinda stuff." He paused for a moment. "Hey, can I ask you something?"

This I wasn't expecting. "Yeah," I said, trying not to sound too suspicious.

"My dad says you guys are headed for bankruptcy or whatever. Is that true?"

I felt my cheeks grow hot. "Well, I have heard my dad talk about it. But he's working hard. I think we'll be okay. Feel free to tell your dad that—so he won't continue to worry about us."

Dalton looked up and glanced at me, just for a second. "I don't think he's the one who's worried. And anyway, Griffin, I think it's better to be financially bankrupt than morally bankrupt." Then he nodded his head toward the dining room.

I nodded at him and headed for the door. "I can't argue with that. Hey, I think I'll go for a walk, maybe talk to Mom a bit. Maybe we can talk a little more later."

Dalton appeared to be seriously considering the possibility. "Maybe," he said finally.

Mom was on the couch watching an infomercial for a piece of exercise equipment that reminded me of our old foldout couch. She patted the cushion next to her. "Sit?" she offered.

I sat down in a large tan recliner to her right.

On the TV, a studio audience began clapping as a model in a belly shirt began folding herself up into something between a sit-up and a carnival feat. She said something about her "rectus abdominus," and I thought what a great name that would be for a professional wrestler: "And in this corner, weighing in at 275 pounds, Rectus Ab . . . dom . . in . . . ussssss!"

"So, Griffin," my mother was saying, her voice laced with annoyance, "it's not that hard of a question is it?"

I swallowed nervously, realizing I had missed a question while visiting the Land o' Wrestling. So I followed the same protocol I used when this happened at school (and it happened with Greenwich-clock regularity): I tried to look thoughtful. I considered resting my chin on my fist, but that could be construed as overdoing the ponder thing.

"I'm just not sure what you mean by the question."

Mom sighed. "When I ask how your father is doing, I mean simply, HOW IS YOUR FATHER DOING?!"

"He's great." I meant to proclaim that statement with confidence, but it came out like a suggestion.

Mom nodded. "How's . . . what *is* her name?

"Rhonda. She's okay. She sure seems crazy about him, that's for sure."

If this were a game of H-O-R-S-E, I would have just made a

behind-the-back, through-the-legs reverse layup.

"Well, he is a truly good man. I can see why, um, Rhonda would be drawn to him. Especially when most men her age are self-absorbed losers."

What kind of a response was this? This was the verbal equivalent of just handing me the basketball and saying, "I'm not even going to attempt to match that shot. What else you got?" It was like she was going to throw the game.

That was fine with me. I'd put her away in short order; I had the rest of my shots all planned:

Shot #2: "So, what drew you to Maxwell the Mediocre in the first place? Back when you were still married to another man—you realized that, didn't you? The man who was the father of your two children? Anyway, back to Max: Was it the saggy face, the man-breasts, or the fact that he writes novels that are the literary equivalent of aerosol cheese?" H-O.

Shot #3: "Does it bother you that your husband, he of the fleshy neck wattle and gray skin pallor, lusts after a vapid reality-show celebrity who's less than half your age? Does it bother you that you just don't 'do it' for him anymore?" H-O-R.

Shot #4: "Do you ever miss me, Mom? I mean, you don't even write, except on my birthday (which is an afterthought, based on your timing) and Christmas. I know you don't want to be my real parent, but I thought you'd at least be my pen-parent. Does the fact that you're my co-creator and I grew inside your body ever make you miss me?" H-O-R-S.

Shot #5: "Or I'll tell you what: Let's forget me. But what about Colby? Do you miss *him*? Do you ever feel guilty that you left him behind? Can you help me understand what it is that allows a mother to abandon a toddler who is everything good and nothing bad? Because if you can, maybe it will help me console him on those nights he starts sobbing and locking onto my eyes and begging me to tell him why Mommy went away.

"He was still in diapers when you left, you know. And you might have thought you got out of diaper duty by ditching us, but I've got news for you: Maxwell looks like he's not far from those golden Depends years, so fear not. All those Colby diapers you missed will be replaced by big stinky Maxwell diapers, the ones he'll fill for you after he gums his creamed corn and mashed taters. And if that ain't poetic justice, I don't know what is.

"Game over. There's your E, Biological Mom of Mine. Thanks for playing. I guess you're more adept with a bowling ball than a basketball. Too bad we're playing H-O-R-S-E instead of Smite the Family Vehicle with a Brunswick Right in Front of God and Most of the Neighbors."

But we didn't finish our game of H-O-R-S-E. I saved up my questions like bullets in a gun, in case I needed to fire them later. Instead, we played Listen to Mom Talk About How She Misses All That Great Kansas City Barbecue and Let's Beg Griffin to Stay the Night Because Lynnette Is Oh-So-Tired and Would Love It If We Could Do Some More Catching Up in the Morning (and She'll Make Waffles!).

I asked to use her phone, and I called Dad on the cell. I knew he would squash this scheme like a grape. I wouldn't even need to lead him (e.g., "Dad, I know this is really asking a lot of you, given that you've already graciously modified your painstakingly crafted travel schedule, but Mom was wondering . . .").

"Actually, Griffin," my dad said, and I had to tighten my grip on the Maxwellian cordless phone to keep from dropping it—or hurling it through their grand picture window—"that modification in plans would serve all of us well. Cole has been invited to stay with some teammates in Denver this evening, and Rhonda and I still have much left to discuss. Things are going quite well, thank the Lord, and, with divine help, we are plowing new ground in our relationship. And we'd like to keep going."

"Oh," I said. *Oh, thank you for sentencing me to what I'm sure will be the most awkwardly uncomfortable evening of my young life. I wish that coyote had bitten me. And I wish he were rabid. I bet if I were foaming at the mouth right now and eating the stuffing out of Maxwell's gray sectional, I could spend the evening someplace more desirable—like the emergency room. I'd even settle for being chained to a pole outside till morning, when the vet could come take a look at me.*

I said goodbye to my dad and turned to my mom. "Great news: I can stay. Waffles for breakfast it shall be!"

You, Griffin Smith, can feign enthusiasm with the best of 'em. You, too, are game show host material. Like shallow mother, like son, I guess.

I woke up without opening my eyes. I felt the marshmallowy couch cushions underneath me and tried to figure out where I was. I could have opened my eyes, of course, but that would have been too easy. No, better to lie there and let reality drift over me slowly, like a fog. What state was I in? What city? Whose house? Whose mushy couch?

The word "coyote" popped into my brain, and all the elements of my reality lined themselves up like little toy soldiers. I blinked my eyes open and saw a large handwritten note on the coffee table parallel to the couch.

Good Morning, Griffin!
Maxwell and I are taking a long walk, enjoying the wonderful Wyoming morning. Bagels on the kitchen counter, if you need something to hold you till breakfast. Plenty of cereal in the pantry next to the refrigerator too. Also, would you mind waking Dalton up? We don't want him sleeping the morning away.
Love (and soon waffles!),
Mom & Max
P.S. Please don't forget to wake up Dalton.
Do know that he'll ignore you if you let him.

Okay, I grumbled, crumpling the note and tossing it across the living room, *that's why some mornings it's just better to keep your eyes shut. That way there's at least a slight chance you'll die a sudden, painless death before you wake up and realize what a crappy place you're in—literally and figuratively.*

I stretched and walked to Dalton's room.

"Dalton," I said to his closed door, "I guess I'm supposed to wake you up. Sorry about that and all, but . . ."

I waited, hoping for a sleepy acknowledgment of some sort. Even a muffled profanity would suffice. But apparently Dalton was a sound sleeper, like Cole. This is annoying to people like me, who crave sleep but can be awakened by the sound of a butterfly lighting on a down pillow.

I hammered on the door with the meaty part of my fist. "C'mon, dude. I guess my mom's gonna be all tweaked if she comes back and finds you still asleep. I'm sure you know how she gets. Look, I know it stinks and all, but . . ." I sighed loudly, as much for Dalton's benefit as my own. "I was thinking I would be at least thirty and married with kids before I'd have to do this kinda thing," I said. Again, as much for Dalton as for me.

I watched a minute slide by on my watch, then gently twisted Dalton's doorknob. I half-expected to find that he'd snuck out. Maybe to go cow-tipping or whatever teens do for fun in Wheatland.

I don't know how or why, but I sensed he was dead the moment I stepped into his room.

He was lying on top of his bed, which was neatly made underneath him. He was still dressed, too. I told myself that he might just have downed a fifth of Stoli or popped a few Vicodins and was just sleeping it off. (I knew that drill.) But I wasn't really listening to myself. I knew myself was in denial. Instead, I was watching Dalton's chest not rising and falling. I was listening to him not breathing. "Dear God," I heard myself say. I wasn't sure whether it was an exclamation or a prayer.

I dutifully checked for a pulse on Dalton's wrist, then the cool rubbery skin of his neck. I noticed he had changed shirts. The night before, he sported a Ramones T-shirt, one more thing that was making him start to grow on me. But now he was wearing a pool-table-green shirt that he might have had custom-lettered—like the ones you can order from the back pages of music magazines. His shirt said, SMILE FOR ME, LITTLE EMO GIRL. I wondered if his ex-girlfriend had been the inspiration for the message. Then I positioned my left ear over the "E" in SMILE, where I guessed his heart would be. Dalton's body was quiet, as I knew it would be. I began to recall that there was something in his eyes the night before. Call it the Hopeless Look of the Lonely Exotic. I know it well. I see it in the mirror sometimes, on nights that are too quiet and too filled with bad memories. Bob Dylan says there are some memories you can learn to live with, but some you can't. And when those latter ones coil around you like a python, you believe they can actually kill you—or if you're lucky, just make you insane.

I kept my head on his chest for a moment, wondering what the scene would look like if I could watch myself from outside my body. I'm a teenager—I can imagine scenarios in which I run sub-4-minute miles barefoot and save both the Olsen twins from a bloodthirsty gang of Crips. But every now and then, reality puts me in a scene I couldn't have made up if you'd injected Ecstasy directly into my brain stem.

Then I looked around for a note or a bottle of pills, but I

didn't see anything. It made sense. If this was a suicide, Dalton didn't seem like the kind of guy who would create a big scene: prescription bottles toppled across his nightstand, cryptic note safety-pinned to his shirt. I figured they might find pill bottles somewhere, but they would have to hunt.

But maybe it wasn't a suicide. Maybe he was sick with one of those TV-special diseases, like the one that took Claudia Koltenbacher. But he hadn't looked sick at all; he'd looked a little sad and alienated, but as far as his RDA of important vitamins and minerals, he'd appeared good to go.

I stood up. Reality Girl smiled, pouted, and teased me from the autographed posters on the walls. Wait a minute. *Autographed* posters? I didn't recall their being autographed. I clicked on the light.

I felt myself smiling, even though it seemed wholly inappropriate to smile. Dalton had conveyed his final words to the world via the media of Sharpie and soft-core porn.

"Dad, Lynnette, and Pam," the words read like a headline at the top of the poster nearest his door, "please don't be hard on yourselves. It's not your fault." Pam, I guessed, must be the ex-girlfriend.

On the next poster, Reality Girl was holding a garden hose. Dalton had made a voice bubble coming from the mouth of the hose. "I just don't fit . . . anywhere," the hose said.

"I feel better already," the third poster assured, despite Reality Girl's pouty lips and crinkled forehead.

I noticed that I was mentioned on the next one. A voice bubble coming from Reality Girl herself this time said, "Griff, you're all right. I wish you well in college. Life, too. Don't go bankrupt."

Finally, across a white pool robe that Reality Girl was struggling to keep closed around her, Dalton said, "Goodbye and peace to all my family and friends. Please don't be sad."

I heard laughter and the scuffing of feet on the front porch. "Goodbye, Dalton," I whispered, wondering how I was going to tell Maxwell the Mediocre that his only kid was dead.

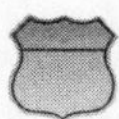

Key Life Lesson #3: In a weird way, death changes the living almost as much as it changes the deceased. It's important to note, however, that the living's encounter with death has to be up close and personal, right there in your face; otherwise, this lesson doesn't really get absorbed. You go right on watching vapid TV shows and drinking light beer and figuring out what you are going to do about those nagging physical flaws that you just know are keeping you out of life's VIP room.

When I was five, my great-grandmother died, and Dad marched me past her open casket. I looked at her for a moment, and I understood, I think, that she was dead. I knew she wasn't going to sit up and ask me if I wanted a shortbread cookie, which was her guest-snack of choice. But she seemed more like a mannequin than a person. My most lasting impression was of how small she looked.

Even Claudia Koltenbacher's untimely death didn't change me the way it should have. I hung my head like all of the other guys and tried not to sob and sniffle like all the girls were, but Claudia hadn't been in school for such a long time that I don't think I grasped the significant difference between her being gone . . . and being *gone*. I didn't do right by Claudia in the grief department. And I liked her a ton. Still do. In fact, I think her death is more profound to me now than it was back in sixth grade, when it was a fresh death.

But Dalton had changed all of that. In those moments before I left his room to find Maxwell and my mom, I studied him like I was going to paint his portrait. I thought of our conversation the night before and how wonderfully twisted and brilliant it was that he scattered the Brandi pictures around his room. It's the kind of thing I wished *I* would have come up with. I wondered how he felt writing his Sharpie captions right before he took his life. I could imagine him smiling, even allowing himself a small chuckle or two. But it all would have been laced with sadness.

Now he was lifeless. I will always remember standing by his bed and feeling the floor disappear under my feet. Kind of like those old Western movies where they build gallows, and a trap-door opens up under Bad Bart, and he plunges through the floor, only there was no noose to stop me. I went into a free fall, praying desperately, "God, please don't let me end up like Dalton, because this is the saddest thing I've ever seen."

And this was a real prayer, certainly an anomaly for me. Yes, I prayed all the time that I would ace a chemistry test, for example, or that I'd blow Ross away with my brilliant analysis of a Thomas Mann short story. But too often these prayers would devolve into Just-Really-God prayers. You know the type: "God, we just really seek your face right now, God, and we just really ask you to help us just really do well in school, God. Because, God, that would just really be honoring to you. Really." And at the same time I was dutifully uttering my autopilot Just Really God's, I was studying like crazy. I did the Required Reading. The Suggested Reading, too. I took every sample test and quiz. In short, I covered all the bases—prayer was just one of them.

But this was different. Get yourself alone with a dead person your age, and Just-Really-God is about the last thing you'll say, because getting up close and personal with death is like taking a bath in turpentine. It strips off every bit of pretense and delusion—pretty much anything that isn't true. And the process hurts, because even as I prayed my "Please, not me" prayer, I knew I was venturing into the Land of the Nonnegotiable. I knew that someday it *would* be me lying dead on a bed. It would be Dad, Colby, Cole, both Amandas . . . all of us.

One more thing about my free fall: I wish I could say that, on the way down, I tore at the air like a wounded bird, trying to find something to grab on to, then Jesus' hand appeared out of nowhere and yanked me to safety—and at that moment, I resolved to change my major from journalism to missions so that I could Make the Most of Every Minute Because Life Is Short and Precious. But none of that happened. Instead, I just let myself fall. I wasn't enjoying the ride, but I was accepting it.

I don't know how much time passed before I felt my feet under me again. It couldn't have been that long, because Max and my mom were still giggling and talking way too loudly. I left Dalton in his room, closing the door softly behind me, out of respect for him, I think.

In the hallway hung a small square mirror. I hesitated to look in it, for fear I'd see deep lines in my face, like they had been etched with sculptor's tools. Lines like the ones that seemed to appear overnight on my father's face after the divorce. I felt older. Getting drunk for the first time didn't make me an adult. Neither did having sex or turning eighteen and registering for possible military service. But this might have done it.

I knew myself well enough to know that I wasn't going to

instantaneously change my life, shed all my bad habits like dead snakeskin. In fact, I really, really needed a drink at that moment. But things would be different somehow. The particulars were vague, but this I knew: From now on, I was *paying attention.* I know this isn't the same thing as changing your destructive lifestyle, but it was, perhaps, a start.

Hand in hand, Mom and Maxwell turned into the hallway and came toward me, swinging their arms like grade-school children. They were both smiling like synchronized swimmers, and I wondered how long it would be before they would smile again.

"Mom, Sir," I said carefully, "I need to tell you something . . ."

It amazed me how fast a remote house on the lonesome Wyoming prairie could fill up with people. At eight o'clock on a Saturday morning. I watched hugs and handshakes galore. I watched people suddenly melt into tears, some of them convulsing and needing to sit down.

At one point, a buff deputy sheriff pulled me into a guest bedroom and scratched notes into a tattered notebook as I answered questions about my time with Dalton. He wrapped up by saying, "Is there any other statement you'd like to make?"

I thought for a moment. "Statement?" I repeated. "How about this: You know why Reality Girl is alive and Dalton is dead? Because, ironically, she doesn't truly have to deal with reality. Dalton did."

The deputy frowned at me, but then he thanked me for my time. I trailed him into the kitchen, where I plucked the cordless phone from its stand, slipped outside, and told Dad the news. "Those poor people," he said. "Griffin, you must pray for them. Please. It's important. This is the thing that a parent dreads more than anything else. It's the kind of thing you plead with God about: 'Please, Lord, anything but that. Take me. I'll accept death. I'll accept any disease, any injury. But please, protect my child.' I pray that for you and Colby every day, without fail."

I wondered if anyone had prayed that for Dalton. I wondered if Maxwell had become so obsessed with his vampires and naked ravens that his son had dropped off the grid. I promised my dad I would pray. Then he said, "Will you ask Lynnette if I may speak to her?"

I found my mother in the kitchen, bear-hugging a pear-shaped woman in a flower-print dress. I handed her the phone and studied her, because I was paying attention now. I watched tears slide down her cheeks as she nodded occasionally and every now and then whispered something into the phone.

After a while, she clicked off the receiver and set it on the counter. She looked at me and said, "Wait here."

Soon she returned and motioned for me to follow her outside. "Walk with me?" she offered.

We headed down a narrow dirt path away from the house. We walked in silence for a while, but then she drew in a deep breath and said, "You need to head back to Denver. Your father was very gracious; he wanted to make sure Maxwell and I had people around us to support us. He wanted you to stay if we didn't. But as you saw, we have a houseful. Some are just Maxwell groupies, and that includes a few of the relatives, but most are real friends. Of course, it will be hard to reach Dalton's biological mother; she abandoned the scene years ago. Anyway, you can go, Griffin. You still have a lot of miles ahead of you. And I know you want to spend as much time as possible with Cole."

I nodded tentatively.

The house was still in view when my mother stopped abruptly and grabbed both of my wrists. "Griffin, please hear what I am about to tell you."

"Okay," I said.

"I am sorry, deeply sorry for, you know, everything."

"It's okay."

"No, it's a long, long way from okay. You see, I tried to be a certain kind of person, the kind of person I thought I should be—certainly the kind my parents and all my friends thought I should be."

I tilted my head toward the sky. "You mean, a mom kind of person, don't you?"

She was crying softly. "Yes. Yes. But as you know, I was lousy at it. It wasn't who I was. I tried—I promise I did—to *make* it who I was, but I just couldn't."

"Well, maybe it wasn't just you. I'm sure I wasn't the easiest kid to parent."

Her head began shaking violently. "That's not it. Not at all. I'm not saying you had no faults, but I don't want you to miss the point here. It wouldn't have mattered if you were the perfect child. The outcome would have been the same, ultimately. I'm telling you this because I don't want you to blame yourself. I got the feeling you were doing that when it all went down. And maybe you're still doing it now. Look, Griffin, there is so much I didn't give you, and there is little I can give you now, but at least I can free you from the guilt. At least I can give you that. Okay?"

"Okay" would have been the definitive answer, but I didn't

have it in me. So I just stood there, silent, even though I knew this was the kind of thing that tugged at my mom's nerves—nerves that were already strung as tight as piano wires.

She released my wrists and crossed her arms. "Don't you have anything to say? Any answer at all?"

I said the only thing that occupied my mind: "I need to get back to Denver." Then I started back toward Maxwell's house.

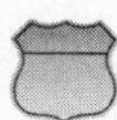

I sat in the front seat of the Durango, staring down the blank sheet of paper in my creatively named Plain Writing Tablet, which I kept stuffed in the glove compartment. *Okay, Mr. Would-Be Writer,* I challenged myself, *it's coming up on fifteen minutes, and your mom will be out here any moment. So if you have anything to say, any words of comfort for two people who have just lost a son, now would be the time to let this pen in your hand bleed.*

I finished writing just as I heard the front screen door bang shut. As my mom drew close to me, I saw that she had applied a fresh coat of makeup. I tore the white sheet of paper from the notebook, folded it neatly in half, and wrote For Maxwell and Lynnette on the outside.

"I wrote this for you and your husband, Mom," I told her. "Please share it with him when you get a chance." This was the kind of thing Amanda Mac would have said in a similar situation, and I'd rather trust her instincts than mine any day.

My mom took the note. "Thank you, Griffin," she said. "You always wrote so well; I know we will be touched by your words. It's funny, you know, your dad just called again. He wanted to make double-sure we were okay. And, of course, he asked about you—were you okay to drive and such. Abi, our little beagle, started barking while we were on the phone, and it got me thinking about King. You remember him, right?"

I forced a smile. "Mom, a boy never forgets his first dog."

She returned my smile, but hers wasn't forced. "Well, when King got so sick and we knew he didn't have long, your Dad resolved to sleep on the floor on a blanket next to the dog. He said, 'I don't want King to die alone. I can't bear to think of that happening to him.' It happened on the second night, which, I guess, given your dad's bad back, was merciful all the way around."

"I remember King dying," I said, "but I didn't know Dad did that. I'm not surprised, though."

"He is truly a good man. Learn from him."

"I better go," I said quietly. I offered my left hand to my mom, and she clasped it in both of hers.

"Be careful," she said. "And I hope that one day you won't hate me. And I hope Colby—"

I watched my mother dissolve into tears. I waited awhile to speak, for fear she wouldn't be able to hear me over her sobbing. "I don't hate you," I told her after she had cried herself out. I wasn't sure those words were actually true until I heard myself saying them. But I felt relief wash over me at the realization that I hadn't lied to my mother on a day like this.

"I hope that's true," she said. "Or that it will become true. Dalton liked you, you know. And he didn't like many people. I know he was kind of pissy last night, but he wouldn't have brought you to his room, even under threat of house arrest, if he didn't like you. And you two were in there a while."

"We could have been friends," I said. "I won't forget him."

My mom released my hand, and I drove away. Through a side-view mirror, I saw her unfolding the note.

I had written this:

Maxwell and Mom,
I hope that the peace that somehow eluded Dalton in this world will be his in the next.
With love and prayers,
Griffin Smith

It had taken me about fifteen minutes to come up with the eighteen words that formed the heart of my message—a pace that would make me pretty much unemployable in the world of words, unless I could find a job carving them into marble. For a while, finding the right words felt like groping for a light switch inside a strange, dark house. I didn't want to resort to some cliché. And I didn't want to say, "I'm sorry for your loss," because that's what the TV detectives and TV doctors say to every dead person's family on every cop show and medical drama on every channel on every cable and satellite network. Pretty soon this trite nugget will become so ubiquitous that it will be shortened to its initials, like chat-room shorthand. Thus, a somber lawman in a suit can approach a murdered girl's mom and simply say "ISFYL, ma'am."

In the end, I'd leaped over my writer's block by imagining Amanda in my situation. I thought about what she would write. I thought about what would come from her heart, because that's what I wanted to come from mine.

I wondered if my words would bring any comfort to Dalton's

father, or to my mom. And I wondered if/when I became a writer for my J-O-B, if I'd ever have to write anything as hard as the Dalton note.

Mr. Ross, for all the fun I poke at him, has taught me a lot about writing. So has Mr. Saunders, and Miss Cavanaugh, the journalism teacher. But the best advice I received in four years of high school was from Justin Wyatt, who is the best writer in the school, maybe the state.

"People talk all day about technique and voice and style," he told me once, "but in the end, it's all about meaning every single word."

I thought about how serious Justin looked when he said this to me, and I wished I had a cup of something to raise in a long-distance toast to him, because I had done it exactly the way he'd said.

The thought of offering a toast to Justin started to make me thirsty, so I stopped again at Sip & Go on my way back to Denver. "Welcome back, darlin'," Sally called to me when I entered. I felt her eyes scanning me for a moment, then her upbeat tone changed. "Tough trip, young man?"

I whistled softly. "You might say that."

"You goin' to be okay?"

I considered the question, really turned it over and over in my mind as though it were an apple I was thinking about taking a bite of. "I'm not sure," I said finally.

Sally didn't reply, for which I was grateful. I didn't need anyone going all *60 Minutes* on me at the moment. I breezed by the energy drinks and found the spigot bearing the tag REGULAR COFFEE. I could almost hear an angel choir burst into song as I filled up my thirty-ounce cup.

I smiled at Sally as I handed her two dollars. As I turned to leave, I said, "Vaya con Dios," remembering her farewell from the day before. But then I realized that *her* farewell had made sense, as I was the one getting ready to "vaya" at the time. I offered my best sheepish laugh. "Uh, I mean, goodbye," I corrected myself. "I guess you're not going anywhere."

"Darlin'," she said, her voice taking on parental timbre, "we're all goin' somewhere, and as for me, I intend to go just as you say."

"You might want to think about getting rid of the porn behind the counter," I started to say, but then I stopped myself, as I realized that would have been something the Old Griffin would have said—the one who didn't usually pay attention. Post-Dalton-Death Griffin noticed that Sally's name tag didn't say MANAGER or even ASSISTANT MANAGER. Just Sally. And she was working on a Saturday morning. She probably didn't have any say in the merchandise. In fact, maybe without her influence, the porn would be down at kids'-eye-level with the Moon Pies and Laffy Taffy.

So instead of busting Sally's chops, I just told her, "Fair enough."

"Stop in, if you're ever up this way again," she said.

"Will do."

I started the Durango, wondering what bizarre convergence of events might bring me back to the vicinity of Wheatland, Wyoming, but it wasn't beyond the realm of possibility. If a coyote that should, by all rights, be dead can rise up and run again, and an eighteen-year-old with a wonderfully wicked sense of humor (and a rich dad) cannot find one reason to continue living and, as a result, kill himself, well, then anything was possible.

I sat in the backseat feigning sleep as we drove west on Highway 36, taking Cole from Denver to Boulder. I knew this was the only way to keep myself from being peppered with questions about Dalton, Mom, Maxwell, and, for all I knew, the Wheatland High School Bulldogs and how they were going to fare in football in the fall.

Cole shared the backseat with me, and every time I risked easing my right eye open to look at him, I found him gazing out his window. He seemed sad.

When we pulled up to Cole's dorm, I slid out of the Durango and did my best to transform myself into Mr. Efficient. I unlocked our small, blessed-by-prayer trailer and informed everyone in the general vicinity, "Cole and I can haul the big stuff. Dad, you and Rhonda can bring the rest. Let's make it quick, though; it's almost noon, and we need to get back on the road soon."

I heard loud barking, and before long, a few thickly muscled football players in cutoff T-shirts jogged up, clapped Cole on the back, made quick introductions to me and my family remnant, then barked some more.

We had Cole moved into his room in less than a half hour. Then my dad hugged Cole, in front of God and football players and everybody. I made a mental note of this, wondering what I could do to ensure that my arrival at Lewis College would happen under cover of night.

Well, I thought, *at least Dad isn't laying hands on Cole and praying over him.* I had this thought approximately eight seconds before Dad took Cole's hands in his own and they both bowed their heads. I edged away from them, wondering if the other Buff gridders would start barking again—or something even more irreverent. But they were silent. In shock, most likely.

Dad gave way to Rhonda, and I turned my back on the scene and walked away. I was tempted mightily to watch the two of them. It would be one of the most awkward goodbyes in the long, storied history of awkward goodbyes. But I knew it would put more pressure on Cole if he knew I was watching him, so I watched a girl in a CU cross-country T-shirt running by at about 5:30 mile pace. *I'm glad I'm not going to school here,* I thought. *I would probably be hard-pressed to make the* girls' *team.*

I was still watching the girl phenom disappear around a curve when Rhonda snaked her arm around my shoulders. "You're up," she said. I sensed it was taking her a lot of effort to sound so nonchalant.

By the time I got to him, Cole's breathing was so forced that it was like he was learning to do it for the first time. "Don't worry," I told him, "you'll get used to this altitude. You'll be breathing just like a normal person in a couple of weeks."

He smiled at me, out of politeness, not because I had said anything in the general vicinity of witty.

"Want to take a little walk?" I offered.

"Not sure if I can move."

"Left foot, right foot. As long as you stick to that pattern, you're golden."

When we were about fifty yards—almost a Cole Sharp discus throw—away from my dad and Rhonda, I stopped. "It'll go fast," I said. "We'll be home, enjoying a long Christmas break before you know it."

"It better."

I studied Cole for a moment. He looked smaller at this big school. He hadn't been the biggest guy at Talbot High, not even close. But only Sal Ernst could out-bench-press him, and Sal had forty pounds and a Mexican pharmacy's worth of performance-enhancers going for him.

"Griff," he said, staring off toward the Rocky Mountains, "I don't know if I can do this."

"You can do this. I know you can."

My best friend didn't look convinced. "I wish you were going here," he said. "Maybe we could still meet somewhere for Thanksgiving, like we talked about. It's too long a time till Christmas, I think."

I was really hoping to visit Amanda at Thanksgiving. "Maybe," I said. "Look, man, let's just do this, okay? Dragging it out is killing me."

I stuck out my hand. Cole grabbed it, then pulled me into a fierce hug. "Stay strong, my brother," he said.

"You, too."

Cole released me, then took a step back. "Run fast," he said.

I looked in the direction of the once-barking football players. "Play strong," I told him. "You're just as good as any freshman out there."

"You're the best friend I've ever had."

"Thanks for saying that. And right back at ya."

"I'm sorry about— "

I shook my head at him and put a forefinger to my lips. "That's over," I reminded him. "Now, I gotta scoot before Dad comes over here and starts another prayer meeting. E-mail me in a couple of days, okay? And I'll call you from the road."

Cole turned away from me, and I knew why. I resisted the urge to run to the Durango and speed away, whether Dad and Rhonda were in the vehicle or not. I just needed to get away from the scene of this farewell. The Colby goodbye and the Cole goodbye had just about killed me. I didn't know how in the wide world of sports I was going to say goodbye to my dad in a couple of days.

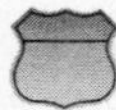

We backtracked toward Denver so that we could jump back onto I-70. When we approached the Eisenhower Tunnel a little while later, I looked over my shoulder and told Rhonda, "This is one of the longest tunnels in the country. You're supposed to see if you can hold your breath all the way through."

"I don't know, dude," she said, smiling, "I can't even see the end of this thing. But I'll give it a shot. You down for this, B.T.?"

My dad, who was in the passenger seat next to me, frowned. I knew he was calculating the probability. "How long is this tunnel anyway, son?"

"I don't know, Dad. Long enough to get us through this ginormous mountain. Now, please don't turn this into a story problem. Just fill up your lungs and see what happens."

I smiled as I heard Rhonda and my dad take big gulps of air. There was no way Rhonda would make it, but at least this would shut her up for a couple of minutes. A week ago, I would have said that my dad had no chance either, but a week ago, I would have said that he'd never hit me. And I'd have bet my liver that he'd never play a game of human Frogger on an interstate highway, all to retrieve a dead Pittsburgh puppy's collar.

I still couldn't see the end of the tunnel when Rhonda began gasping and coughing. "No way," she said. "I'm sorry to purse out, but I don't have the lungs for this."

My dad began wheezing and sputtering about ten seconds later. "My goodness, what a lengthy tunnel," he managed to say before erupting into a coughing fit of his own. I saw a pinprick of light ahead of me. *Relax,* I told myself, *you can do this.* I felt pressure behind my eyes, as if two little cartoon guys were inflating them with hand pumps. I knew I was going to have a dandy cranium-in-a-vise headache as a result of holding my breath for what had to be coming up on two minutes, which was my record. I let a little air escape through my nose, but I didn't inhale. (Really, I didn't.)

At about two hundred yards from the end of the tunnel, I knew I wouldn't make it—at least not without passing out. Then, for some reason, I heard the voice of the genius Nina Majors in my head: "Speed up, you idiot!" I stomped on the accelerator as if I were trying to kill a spider. I was flirting with 100 when the Durango entered sunlight again, and I allowed myself to breathe.

"Dude, you are crazy," Rhonda laughed. "That is some serious lung capacity you're packing in that bod of yours!"

I looked into the rearview mirror and grinned at Rhonda. She was right; my lungs were well-developed. If only I could say the same of my conscience, my soul.

"Son," my dad was saying, shaking his head in disbelief, "how in the world did you develop that kind of breath control?"

"Making out with Ally Long for hours on end," would have been the most honest answer. That would have been "keepin' it real," as Rhonda is so fond of saying. But I think it was T. S. Eliot who said that people can handle only so much reality, and I was quite sure the Ally Long revelation would have filled my dad's cup o' reality to overflowing. I didn't know what Rhonda would think, but I didn't spend a lot of time worrying about that. Because I also didn't care.

When we entered Glenwood Canyon, about sixty-five miles from the Colorado/Utah border, I heard Rhonda sigh. I swung my head over my shoulder. I thought she might be admiring the towering rock walls of the canyon, but she was asleep and, apparently, having a pleasant dream. I hoped like crazy it wasn't about Cole.

When we popped out of the canyon and into the town of Glenwood Springs, Dad suggested that we stop for an early dinner. I thought Rhonda would start whining about how she wanted to soak in one of the natural hot springs that dot the town, but she ate in near-silence, picking halfheartedly at some bizarro salad that appeared to feature both raisins and cubed chicken—an unholy pairing if ever I saw one.

I wondered if she was starting to miss Cole and that was what had deflated her spirits. *If that's the case,* I thought, looking at her as she tried to spear a raisin with one tine of her fork, *it serves you right. But look on the bright side, girlfriend, abstinence makes the heart grow fonder*.

My dad held the back door for her as she climbed back into the Durango. "Are you okay, Rhonda?" he asked.

She closed her eyes for a moment, then opened them slowly. "I'm just missing Colby. He's such a cool little dude."

Colby? Did I hear that right?

"Bryant," Rhonda was saying now, "couldn't we please try to call him? I know it'll be roaming charges and all, but . . ."

Dad plucked the cell from one of the cup holders and poked his way through Aunt Nic's number. "It's her answering machine," he said after a while. "Colby probably talked her into taking him to a movie. We'll try again later; I promise."

I heard Rhonda slump back in her seat. "Do you miss him too, Griff?" she said.

"Yeah, I sure do." *A lot more than you do. If we were to have a Who Misses Colby Most contest, I would own you. You're a newb when it comes to this. You might be older, but I was missing Colby back when you were prancing nearly naked around some* other *middle-aged guy's apartment swimming pool. So don't even start with me, woman.*

Rhonda started crying softly, and for a moment I feared that I had inadvertently broadcast my ungracious tirade out loud. But Dad wasn't glaring at me or punching me in the shoulder, so I knew I was safe on that count.

The alternative explanation for the Rhonda tears, however, was equally disconcerting: What if she really did miss my little brother that much?

The first thing you notice when you close in on the Colorado/Utah border is how much the terrain flattens. It's like God grabbed the end of a lumpy rug and gave it a couple of mighty tugs. I felt like we were back in Kansas again.

It was almost four thirty when we entered Utah. This was my first foray into the Beehive State, and I was immediately struck by how most of the cities would make great names for old white guys: Ogden, Brigham, Roy, Orem, Vernal. I wondered if this was just a coincidence or if the towns were, in fact, named after old white dudes. I thought about asking one of the highway patrolmen, who were so plentiful that I wondered if they were staking out the whole state.

A half hour after we crossed the Utah border, my dad stabbed his left forefinger across the top of the steering wheel. "Up there, in the median," he said. "Better slow down."

I fought to keep exasperation from seeping into my voice. "I see him, Dad. Saw his twenty-eight friends before him, too."

"I'm just trying to keep you from getting a ticket."

I started to say, "Well, if you frustrate me to such a degree that I go temporarily blind, lurch off the road, and clip an Osmond with my bumper, I'm gonna get a ticket for sure. So maybe a moratorium on the pointing of fingers and clearing of throats is in order." But instead I just gripped the steering wheel like I was trying to choke it.

"Are you okay, Griffin?" my dad asked. I felt him studying me. "Anything I can get you?"

I felt my frustration melting away with a realization: What I needed was a drink. Preferably vodka, but I'd settle for absinthe, Pabst Blue Ribbon, even Nyquil. I had a small bottle of Smirnoff, a parting gift from Sal Ernst, tucked into my toiletries bag, which was tucked into my suitcase. But my suitcase was buried somewhere in the back of the Durango, under one of Rhonda's eighteen bags and suitcases and satchels and knapsacks. And I knew that if I insisted on excavating my suitcase from under Rhonda's rubble, I would be forced to provide a solid reason. And I knew that, "I'm just dying to floss," wouldn't quite cut it.

"Griffin," my dad was saying, "are you failing to respond because you're angry about something, or have you gone somewhere else again?"

I chuckled. "Sorry, Dad. I know I'm a little tense. It's not you; it's just that these last couple of days have really knocked me around, you know?"

"Anything you want to talk about?"

"Uh, no. I don't want to talk about any of what went down. I don't even want to *think* about it."

"Well," Rhonda began slowly, "let's talk about something completely different, then."

I fought to keep my eyes from rolling. "Such as?" I queried.

"Let's talk about school. As someone who never went to college, I'm wondering how you feel right now. Are you scared? Do you feel pressure to get good grades? I mean, you and that Nina Majors really tore it up in high school—"

"Stop right there," I interrupted. "Rhonda, you need to understand something: I'm not like Nina Majors, not even close."

"I can't agree with that," my dad said. "You were number two in your entire class. And your GPA was 3.9 something or other. What was it exactly again?"

"I honestly don't know, Dad," I said. "And I really don't want to talk about this anymore."

My poor disillusioned father. He still thinks I am the kind of guy who would know his GPA, right down to the twenty-third decimal, better than pi. But the truth is that once I sacrificed my 4.0 like an Old Testament lamb, I ceased to care. It wasn't that

I couldn't remember all of those numbers, because with enough practice, I knew I could. I simply chose not to. Late in my junior year, I tired of the pressure to be perfect. It was like having my guy parts in a vise 24/7. And the Magic Happy Power that each straight-A report card brought to the Smith home was getting progressively weaker. It got to be like those little leaf-shaped air fresheners you hang from your rearview mirror. For a day or two, your car smells like vanilla or a lush forest. Then it goes back to smelling like . . . car.

So I opted not to turn in a major paper, thus lowering my Advanced Research Writing grade to a B-plus. Mr. Ross did everything but come over to my house and let me dictate the thing to him. But I told him I was having personal problems and finding it impossible to write anything more creative than my own name. When grades were posted, I was depressed for about ten minutes, but after that, I felt like I had come up for air after being tangled in seaweed at the bottom of the ocean.

You see, I'm not like Nina Majors, Ms. Class Valedictorian. Her final GPA was 4.27, better than perfect. If you doubt someone can be better than perfect, you've never met Nina. She started taking college classes as a ninth grader. She taught herself Japanese just for kicks.

She has world-class Google-fu. I've known her since sixth grade, and I've never heard her answer a question wrong or say anything that wasn't smart and insightful. A disclaimer here: I can judge only the stuff she says that I can actually understand, which is roughly 65 percent of what comes out of her lipstick-free mouth. Sometimes she starts talking about "String Theory" and loses me at about Sentence 1, Word 3.

String cheese I know. String Theory I am not capable of knowing.

It's incomprehensible to me that Nina and I were voted "Class Brains." Sometimes we'd be walking down a hallway at school together and one of the teachers would say something like, "Make way: Here comes the Talbot High School brain trust." Or if we were divided into quiz teams in a science class, Amanda Sandwich would always protest, "If your team gets Nina, then we have-have-have to get Griffin! It's only fair."

To me, that's like hearing this: "Tonight our A&E special will examine the parallel lives and crafts of two legendary actors, Sir Laurence Olivier and Sir Steve Guttenberg."

You might factor in my GPA and think I'm sandbagging here, but trust me on this. Often, I will stretch the truth like Laffy Taffy, no problem. But not on this subject. The difference between me and Nina Majors is simple: She is a genius, whereas I am a guy who knows how to get really good grades. People confuse that with being smart.

My mom did all the time. She invariably introduced me to strangers as "my smart boy." Never my good-looking boy or my athletic boy. And as I've noted before, it didn't escape my notice that she always put up my report cards on the big old Kenmore refrigerator/freezer, but never my class pictures. Once, she mentioned something about my "awkward phase," which I think has spanned kindergarten to the present moment.

I was navigating I-70, playing Spot the Highway Patrol Car, when I started thinking about Nina Majors and wondering if she ever found it burdensome to be so smart. I wished I had talked to her more about things that weren't school-related. I wished we could have been better friends, but it was hard, given that we were often pitted against each other, being the No. 1 and No. 2 students in our class.

But the rivalry that the teachers and a few of the students tried to stir up between us was laughable. Nina was like Tiger Woods. I was like All the Other Golfers Who Wish They Were as Good as Tiger Woods. In seventh grade, we were the last two spellers standing in the all-school spelling bee, and I spelled G-e-d-d-y L-e-e when given the word "bassist" because I just couldn't take the pressure. Besides, why prolong the inevitable?

My musings about Nina were interrupted by the sound of Rhonda doing . . . what was this, practicing the alphabet?

As I paid closer attention, I realized that she was giving my dad her professional, psychiatric diagnosis of one Griffin Smith, a diagnosis based on her professional standing as a waitress with a high school diploma. "I'm telling you, Bry," she was saying, "it's classic AD/HD/OCD. Adderall is really good for that. He might need some Zoloft, too.

Now, I wouldn't mind checking out Zoloft, just because their little spokes-character is so cool. But I wished I could have told Rhonda that I had done just fine handling my own medication needs. No psychiatrist needed. I had just needed Sal Ernst to continue poaching pills from his grandparents and meeting gang-bangers late at night in Theale Park, which is a great park—if you're a gang member, sexual predator, or syringe.

Of course, I was nervous about what would happen when my meager supply of white pills ran out—something that I estimated would occur shortly after Thanksgiving break. Sal hadn't expanded his business to include a mail-order division, and besides, it was only a matter of time before he got himself incarcerated—again—for something. And I figured that the prison officials would frown upon his distributing anything other than clean laundry.

However, there was always the possibility that education — and perhaps even life in general — would start to be less painful once I began college, but I didn't want to count on this. I had counted on my parents' staying married, my romance with Amanda Mac sprouting and then flourishing, and death remaining some vague and distant concept that I wouldn't need to concern myself with for another seventy years or so. And just look what happened. If the past few years had taught me anything, it was that you shouldn't keep your hopes up. In fact, you might be well advised not to keep them at all.

My dad and Rhonda were asleep by the time we were two hours into Utah. I slid an Al Green best-of CD into the player and found myself in a great zone for driving. I drifted deep into thoughts and memories, and the Utah towns just slid by.

When "Let's Stay Together" came on, I smiled with sad recognition. Often when my mom and dad's arguments escalated to full-volume shouting and screaming, I would play on my iPod a song that was the antithesis of marital strife. I found the irony soothing. And if a plate or coffee cup happened to shatter on a downbeat, I would take that as a sign that God was in on the joke and was providing me a little signal as if to say, "Yes, I know this is hard on you, but if you can just keep your sense of humor, you can survive this."

I have no idea if this is true, but when the people who brought you into the world are indicating their regret that the other was ever born, you hang on to whatever you can.

About an hour from Richfield, it began to rain. I clicked off the CD player and listened awhile to the pleasant whisper of road spray against the Durango's undercarriage.

Dad woke up a few minutes later. "The road slick, son?" he yawned.

"Nah. We have good tires. The rain is kind of a nice change of pace, actually. Plus, it helps get the mashed bugs off the windshield." I leaned forward and focused hard on the road so Dad would feel guilty about trying to embark on an actual conversation and let me go back to enjoying my Interstate White Noise.

"Thank you for driving so much, Griff. You've really been our road warrior. I feel rather bad. I don't know why I've been so sleepy."

"It's okay, Dad. I know you're going to have to drive most of the way back. And, hey, thank you for coming out here with me. I know it's a chunk of your vacation time."

"Well, perhaps I should have listened to you. Things sure would have been less, uh, complicated if we'd just flown you out."

"Maybe, but they'd have been . . . uh, less interesting, too. Whatever you want to say about this trip, it's certainly not something I'll ever forget. So, like I said, thanks."

"I appreciate your saying that. It really means a lot to me."

I thought the conversation might actually die at that point and I could resume listening to the sounds of the rain, feeling the road vibrating up my spine. But my father was kind of leaning toward me, and the way he was smiling told me, "I'm enjoying this father/son talk. Please don't let it end."

Okay, I urged myself. *Do this. For him.* "Dad," I began, "is your job going okay? You miss being an entrepreneur, your own boss and all of that?"

He laughed softly, and I realized I rarely heard this sound from him. "Well, I wasn't much of an entrepreneur. It's not like everything I touched turned to gold. More like it turned to something else—something which a gentleman doesn't mention by name. I'm afraid I didn't set a very good example for you and Colby. I grew desperate. I made some bad decisions. But I would try one thing, and after a while it would feel like I was beating my head against a wall. Then something else would present itself, and in the back of my mind, I would think, *This is just another brick wall.* But at least it was a *different* brick wall. And I was so desperate that the subtle difference was enough."

"But at least you kept trying, Dad. I wasn't always sure about the choices you were making, but you never quit. And that was a good example for Colby and me. Especially because we both know you were doing it for us."

He leaned even closer to me. "Really? Colby knows that too? How can you be sure, Griff?"

I smiled at my dad. "Because I told him so."

He shook his head in disbelief. "You're a good son," he said.

Not really, I thought, *but I guess I do have my moments.*

Then he was asleep again. It was as if just talking about Pizza On the Move and all the others had exhausted him.

It was past 9 p.m. when I nudged the SUV into the parking lot of the Kountry Inn in Richfield, not far from where I-70 droops south and becomes I-15. I had protested our staying at an establishment for whom even basic spelling was a challenge, but Dad and Rhonda countered that the place looked quaint.

"Quaint," I had said. "And to you, that's a *good* thing?"

"Oh, Griffin" was all my dad could manage in response. But he said those two words with a weary smile on his face, and that told me that he was something other than disappointed in me. And that made me happy enough to agree to eat delivery pizza with him and Rhonda, in their room, before retiring to my own room and doing my part to support the Russian distilling industry.

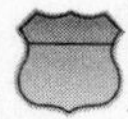

You can determine immediately if any hotel room is high quality, provided you know the signs. Here's the first thing you do upon entering your room: Find the remote control for the TV. If you find yourself asking, "What remote?" or worse, "What TV?" then you have your answer right there.

Once you do find the remote, take a close look. If it's sleek and modern and has a sticker on the back listing more than fifty channels, you're in for a pleasant stay. However, if the remote is large and clunky, like those clumsy, prehistoric cell phones that rich guys used to have in their convertibles in the early 1990s, you're in serious trouble. There will be hairs—long black ones, most likely—on your supposedly freshly laundered towels. There will be faint but still troubling stains on the sheets; a strange odor, not unlike stale chicken broth, in the bathroom; and wafer-thin walls and noisy neighbors in your immediate future.

I nodded approvingly at the slim remote control that I found on the nightstand next to my Kountry Inn queen bed. The bedspread portrayed an army of ducks, but it smelled clean, with a faint hint of hospital-grade disinfectant. Yes, the Kountry Inn was Kwaint, but it was also Klean and Komfortable.

I found ESPN on the TV and fished the small bottle of vodka out of my toiletries bag. I stared at it awhile. Then, with a sigh of resignation, I placed it back in the bag. I determined I would save it for later.

Despite all that had happened so far, despite all that I had seen, nothing really hurt—at least not at the moment. And I hadn't needed to be smart or well-informed or well-prepared during the entire trip, so conversely, there was no need to be stupid or slow to balance things out.

Besides, I worried about exhausting my vodka supply. It would be a challenge to find a new source. Since Lewis was, as the catalog said, a "faith-based institution," I knew there would be a sizable population of preacher's kids, and at least half of them would be covert drinkers like me. But it could be tough to find them. And if you latch onto the wrong preacher's kid, you could end up having to deal with a Concerned Friend who doesn't have the decency to let you go ahead and destroy yourself.

But I couldn't let myself start to obsess about that now. I stacked three pillows in the center of the bed and lay back to watch a recap of the day's Major League Baseball action. Once the sports coverage drifted from baseball to golf, I went to get the cell phone from Dad so that I could call Cole.

"Hullo," he said, raising his voice over the barking in the background, "is this you, Griff?"

"Yeah. You settling in okay?"

"I guess so. It's kinda crazy here. There was this big lineman passed out on our bathroom floor. I really needed to get in there, so I just kept driving my shoulder into the door, over and over, kinda like hitting the blocking sleds. I could move him just a couple of inches each time. I could hear his skin squeaking against the tile floor. He didn't even really wake up. Just kinda half-moaned every time the door hit him. Eventually, I got the door open enough so that I could squeeze in."

"That's pretty funny."

"Not really."

"Well, some of the parties back in Talbot got pretty crazy."

"Yeah, I guess so. But not like this. Seems a lot more, I don't know, dangerous here."

"Well, maybe we can have a nice low-danger party over Christmas break. I know Amanda Sandwich is going to try to put something together."

"That'd be good, I guess. That last party at her house was cool, in a weird sorta way."

"You got that right. Hey, I'm feeling pretty tired, Sharp. I just can't seem to get much sleep on this trip. And I mainly just wanted to check in, see how things were going so far. I'll call you again from the road tomorrow, okay?"

"Okay. Cool. Hey, Griff, thanks for calling."

I returned the phone to my dad and went back to my room. I wondered if the Christmas party at Amanda Sandwich's would be anything like the last one, the one on graduation night. The one I could still play in my head like a DVD. It's still untitled, but if pressed, I guess I'd call it *A Tale of Two Amandas* . . .

Cole and I spend about twenty minutes at the old-school keg party at the Radcliffe's barn. But after the fourth or fifth time one of my intoxicated classmates slings an arm around me and slurs something about "tappin' all those California girls," I nod at Cole, and we head for the invitation-only event at Amanda Sandwich's.

Nina Majors answers the door, cradling a bottle of Beck's. "Can you believe Amanda's parents cleared out so we could have the run of the place?" she shouts over some crappy pop song. It's by a group with a number and part of a house in its name. Three Broken Windows, maybe, or Five in the Attic? I can't believe that I even *almost* know this information.

I spend the next hour deflecting even more lascivious Cali-girl inquiries and searching for Amanda Mac. My Amanda. Or more accurately, my would-be Amanda.

At ten past eleven, she shows up, a bottle of unfiltered apple juice in hand. I can't believe how much I love her. I feel drawn to her, as if she's an electromagnet and I'm a hunk of scrap metal. (Make of that metaphor what you will.)

"Amanda," I say over some new crunk artist, "I'm glad you're here. Can we go somewhere quiet?"

She shrugs helplessly and smiles. "I don't know. Can we?"

I offer her my hand, half-afraid she will spit on it, but instead she frowns for only a second before taking it. I lead her to the

Carlisles' back patio. Carlton Tucker and Linda Little are vacuum-sealed to each other's mouths. A few other couples are giggling and groping each other in the backyard. A large figure, Sal Ernst, maybe, appears to be relieving himself against the back fence.

"Okay," I tell Amanda, "Plan B."

I lead her to Mr. Carlisle's home office on the third level. The door is locked, but it's one of those safety locks that can easily be opened with a dime, which fortunately I have three of in my pocket.

"We'll be safe in here," I tell her, closing and locking the door behind us. "There are books in here. Nobody is coming in — too much of a risk of learning something."

Amanda laughs politely at my feeble sarcasm.

I gesture to Mr. Carlisle's calfskin chair, which Amanda probably wouldn't sit in if she knew what it was made of. She sits, and I try to position myself in a cool-yet-comfortable pose on the polished surface of Mr. Carlisle's oak desk.

"I kind of need to talk to you," I say, "because I know we'll both be working over the summer. Plus, you've got that missions trip."

"Yeah, I'm afraid the summer is going to fly by too fast."

"Yeah."

"So . . . talk to me, Griff. I'm all yours."

You have no idea how hard it is to refrain from asking Amanda to repeat that last bit, maybe a hundred times or so.

"Well, Amanda, it's just weird, you know?"

She shakes her head. "Um, not really. What's weird?"

"Lots of stuff. But specifically . . . uh, in some ways, you see, high school went pretty much how I thought it would, but in others . . ."

I look at her and realize she's not going to prompt me anymore. She's not being impatient, but she's not going to do this little verbal dance with me either. Crap.

"To get right to the point, then, uh . . . Well, I just want you to know that I guess I wish things could have been . . . I don't know . . . different. With us."

Still no assistance from Camp Amanda.

"Don't get me wrong; I am thankful we're such great friends. But what I'm trying to say is that for a long time I have hoped we could—if you wanted to—be more than that. Bottom line is . . . I guess I really like you. Have for a long time."

"I know," she says with a soft laugh.

This information is not helpful or assuring in any way. I was hoping for, at the very least, an "I really like you too, Griff." But maybe I can get to that if I can just ask the right incisive question.

"Uh, oh . . . um, you know?" *Great job, Griffin. You are Mr. Loquacious. What? You couldn't have thrown in a "duh" or "hmmm" amid all of your stumbling*?

She laughs again, and I think of how great it would have been to hear that laugh over dinner at the Big Bear or Grandma Brooks, during midnight phone conversations, or between vintage movie-esque saying-goodbye-at-the-train-platform kisses.

"Zeke, my little brother," she explains. "He'd come up and knock on my door from time to time and say, 'Hey 'Manda, Griffin Smith is parked across the street *again*, watching our house like the police!'"

I feel my face growing hot. "Look," I say, "it wasn't like I was stalking you or anything. It was just that I kept trying to pop over and see you, then I'd get . . . nervous or something. So I'd sit there in my car awhile, trying to think of something to say. Trying to think of a good reason to actually . . . you know."

She raises one thin eyebrow, and I realize that she doesn't "know." Or if she does, she isn't going to acknowledge it.

"The main thing," I say eventually, "is that I want you to know I wasn't being all stalker-like or anything."

She frowns a little, and it occurs to me that to keep asserting, I AM NOT A STALKER! I AM NOT A STALKER, is perhaps not an effective way for a guy to persuade a girl that he's not stalking her.

"Anyway, Griffin," she says at last, "it's all water under the bridge at this point, isn't it?"

I hear myself exhale, too heavily, like I've just completed a bench press. "I guess so, Amanda. I just felt like this was something I needed to do. I want you to know that I think you are an amazing person. And I hope we can stay in touch this coming year. So, do you know your e-mail address at school yet?"

She flashes me a teacher-esque smile. "I gave it to you, remember? I sent an e-mail to all my closest buds from school and church."

I remember as soon as I see her smile. Several excuses parade their way through my brain, but they all seemed too poorly disguised to fool Amanda Mackenzie.

"That's right. Sorry."

"It's okay," she says. And for the life of me, I cannot read which kind of "It's okay" I am getting:

A) It's okay. I'm sure you get a lot of e-mails from girls and you can't remember them all. I'm just glad for the chance to be able to remind you so that we can ensure our future communication.

B) It's okay. I know that you are scatterbrained, and I find that charming.
C) It's okay. I know that you are scatterbrained, and I find that inconsiderate, annoying, and immature, thus making you the kind of person I will never marry, nor even kiss in a weak "goodbye" moment.
D) It's okay. I don't like you anyway.

I have narrowed the choice to C or D when Amanda stands up. "I want to hug you," she informs me.

I fear it will be one of those Hollywood lean-forward-and-pat-each-other-on-the-shoulder-blades hugs, but Amanda Mackenzie gives me a genuine last-day-of-summer-camp hug, and I feel my knees turning to gelatin. I force myself to think about the Periodic Table of the Elements, specifically the Noble Gases, to keep from getting, uh, romantically inspired.

She taps an unpolished fingernail against her now-empty apple juice bottle. "Do you know if Mr. and Mrs. Carlisle recycle glass? Or do I need to ask them?"

"Actually, you can't ask 'em. They're not here right now."

Amanda is frowning. "Then where's the adult supervision?"

"There is none. I mean, they'll be back in a while, but since this is a private party and we're all seniors, I guess they trust us."

She stands. "I've got to go. I can't be here. I promised my parents. It's kind of a rule we have."

"But it's not like we're at a kegger out in the boonies. We're in a house. There are neighbors around. I'm here. You're safe with me. And like I said, Amanda's parents will be home soon. Please don't go." I can't believe how shrill and whiny I sound. Colby sounds less mewling when he begs to stay up late and watch one more rerun of *Cow and Chicken*.

"A promise is a promise, Griff. I need to go now. Please give Colby a hug from me. And say hello to your dad and Rhonda, okay?"

I walk her to the door, past Carlton, who is now freak-dancing with Lisa in the living room. I'd like to say I walked Amanda to her car too, but I was more like a golden retriever following its master to the dog run.

"Hey, Amanda," I venture as I open her car door for her, "about what I said?"

"Yes."

I can't read that yes. Is it "Yes, please elaborate on what you said. Hearing of your long-repressed fondness for me gives me new life. It's like a B-12 shot for my very soul." Or is it, "Yes, I heard you. Thanks for sharing. Now, if you'll excuse me, I need to get home and watch the cooking channel because they're featuring this intriguing soufflé."

I study her. She isn't going to indicate one way or the other. She is simply letting her yes be yes. I hate when people go all biblical on me.

I find myself trying to loosen a piece of asphalt from the street with my toe. "Okay, I'll just say it: Do you have any response at all to what I said? I mean, I kinda went out on a limb, you know."

Amanda is smiling at me, but it's not a you're-charming-when-you're-nervous smile. "Griffin," she says so softly that her voice is almost a whisper, "do you know that a girl dreams for years about her first kiss? My first-ever kiss was on stage, with Dusty Redmond during the one-acts last year. And my second-ever kiss was also on stage, with Rick Fletcher this past spring. *The Sound of Music*. You were there. There has been no third kiss. So please don't talk to me about *your* regrets, okay?"

Dusty Redmond auditions for the one-acts with the express purpose of finding an opportunity to kiss otherwise unkissable girls like Amanda Mackenzie. And as Amanda would diplomatically put it, "The boy has hygiene issues."

Rick Fletcher has an ego even larger than the World's Largest Concrete Prairie Dog. He is certain he will become the greatest entertainer since Sinatra. "You know how I'm going to introduce myself once I've hit the big time?" he asked me after portraying Henry Higgins in the fall musical of our junior year.

"Uh, 'Hello, Branson!'" I offered.

I thought for a moment that Rick/Henry might take a swing at me, but he was standing there in his thick makeup and big-boy English clothes, and he must have realized that you can't rumble when you're dressed as Henry Higgins.

I play the Amanda/Rick kiss in my head, for roughly the five-hundredth time. Thank heaven the nausea went away after number four hundred or so. Then I study Amanda standing in front of me and grope for words I know I won't find in time.

Soon Amanda shakes her head slowly and slides into her car. Her taillights get smaller by the second. I notice that I've managed to dislodge a marshmallow-sized chunk of asphalt. I pick it up and fling it playfully at Amanda's rear bumper, but I can't throw anywhere near that far.

At this point in A Tale of Two Amandas, *the screen would fade out to black and then fade in again . . .*

It's 1:37 a.m., and the Carlisle parents still aren't home. Amanda Sandwich, who can barely speak or stand, says they've probably stopped for drinks. Then she grins at me and collapses to the floor.

Cole helps me carry her slumping weight to her bedroom, where we lay her across her bed. I go to remove her shoes but realize she's not wearing any. Then Cole and I begin clearing out the house. I fear there will be some protests, but even under the influence of a variety of chemicals, no one dares to defy Cole.

At the front door, Cole slaps me across the back like he's trying to kill a mosquito. "I can't believe it's over," he says.

"The party, or high school?" I ask.

"That's a good point."

I nod, but Cole is being too kind. I wasn't aware that I was trying to make a point.

"Call me tomorrow, okay?" he says. "We can run together."

Cole heads for his Civic, and I start to follow him, but something stops me. I can't remember ridding the Carlisle home of Carlton Tucker.

I half run toward Amanda's room. I can hear Carlton's eager, raspy breaths before I get there. Carlton is straining to pull his Abercrombie hoodie over his head.

"You need some help with that?" I ask him, keeping my voice low so as not to wake up Amanda. Why I want to avoid disturbing her slumber, I can't be sure.

Carlton freezes for a moment, and I can guess what he's thinking: *Do I doff the hoodie, anticipating that I can get rid of Griffin Smith and proceed to my debauching of my unconscious prey? Or do I leave it on for the moment so as to maintain my decorum, in case this situation escalates to violence?*

(I must admit, this is only a general guess. I know I'm off on the specifics. Carlton probably thinks "decorum" is part of the digestive system, and it's probable that he thinks "doff" is a British euphemism for "doing it.")

I feel relief wash over me when Carlton lowers his hoodie back over his small but promising beer belly. I don't want to fight a shirtless opponent. There is something way too Brokeback about the prospect.

"Go away, Smith," Carlton is saying. "This has nothing to do with you."

I wag my head. "Yes, it does. I'm the Nightwatchman." Thank you, Tom Petty. "I'm going to stay here, make sure Amanda is okay. Safe, you know."

Carlton is trying his best to give me a Billy Idol fishhook sneer, but he looks a little like my dad when he's trying to get a popcorn shell out of his teeth with his tongue. "I mean it; you better bounce," he says finally.

"What, Tuck? Is there no one conscious who wants you? And come on, she's not even your girlfriend anymore."

He takes a step toward me, and it's all I can do to hold my ground. He probably has twenty pounds on me, and there's the small matter that up to that point in my life, I've never been in anything more than a shoving match or two.

"This is your last chance," he says through gritted teeth. "Get out or die."

I manage a yawn. The yawn is good. I must remember the yawn. "I'm not going anywhere. You're not going to force yourself on an unconscious girl. I think they have a name for that: rape. Not to mention pathetic."

"Shut up!"

"Go home, Tuck. Please. I'm prepared to stay here all night if I have to. I'll even fight you if it comes to that. I don't want to, but I will. And you know that I never get tired. Besides, I'm not clumsy-drunk."

"Hey, bein' drunk just means I won't feel no pain."

"Not tonight you won't. But in the morning . . ."

He snorts. "You're just doin' this because *you* want her. How do I know that if I leave, you won't be all over her?"

"Uh, because I'm not a disgusting, lecherous pig?"

He doesn't have an immediate comeback; I probably lost him at lecherous. But he folds his arms across his puffed-out chest. "Tell you what," he says. "You want me outta here? You move me."

I sigh and fish my cell out of my pocket. "Okay. I think I can arrange that. I'm calling Cole. He will come back here and beat you like a piñata on Cinco de Mayo."

Carlton snorts again. Big snorter, this Carlton. "I can't believe you're gonna wuss out, get someone else to fight your battle."

"No, Tuck, it's called 'delegating,' and it's an effective thing to do." I hit a speed-dial number—the church information line—and Carlton stumbles out of the room. I follow him. He's swearing at me and vowing, "I'm not gonna forget this," but his 80-proof breath wafts over me, and I think he's wrong. I lock the front door behind him and go back to check on Amanda.

She's snoring softly, like a kitten purring. She told me once that she snores only when she's drunk. She'll probably have a head-pounding hangover tomorrow, but for now she's safe with me. I look at my watch. It's past two now, and I wonder if the Carlisle adults will be out all night. It's okay if they are. I'm the Nightwatchman. I am Security. I'll stand guard here as long as I have to. It strikes me that I wish *this* could be my job: protecting the Amanda Carlisles of the world from the Carlton Tuckers. I'd be good at it. And there's no way I would ever take advantage of the situation. Maybe under different circumstances, but not when I'm on the job. No chance.

At 2:32 I hear the moaning of the garage door, then muffled laughter. Adult-stupid "My, oh my, could those margaritas have *been* any *stronger*?" laughter.

There's a quilt draped over the footboard of Amanda's bed. I draw it up to her neck, then bend down and kiss her forehead. "Sweet dreams, Amanda," I whisper.

I keep my head near hers for a while. Her hair smells like herbal shampoo—and beer. I raise myself up and shake my head. "Five years you've wanted to do that," I scold myself softly, "and you go and kiss the wrong Amanda."

And we fade to black again.

Lying on my Utah Kountry Inn bed, I studied my watch. It was half-past midnight. An hour later back in Talbot, where Amanda Mac was probably sleeping. There was no way I could justify calling her. You are required to have won a couple million dollars in the lottery or be in the garage, a noose around your neck and ready to leap off the hood of the family Pontiac to your death before you can call someone at this late hour. Even Amanda, who shares with my dad the title of Most Understanding Person in the World.

But if I could call her, I'd tell her I was sorry for keeping my feelings hidden away, not unlike my hard liquor and my pills. I'd tell her that I was afraid to plunge into a relationship with her because I knew she would be too smart to fool, too perceptive to dupe, and thus at some point she would realize what a mess I was. And at that very point, she would dash away, just like that Wyoming coyote. Just like my mom.

I removed the two superfluous pillows from behind my head and closed my eyes. Almost as if on cue, the person in the next room began snoring like a farm vehicle.

"Great," I said. "I think I could have actually slept tonight, I'm that freakin' tired."

I sat up and covered my face with my hands. *Well,* I told myself, *you can either go for a walk or try to find some of those breathe-right nose-strips and slide them under the guy's door, then knock real hard and run away.*

The Kountry Inn sat apart from a row of gas stations, convenience marts, fast-food restaurants, and name-brand hotels. It was as if the old KI were being ostracized. I walked behind the hotel to the edge of the parking lot, where asphalt gave way to thin, waist-high stalks of some kind. In the meager light, they looked like weeds. But I noted the smell of freshly turned earth in the night air, so it was possible that the KI backed up to a farm of some sort.

The sound of someone clearing his sinuses, which never fails to turn my stomach, startled me. I looked to my left, to the opposite side of the parking lot, and that's when I saw the guy with the rifle.

It was small relief that the rifle wasn't trained on me—at least not yet. It could be that, once the guy realized there was something more interesting to shoot at than whatever was out in the Field of Weeds/Wheat/Whatever, I would be diving behind the nearest SUV for cover.

"Everything okay there, sir?" I heard myself asking, somewhat amazed I was able to speak at all.

"Hush!" came the response. "You'll spook him. I think I've got a bead on him."

"Uh, on whom?" I asked, dreading the possible responses:

My dad-burned-brother-in-law

The cheatin' sleazeball I caught with my wife

My abusive former priest

That annoying Anderson Cooper. Dude grates on my nerves somethin' fierce.

"Stinkin' coyote," the armed man said, then muttered, "I hate them friggin' mangy coyotes."

"Are you sure?" I heard myself asking, shocked that I was eschewing the timeless axiom, THOU SHALT NOT ASK DUBIOUS QUESTIONS OF THE MAN WITH THE RIFLE.

"What do you mean?" The voice was irritated. "I know a friggin' coyote when I see one."

"But it's dark," I noted, "and it looks like there are houses out there beyond the field. See those dots of light? And think of all the hotels around here. Maybe some kid's dog got away or something."

"Well, you can go ahead and find that out if you wanna go out there and fetch the carcass in just a second."

I looked around near my feet. I found a piece of concrete about the size of a hand grenade. I launched it in the direction the rifle was pointed. It wasn't a Cole-quality throw—he can hurl a baseball to the moon—but it was enough to send a dagger of pain into the front of my shoulder. I heard a soft thud, then the rustling of weeds/wheat/whatever as something bounded away.

"What'd you do that for?" the man asked accusingly. But I said a silent prayer of thanks at the fact that he was saying it with the butt of his rifle resting on the ground. In fact, the guy looked like he was posing for the cover of *Coyote Shooters Monthly*.

"As I said," I informed him while backing slowly toward a Chevy Tahoe that I sincerely hoped was bulletproof, "that coulda been some kid's dog. Besides, isn't it risky to be shooting a gun in the dark? Is it even legal?"

"Boy, are you lookin' for trouble? 'Cause if you keep runnin' that mouth— "

I bumped into the Tahoe—and jumped like I was on a pogo stick when the vehicle's alarm began to sound. But when you're looking to excuse yourself from the company of a gun-wielding coyote hater, the staccato blaring of a horn and the strobe-like flashing of the head- and tail-lights can really grow on you.

The man cradled his gun with one arm and speed-walked away.

I knew I didn't have much time before someone, probably the Tahoe's owner, came outside to investigate. So I angled my body toward Wyoming and said, "Okay, we're even now. You got that?" I wasn't sure if I was speaking to the Wheatland Coyote in particular or coyotes in general, but I hoped the appropriate target got the message.

I wish I could tell you about the last day of our trip, about the terrain and roadside points of interest along I-15, about whether you can feel the difference when you hit the desert climate of southern Utah. I wish I could report whatever clever put-downs Dad came up with when we sliced through Las Vegas (although I'm sure the phrase "Las Vegas—more like Lost Wages!" was involved). But after getting only about three hours of sleep during our night in Richfield (just *try* to sleep after saving the life of your brother-animal; that kind of rush doesn't soon wear off), I went into a fairy-tale quality slumber after about fifteen minutes in the SUV and didn't wake up until I heard Dad say, "I do believe that's Lewis College up there, Rhonda. Hey, Griff, wake up, buddy; we're in San Bernardino—almost to your school!"

Dad followed a series of handprinted signs noting Parking—This Way, and soon we arrived at a football-field-sized lot full of mammoth vehicles. I strained to focus my eyes on all the crying and parent-on-student hugging that was going on. I noticed a few awkward handshakes and tentative pats on the shoulder, too.

I was grateful that my own goodbyes were at least an hour or so away, but at the same time, I kind of wished I could get them over with right at the moment—while I was so groggy that my emotions would be numbed.

I looked around as we walked to the administrative building, feeling curious eyes on me and hoping that Rhonda was passing as my older sister, not my dad's tight little package of Middle Age Helper.

After obtaining two pack-mule-worthy folders and the keys to my dorm room, we went to the athletic center to meet Coach Freeman.

Coach Freeman wore a baseball cap, a white Adidas soccer shirt, red sweatpants, and top-of-the-line Asics running shoes. From the school's website, I knew he had been a tough half miler in his day, but his day was about twenty years ago. He was carrying the requisite middle-aged gut, and, unless they were brand-new, his running shoes didn't look like they had seen much actual running.

"Ah, Kansas," he was telling my dad, "Jim Ryun country. You ever get a chance to meet Mr. Ryun?" Coach asked, turning his attention to me.

I wondered if my run with Imaginary Ryun would count. "No, sir," I said. I could hear disappointment in my voice. "But maybe someday."

"Well, if you do," Coach said, "shake the man's hand for me."

Then my coach went into public-relations mode, telling my dad that I was already preregistered for all of my classes, that my books had been purchased, and that I would be living in the "jock quads," a series of four-bedroom units inhabited, for the most part, by Lewis College's soccer, cross-country, basketball, track, and baseball teams.

". . . and the jock quads," Coach said, winking at me, "are right across from Stewart Hall, one of the girl dorms."

I wondered if The Carrot was a Stewart Hall resident.

Next, Coach began a homily on training camp, which would start in a couple of days. I was so tired that most of his speech seemed to be in Latvian, but my mind did spring to life when I heard him say "fartlek." I knew this word, Swedish for "speed play," would make my dad wince. It sure did every time I tossed it into a conversation, which was as often as possible.

Coach concluded by inviting me to some kind of huge snack-fest in the school cafeteria that night, then excused himself.

The jock quad, officially known as Hill Hall, was our next stop. In almost total silence, we moved Griffin Smith's half a small trailer's worth of portable worldly possessions into my dorm room, which I would share with a sophomore point guard named Elden Thomas.

Thomas's stuff was in the room; he was not. I looked at the posters on his walls and tried to get a read on him. There was a poster featuring the current incarnation of the Duke Blue Devils, and another showcasing power forward Les Ford—who'd torn up the NCAA as a Wake Forest freshman the previous season—dunking over some lumpy and scared corn-fed white center.

It didn't escape my notice that all of Mr. Thomas's posters were of big men—power forwards or centers. Given that my new roomie was a point guard, this spoke volumes. I would have bet Dad or Rhonda fifty bucks that Elden Thomas was a short, trash-talking white guy with a Napoleon complex and a dream to play in the NBA—a dream that, in reality, would be fulfilled only if he could find a team that needed someone to fill a size Small mascot costume.

I shook my head in disgust. *I won't be surprised,* I thought, *if the first time I meet this guy, he's hanging upside down from gravity boots in the closet and practicing answers to NBA courtside interviews that will never, ever happen.*

My move-in took about as long as Cole's, roughly half an hour. Dad offered to take me to dinner before he and Rhonda ventured back to Kansas. We went to a burger place just a half mile from the school.

We ate in almost complete silence. I tried to coax some kind of reaction out of Dad, wondering aloud if the fartlek to which Coach Freeman had referred was Lydiard or Holmer fartlek. "As you know," I said, letting my eyes fall on Dad, then Rhonda, "not all fartlek is created equal."

"Griffin," my dad said softly, "would you like some of my fries? I'm finding that I'm not very hungry."

When Dad nudged the Durango next to the curb in front of Hill Hall, Rhonda leaned forward, poking her head between the two front seats. "Griff," she said solemnly, "how about a little walk?"

"Sure," I heard myself say. My voice sounded strange to me, like when I heard it on the family answering machine, leaving Dad some bogus story about where I was and what I was doing. I had intended to tell Rhonda, "A little walk? Sounds good, Rhonda. Have a good one. Dad and I will wait here for you." Why I didn't follow through on my intention, I had no idea.

I noticed a few pairs of eyes on Rhonda and me as we strolled away from my dorm. A couple of guys nodded at me, and I knew what they were thinking: *That's one hot older woman you got there, skinny dude.* I drew myself closer to Rhonda, just so they wouldn't begin to suspect she was my sister. I wondered if any of them was paying close enough attention to note the ring on her left hand. Just in case, I made a mental note to come up with a great story about my engagement to this woman they were seeing me with—an engagement that transcended age, miles, and even our two different spoken languages. I decided that Rhonda's engaged-to-Griffin name would be Sondra, and she would be from someplace a little more exotic than Wisconsin.

"Griffin?" Rhonda/Sondra said as we veered up a slight incline toward the Lewis gymnasium.

"Rhonda?" I parroted.

She stopped and turned to face me. I could tell she was nibbling on the inside of her lower lip. I was glad it was getting dark. That would make her impending tears less embarrassing for both of us. "This is so hard," she said.

"Look," I said, injecting all due magnanimousness into my voice, "you don't have to apologize anymore. It's okay, really. I don't hold anything against you. Believe it or not, I am still trying to learn a few things from Dad. I haven't forgotten his forgiveness speech."

She was wagging her head slowly. "I wasn't going to apologize again. I can tell you have made it to a place of forgiveness. The tension that was between us a couple of nights ago—I can feel that it's gone. When I said, 'This is so hard,' I meant leaving you."

"Huh?"

"I mean it, Griffin. My heart goes out to you. I'm not totally sure why, but you've found a place in my heart. I think about the pain you must be in, and I truly, truly want to help."

I could see the tears sliding down now, one chasing another. "You don't have to help," I said, making sure to soften my voice so she would know I wasn't being petulant. "You've got enough to worry about. Besides, I'll be okay."

Her eyes widened. "Do you promise? Will you *promise* me that?"

I can spot fake emotion, given that I'm a master of it myself. I imagine it's the same as a toupee maker being able to spot a bad rug at fifty paces. Unfortunately, Rhonda's concern was the real deal. That was going to make it really hard for me to lie to her and promise her I was going to be okay. I had a feeling I was going to be a couple of country miles from okay. Especially if Elden Thomas got himself a girlfriend and didn't spend much time in our room. I could take my brain to new levels of numbness, then get downright medieval-punitive on myself in response. Toss in a Cali girl with Amanda Carlisle's body and Ally Long's flexible morals, and it could be a blog-worthy year.

Of course, I had no intention of keeping a blog. I intended to do only whatever was necessary to cloud the vision of Dalton lying dead on his tidy bed, of my little brother's teary, wounded eyes looking up at me from a Topeka sidewalk. And I knew I was going to need to numb myself against the regret of losing Amanda Mac—of wasting at least four stupid years and not asking her for one stupid date. A couple of burgers at the Big Bear. Would that have been so hard to do?

"So . . ." Rhonda was saying, "I guess I can take that as a no, then?"

I shrugged.

"I wish you would promise me. For your dad's sake. For Colby's sake. But I think there's a reason you won't. I'm scared for you, Griffin. But I do appreciate your honesty."

"Thanks," I said. By this time, I had completely forgotten

what I was supposed to promise.

"Well, I guess we should just say goodbye then. This isn't going to get any easier by dragging it out. But I want to tell you something important, okay?"

I shrugged again. "Sure."

"I asked Bryant once what his life's dream was—what he fantasized about when he was back in high school, or even before. He told me that he always wanted two sons and that he wanted a woman who truly loves him. And Griffin, that's exactly what he has. And if I have anything to say about it, that's what he'll always have."

"Thank you for saying that."

"You believe me, then? I mean, I am being real with you, and it is so important to me that you know that."

"I know it." I smiled at her. "I know it because you haven't spoken hip-hop this whole conversation."

I thought she might hit me then, but she just stood there and cried quietly.

I closed my eyes for a minute because I felt myself growing dizzy, and that's when Rhonda wrapped her arms around me and kissed me on the cheek, the way I imagined a sister would. My point here is that it wasn't weird, and it wasn't all that awkward, except that I wished I hadn't gone two days without shaving. It must have been like kissing the business end of a whisk broom.

Rhonda curled a hand around the crook of my elbow as we walked back toward my dorm. When we were about forty yards from Dad, he called to me, "Wait there, Griff. I'm coming to you."

Rhonda slid her hand from me. She took her shirtsleeve and dabbed at both eyes. "Come home soon," she sniffed.

I nodded. "Vaya con Dios," I told her.

My dad began walking toward me as Rhonda walked away. When their paths intersected, they stopped and he hugged her and whispered something to her. I saw her nod, then head for the Durango.

Dad reached me but kept walking. "Follow me," he said. He led me up to the gym, but not to the front door. We moved to the east side of the squatty red-brick building. On the other side of the gym was the swimming pool, and we could hear an occasional Tarzan yelp, followed by the smack of a body against the water.

Our side of the gym, however, was quiet. We were alone.

"Griffin," my dad said, "these are going to be four very important years. Use them wisely. I didn't. I got lazy. And when I finished, I walked out into a world of very limited options. I paid the price for that, and sadly, so have you and Colby. Learn from that, son."

"Hey, Dad," I said, putting a hand on his shoulder, "you did a lot for us. I wouldn't want to go through all that we faced with anyone but you. I mean that."

I saw him draw in a deep breath. "Thank you, son."

"You're welcome." I let my hand drop back to my side. "Dad, look, I need to tell you something. I am kinda goodbyed out, you know. I mean, it's been Colby, Cole, Rhonda, and Amanda, back home. Then there was the whole thing up in Wheatland with Mom and all."

Dad was nodding. "So let's just hug and get this over with. Maybe enough with the speeches, huh?"

"Thank you," I said. And I meant it.

We did our trademark awkward judo hug, and I almost sighed audibly with relief when Dad released me without breaking into a hymn or a passage from the Psalms.

"You care to walk back with me?" he asked.

I thought for a moment. "Nah. You know, I think I'll stay up here for a while. Maybe go walk around the campus for a little bit, go check out the track. They resurfaced it this summer.

"Fair enough," he said. "I love you, Griffin."

"You too," I said.

I watched my dad start walking away, and I could tell his back was still bothering him. I knew Sal Ernst had some pills that would really loosen him up. Maybe if Sal stayed out of jail and in business, I could sneak something into Dad's coffee over Christmas break.

When Dad disappeared around the corner of the gym, I began walking slowly, following his path. But only for the moment. When I cleared the corner, I would head for the west side of the building, where the swimming pool was. "California girls in bikinis," I whispered to myself, "now that's what I call higher education."

I nearly flattened my father when I rounded the corner.

"Uh, hi, Dad," I said. "You lose something?"

He was smiling at me. "Well, Griffin, there is just one more thing."

Noting the smile, I returned it with one of my own. I knew what this was: This was the part where he handed me a hundred bucks in cash and made a joke about "a little extra beer money."

I tried to appear puzzled when he slid his hand into his front pocket. I couldn't tell for sure what was in his hand at first—only that it wasn't cash. Then came the familiar scratchy-click, and the tiny flame danced above his hand.

I stared at the flame, following its dance, which seemed in

slo-mo to me. Watching that flame made me feel every burn again. I fought against the urge to wince and shake my arms and legs, the way I tried to shake off the pain of each fresh wound. But it was better to look at the flame than at my father's face.

Finally, he extinguished the flame and handed me the lighter. I took it, still without looking up. Even in the dark, I knew it was one of mine. Where had I left it? On top of the refrigerator, maybe.

"Griffin," he said sadly, "when you hurt, I hurt. God hurts. Much more than I do. You need to understand that. And listen, son . . . I've made mistakes in my life. Like not noticing this problem sooner. And I felt bad about them, angry at myself. But I have learned something: It's God's kindness to me that always leads me to sincere repentance."

I saw my right hand waving in front of my face like I was trying to shoo away mosquitoes. But there was no shooing this away. "Look, Dad," I said briskly, "I think you have the wrong— "

"Please, don't, son. Don't tell even one more lie. Look, I know this must be uncomfortable for you, so I'll make this brief: Perhaps you're obsessed with following rules, with not breaking them. Maybe you should focus on following Jesus, instead. You do that, and I believe you'll find that the rules will take care of themselves. Remember what I am saying to you. And know that I will be praying for you."

Then he turned and walked away.

When my dad left me standing by the gym, my desire to do a recon of the pool area must have departed with him. I went back to my room and plopped onto my bed. I tried to think of reasons to resist finding my vodka and giving my troubled brain cells a rest. I thought about Colby and how if he turned out like me, that would have to be one of the saddest things in the world.

Five minutes later, my roommate entered, and I discovered another of the saddest things in the world: I was going to be sharing a room with perhaps the world's most annoying human.

Elden Thomas was talking like a tour guide when he crossed the room to my side. Two giggling girls in stretch pants followed him. "And here in the other half of the Thomas Estate," the five-foot-eight-inch point guard was saying, "we find my roommate, relaxing upon the thin mattress of his bed. Looking at this wiry young gentleman, I'm sure you have guessed that he's an athlete of some sort, though clearly not a heavyweight grappler or a center on the basketball team. So, what say you, girls? Any guesses as to this man's sport of choice?"

"Um, a swimmer?" the more tanned but less cute of the Thomas sycophants guessed.

"I dunno, Ash," the other countered. "I ran track in high school, and I think he's a track guy. Distance."

"Ah," said Thomas, smiling like a politician grubbing for votes, "the lovely Shannon is correct. Mr. Griffin Smith here is indeed a track man. Cross-country, too, if I'm not mistaken. Right, Mr. Smith?"

I stared up—although not that far up—at Thomas. His thick, hairy arms and legs were short in relation to his torso, giving him the appearance of a circus bear. "Yeah, I run cross-country," I said. I didn't like the way my voice echoed in the room. I glanced down at the scuffed hardwood floor. Thomas and I might need to go halves on an area rug. Or I could just strangle him in his sleep and eliminate the need to converse.

Thomas was extending one of his stubby paws to me. I sat up and extended my hand, which he grabbed and proceeded to work like a pump handle. "I'm Elden Thomas," he announced, too loudly, "just in case you didn't read the info the school sent you this summer. Basketball is my game. And I'm making varsity this year. You girls gotta check me out this season; I'm gonna light it up."

"I do love basketball," the copper-toned Ash proclaimed, saying the words as if they were part of the Pledge of Allegiance.

Ash, I pondered. *Short for what . . . Ashley, Ashton, Ashtray*?

Thomas started talking about his shooting prowess from, as he put it, "beyond the arc," and I started thinking about where I could find a liquor store where I might find a cashier susceptible to the old "I've been playing softball with some of the guys from work, and I don't have my ID on me right now" excuse. Because now that I had met my roommate, I knew that my meager supply of vodka and pills wouldn't even get me through the next twenty-four hours.

After detailing to Ash and Shannon why he was "just the kind of guy who needed to have the rock in his hands at crunch time," Thomas paused for a moment to invite me to the pool.

"It's still open for another hour," he said, tapping his watch with a fat forefinger. "And it's a great place to meet people."

I flopped back on the bed. "I don't know, guys," I said, manufacturing a convincing yawn. "It's been a long, long drive. Kind of a hard trip. I need to get some rest. Maybe tomorrow, okay?"

Now Thomas was giving me a grating, senatorial smile. "I'm sorry, my friend, but I'm just not going to take no for an answer."

I stared at the ceiling. "Oh. Well, would you take, 'Get out of my face' for an answer? Or how about, 'Bite me'? I have some other responses, too. We can keep going if you want."

I turned my head so that I could see Thomas's face. He was still smiling, but it was a strained smile, like he was trying to look cheerful while passing a kidney stone or something.

"Apparently," he said, addressing his mini-entourage but looking right at me, "they don't teach science *or* manners down in Kansas."

I smiled up at Thomas. And my smile was as fake as his, but I knew it looked natural. I was the master of the real, fake smile. "Maybe you're right," I said, tapping my own watch just the way he had done. "But they do teach how to tell time. And now you've got only fifty-one minutes to swim. Maybe fifty-two if you leave right now and run, run, all the way to the pool."

"What-ever!" Shannon said with a roll of her green eyes. "El, let's just go swim, okay? 'Cause your roommate is obviously on the rag."

Thomas placed one hairy tarantula hand in the middle of each girl's back and ushered them toward the door. Just before he exited, he whipped his head around. "We'll talk about this later," he said ominously.

"Well," I whispered after I was alone again, "I'm sure *you'll* talk later. But I'm equally as sure I won't be listening, because I'll be either drunk, asleep, or gone."

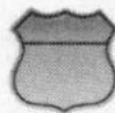

I was in bed, with the lights out, when Thomas returned. He asked if I was still awake, and I gave him a convincing, raspy, "Barely."

Apparently, my answer was encouraging enough for him to talk incessantly, albeit more quietly than before, as he got ready for bed. I thought he might shut up after I heard the faint creaking of his bedsprings. But after tucking himself in, he picked up the conversational ball and started dribbling it furiously, just like the point guard he was.

He offered a quasi-apology for his role in our "less-than-positive first encounter" and noted that he was sure I wouldn't have been so rude if not for the long, arduous drive from "all the way over in Kansas."

I lay there, wondering if Thomas could even find Kansas on a map of the United States.

My loquacious roommate was relating to me the riveting tale of how "a for-real basketball insider at Duke" had urged him to walk on, when I must have fallen asleep. The last words I remember hearing were, "Blue Devils, baby!"

I awoke the next morning to find Thomas tugging at my pillow. I forced my eyes open and gazed up at him. Had this putz been yammering all night and now he was waking me up to torment me some more?

"Smith," he said with a sly smile, "phone's for you."

"Phone?" I asked, frowning.

"It's in the hall. Most of us just use our cells, but . . ."

"I don't have one," I said. "My family is poor."

I stumbled to the hallway and saw the receiver dangling only an inch or two from the floor. I cleared my throat. "Hello?" I said.

"Griffin Smith!" a female voice said emphatically as if my name was the winning answer on a game show. "This is The Carrot. Let's meet for breakfast. But not at the cafeteria. There's a coffee place called Common Grounds. Isn't that hilarious?"

"Sure is," I said. Never too early in the day to start lying.

"Do you know where it is?"

"Yeah, by the admin building, right?"

"You got it. I'll wait for you by the front door. I know what you look like, from your picture, you cutie. Be there in a half hour?"

"Okay," I said cleverly.

Even though the walk to Common Grounds was mostly uphill from my dorm, I felt as though I were walking downhill, aided by a strong tailwind. I ran the fingertips of my right hand along my carefully shaven jawline. That's the spot I miss sometimes, but I couldn't meet The Carrot with any kind of weird facial-fringe thing happening. So I had shaved twice. And I'd even completely obeyed the shampoo bottle this time. Lather. Rinse. Repeat.

I patted the back pocket of my jeans for the tenth or eleventh time, just to make sure my wallet was still there. I forced my eyes downward once the coffee shop was in sight. If The Carrot was already there, I didn't want to appear too eager. And it would be nice not to stumble on a rock or step in a huge pile of mastiff dung—two more good reasons to pay attention to my route.

When I felt myself within the shadow of Common Grounds, I allowed myself to look up and see a stunning five-nine runner. I knew The Carrot was a runner. She wore black Nike running shorts that hit her mid-thigh, not those short-shorts favored by females who serve burgers, onion rings, and alluring smiles at Carlton Tucker's favorite restaurant. And she had the kind of tan you can't get from a can or a space-age blue-light pod. I knew that The Carrot had earned her tan by racking up miles, not tanning-session bills.

She had a runner's legs, too. Lean and sinewy—the kind of muscles you can't build in a gym. You can do all the leg curls and leg extensions you want, but it's not the same as ten-mile runs and hill sprints and mile repeats at 5K-race pace. I wondered if The Carrot and I would be going on running dates together. I hoped I could keep up with her; she looked fast.

"Carrot?" I said, smiling at her, because Amanda Mac always tells me I don't smile enough.

"Griffin," she said. She was smiling back, but there was something about her smile. It was like tiny invisible elves with ropes and pulleys were trying to make her smile, but the elves on the left side of her face were stronger, or perhaps more skilled, than those on the right. And neither elf team was strong enough to pull the corners of The Carrot's delicate mouth up from Grimace to Grin.

Then she gave me one of those leaning-forward/one-armed hugs. The kind that sends a clear message: "I'm sorry, but you're worth only half my arm total."

"Um, you want some coffee?" I offered, tilting my head toward the front door. *Brilliant so far, Griffin. Boy, asking somebody—while standing in front of a coffee place— if she wants some coffee. Next why don't you ask her if she's at college to learn?*

"Sure," The Carrot said unconvincingly. I followed her inside. She ordered a white mocha, which I quickly offered to pay for. "No, that's okay," she said dismissively. "Save your money; I remember what it was like to be a freshman."

As we stood waiting for our drinks, I felt The Carrot studying me. I felt like I was Exhibit A in a murder trial. I wondered what was wrong with me. It couldn't be the remnant of a zit on my chin. It was practically gone. And I'd put on two good solid coats of Red Zone under each arm and gave myself a swipe across my stomach and chest, just for good measure. If there was any guy in the world who smelled just like Cool Morning Frost, it was Griffin Smith.

We sat down at a wobbly table. The Carrot sipped her white mocha and finally managed a smile. Somehow I knew she was smiling about the coffee, not her companion.

I started counting in my head. It was either that or grab the bread knife someone had left on our table and plunge it into my neck.

"So," The Carrot said as I reached thirty-seven, "you really don't look anything like your picture."

If I were to write a paper about my Carrot encounter for Mr. Ross, this is the moment I would refer to as the epiphany. I knew the pic I e-mailed for the school directory showed me in my best light. Hello, that's why I sent it. But it still looked like *me*. A good version of me, but still me. I didn't photo-shop it one bit. Believe me, my pic looked much more like living, breathing Griffin than any of Maxwell the Mediocre's publicity shots resembled him.

It didn't make any sense. If Photo Griffin inspired the grammatically challenged Carrot to write, "Your a cutie," then Real Griffin should have elicited a similar response. In fact, I had actually expected my stock to go *up* once I met The Carrot in person, because I planned to be charming, sincere, and kind. You know, the opposite of the way I typically behave.

The Carrot was drumming her fingers against the side of her coffee mug, and I wondered how long I'd spaced out. I forced a laugh. "Well, you know pictures," I said abruptly. "They're kind of hit or miss." I thought about how, if I were writing this message to The Carrot, I would render it, "Their kind of hit or miss," just to put us on the same communication wavelength.

The Carrot returned my fake laugh with one of her own. Then we sat a while, just two wacky college kids with two big coffee drinks and only one thing to say. But neither of us cared to say it.

I was relieved when a wide-eyed blond with a prematurely receding hairline entered the shop. "Kenneth!" The Carrot shouted emphatically. "Get yourself over here, you hottie!"

Then she ejected from her seat and gave him the kind of hug that Carlton Tucker would have been grateful to receive. She buried her face in his Tour de France-yellow Lacoste shirt and gave a satisfied sigh. Apparently, she was extremely attracted to Kenneth. Or at least his fabric softener.

I sat there waiting for The Carrot to lick Kenneth's face or maybe offer to retie the laces of his Nike running shoes into a more-festive bow. When she did neither, I cleared my throat softly, then she pushed back from someday-to-be-bald Kenneth and nodded in my direction. "Oh, Kenneth," she said, "this is, um, Griffin." She might as well have said, "This is a dog turd I almost stepped in a few minutes ago."

"I didn't mean to interrupt you guys," Kenneth was saying. "I should just grab some coffee and go."

I could almost see the life draining out of The Carrot's indigo eyes. I scooted my chair backward and stood up. "Actually, Kenneth," I announced, "I need to go now. I have a lot to do today." I gestured to my chair. "Please, sit."

He cocked his head. "Are you sure?" he said.

I smiled at him, then at The Carrot. "I'm very sure."

She frowned at me. It was the kind of constipated-face frown I sometimes get from Rhonda. "Thanks for meeting me, Ms. Carrot," I said. "I guess I'll see you at practice?"

"Actually," she said, "I've decided not to run cross-country this fall. I need to concentrate more on my studies. Plus, I have really bad shin splints right now."

I nodded and left Common Grounds.

As I walked back to my dorm, where I planned to compare my directory pic with my reflection in the mirror, I decided that I couldn't blame The Carrot for her desire to concentrate on academics. I hoped she would put extra effort into her English as a First Language course. I did regret not seizing a chance to ask her about her nickname, given that she didn't have carrot-colored hair or freckles or even giant front teeth like Bugs Bunny. But that was okay. I didn't learn the secret of her name, but I did learn **Key Life Lesson #4**: Where there's a carrot, there's usually a stick.

As I stood before the mirror, holding my freshman directory next to my face, I conceded that The Carrot might have had a point. In the picture, my chin didn't appear quite as anemic as it did in real life. I recalled that I had been struggling with razor irritation in the chin area when the photo was taken. Perhaps the swelling had granted me some extra fullness and presence.

Also, Photo Griffin's eyes seemed wider and more alert than did Mirror-Reflection Griffin's eyes, which were squinty and sleepy. I smiled at the recollection of Amanda Sandwich's blurting out a scatological profanity just before pressing the button on her digital camera. "This one's gonna be a keeper," she told me. "You got this wide-eyed wonder thing goin' on — the perfect expression for a college freshman."

I had been unsure as to whether I was going to miss Amanda Sandwich while at college. After all, it's hard to respect someone who would date Carlton Tucker. But standing there in my California dorm room and holding the picture she took, I felt some kind of weird Amanda Sandwich nostalgia sweep over me.

I had seen her at the Big Bear a couple of days before the Road Trip/Debacle began. We shared sips of a strawberry shake, from two different straws. (Amanda has beautiful, full lips, but those lips have kissed Carlton Tucker. Need I say more?)

As I rose to leave, she had looked up at me with pleading eyes. "Sit down for just a sec, okay?" she asked.

I shrugged, then obeyed.

"I just want to tell you something," she said, leaning across the table until her head was almost touching mine.

Don't look at her breasts, don't look at her breasts, don't look at her breasts, I chanted in my head. *Don't be a Carlton Tucker perv.*

"What's on your mind?" I asked her, studying a small blackhead near her hairline.

"Well, you know my graduation party?"

"I know it well."

"Yeah. Well, I was kinda out of it then."

I smiled at her. "I seem to remember that being the case."

She smiled back, sheepishly. "Uh-huh. But I want you to know that I was level enough to know, at least somewhat, what was going on. I remember looking up once and seeing somebody. And I was so weak and tired and drunk, and that made it *so* good to look up and see it was you standing there. Not Carlton. Or Sal. Or anybody else, really."

I trained my eyes on the Big Bear's ceiling. Better to give my gaze a longer way to fall. "You know I've got your back, Amanda," I said, trying to sound at once nonchalant, sincere, and confident. Try that sometime. It takes almost as much self-discipline as *not* staring at Amanda Sandwich's pectoral region when she's wearing a form-fitting white T-shirt.

"I know you do," she was saying. "And Cole told me what else you did, too—with that perv Carlton. Carlton told me too. His version was mostly a lie, but there was enough truth to it to confirm Cole's version. Griff, I guess I just want to say thank you. You know, whenever I think of you, I'm gonna think of you as kinda my guardian angel."

It was all I could do to refrain from snorting and blowing a snot bubble the size of an ostrich egg. Thank goodness I prevailed; it's simply bad form to snort at a compliment like that, no matter how off-target it is. And while Colby would be impressed by a giant snot bubble, I doubted that Amanda would feel the same way.

"I was just being your friend, Amanda," I said. "I'm sure you would do the same for me, if I were passed-out drunk and Carlton was trying to molest me."

Amanda released a little rat-a-tat-tat giggle and said, "You're so weird."

You have no idea, I thought.

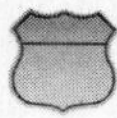

For a moment, standing in front of my dorm mirror, I feared my mental playback of my Amanda farewell, mixed with the recent rejection by a Carrot, would coax tears from my eyes. Then Thomas stormed into the room with a slouchy, loose-limbed guy who had to be six foot ten—and could be a seven-footer if he practiced better posture. "This is Hartley," Thomas said, poking a thumb toward Hartley's breastbone. He's our center on JV. Of course, we're both making it to the big show this season, aren't we, big dog?"

"Yup," Hartley said, but I could tell his XL heart wasn't in it.

The hall phone rang, and I dodged past the two basketball players.

"Hill Hall," I called into the receiver.

My dad's voice sounded far away. "Griffin, is that you?"

"Pretty much. Where are you, Dad? Utah by now?"

"Yes, son. Headed for Colorado. And that is why I am calling."

"Is there something wrong?"

"Well, not per se. But I need to tell you that we'll be picking up Cole on our way home. Listen, son, he is so embarrassed that he asked me to call you. I doubt he'd use the word, but he's having a homesickness problem."

"Cole? You gotta be kiddin' me."

"I'm afraid I'm not kidding, Griffin. He called me shortly after we left your campus last night. He said he just can't stop thinking about home. He says he's just not ready to go away to college yet. So he's coming back with us. He'll reevaluate things once he gets back home. But if I had to guess, I think he'll end up in Lawrence, or maybe Avila or UMKC."

"Whoa. That is some crazy news. But I can't believe he didn't call me."

"As I said, he is humiliated by the whole thing. He is deeply concerned over what you'll think of him."

"Dad, he could dig ditches and that wouldn't change anything. He's still my best friend."

"Mmm. You should tell him that. But don't call him right away, okay? Give him some time first."

"Okay, Dad. How are you doin'? Keeping the Durango between the white lines?"

"You know that I am a careful, attentive driver, son."

"I know, Dad. Just checkin'."

"Griffin, I think the cell battery is going to die soon. I'm down to one bar. But I wanted you to hear the news so that you wouldn't call Cole and stumble into an embarrassing conversation."

"I appreciate that. You take care, and call me later, okay?"

"Will do, son. And don't forget our talk last night."

Yeah, right. As if I could.

I hung up the phone. I wanted to pick it right back up and call Amanda Mac. The Carrot had turned out to be as shallow as she was beautiful. My roommate was like the bellicose senator that TV fake news shows always feature on their clips. And Cole Sharp, all-state in three sports and undefeated in street fights for five years running, was running home because he missed his *mommy*?

Then I realized I *couldn't* call Amanda, because if I did, I would learn that she had joined a cult that worshipped peat bogs and that she was also now smoking crack and eating spotted-owl burgers by the half dozen. I couldn't even call Dad back because his cell was dead, and even if it wasn't, I couldn't converse with him because the first words out of his mouth would be, "Griffin, my boy, I've found the answer to our financial woes. What's best is that you can quit school and help me. C'mon now, repeat after me: 'Hello! Would you be interested in an earning opportunity with Amway?'"

And if I called Colby, he would brush me off in two minutes. "Bro," he would say, "I'd really love to talk, but Aunt Nic and I are going to go toss the football around now. She has a way better arm than you do. And in general, she's just more fun. She's not moody like you are, and unlike you, she's never called me an ugly little freak. You know that you've called me that eighteen times? And each time you said it and made me cry, you promised you'd never do it again. Keep it up, and maybe you can break the world record for broken promises."

On that cheery note, I headed back toward my room, but I stopped when I heard Hartley laughing obsequiously at Thomas's impression of somebody—maybe me.

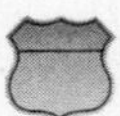

I decided to wander around campus until lunchtime. I went into the school library for a while but couldn't find anything I wanted to read. On my way back to see if Hartley and "Senator Thomas" were still parked between me and my vodka, I passed a small white building with a sign on the door, indicating it was the prayer chapel. *Honey, I shrunk the church,* I thought as I tried the door handle. It was open. I pushed open the door and leaned my body inside. If there was anyone present, either praying or chapeling, I planned to reverse directions like a ricochet.

But the mini chapel was empty. I closed the door behind me and turned the dead bolt. I thought about Amanda Mac and how she would be proud to see me walking into a prayer chapel. But her pride would turn to shame when she learned the truth.

I wasn't going to pray. I was going to shake my fist at the low ceiling—at God. That's how mad I was. Because you can't just jackhammer away a guy's hopes, his foundation, then put two JV basketball idiots between him and his vodka.

Unfortunately, I quickly discovered that there's a big problem with the whole shaking-your-fist-at-God ritual. Have you ever thought about *actually* shaking your fist at the Lord Jehovah? I mean, what technique do you use? If it's the fist with your fingers facing you, you look like a thespian in a really bad high school play—or an old-style British boxer.

And if you make a fist with the back of your hand facing you,

you look more like you're doing the Black Power salute, like those guys at the '68 Olympics. And that's a problem if you're a skinny white kid from the suburbs of Kansas.

So I decided the fist-shaking was out. There's always yelling and screaming, of course, but I'm not much of a yeller, nor a screamer. So I slumped into a mini-pew and heaved a heavy, Bryant Thomas Smith Dad-sigh. "It's too freaking hard to rage at God when you're second-guessing and critiquing yourself all the time," I conceded to myself. "It's a real problem that you're going to have to address."

Then I looked up at the mini-ceiling. "Okay, okay," I said quietly but not softly, "you've made your point. You broke me down. Are you happy now? Please know that I'm not being disrespectful here, but I am angry. Look, I'm pretty sure I have just three things to say. Then I'll vacate this place so some truly worthy people can use it.

"First, I'm sorry. For everything. And I do mean everything. I never meant to hurt you. I never meant to hurt Dad or anybody—except myself. I just didn't realize it was a package deal.

"Second, I'm realizing that I can't do this without you. 'This' being life and such. I'm not happy about this realization, to tell the truth, for once, but it is what it is. So whatever it is you do for people like Amanda Mac and my dad and Youth Pastor Ted, I could use some of that. Whatever you can spare. What I'm saying, I guess, is please don't give up on me. Don't let go, okay? No matter how hard I thrash around.

"I feel guilty about this one last thing. This request. I need to know, sir, that I'm okay. As a person, I mean. Because I'm honestly not sure. So please . . . I don't need a burning bush type of sign—don't deserve one either—but anything would be nice."

I left the chapel and headed for the cafeteria. It was only eleven fifteen, and I hoped I'd be early enough to eat and get out before the place was invaded by the Collegiate-Friendly People. You probably know some Friendly People. They spot any loner anywhere and start waving their arms like desert-island castaways about to be rescued. "Yo, there," they cry, showing their mouths full of ivory teeth. "Come join us!" They punch up the word "join" the way sportscasters give extra vigor and volume to words like "victory," "touchdown," and "slam dunk."

What can you do in the face of such unfettered enthusiasm? It's like trying to stand on your feet when a tidal wave crashes over you. So you stagger over to the Friendly People as if pulled by magnetic force. En route, you close your eyes and say a silent prayer for the patience not to stab a fork into any of the happy faces. Then you sit down among them and wait to be peppered with questions. And it won't be long before The Big Question will come at you like a spear: "So, Griffin, tell us all about your *family*!"

Fortunately, on this day, all of the Friendly People were either already pestering some other exotic loners or still in their Friendly Cottages, flossing their teeth and practicing their used-car-salesperson smiles.

I found a table near the back of the lunchroom. An empty table. I love empty tables. At the table next to mine sat a lone girl, hunched like a question mark over her tray. She was thin and plain, wearing an old army jacket. I liked her instantly—but not enough to sit at her table. And if I was judging her demeanor correctly, she was uttering a fervent, silent prayer that I wouldn't sidle up next to her, smile, and ask, "So, baby, what's your major?"

Soon, though, the Senator and a bunch of his idiot buddies, Hartley included, invaded her table. I could almost feel her insides squirming. Senator and Co. commenced yapping and laughing, and one of them tossed a half-pint carton of milk across the table to the Senator, who, inexplicably, tried to catch it in his mouth. When it bounced off his chin and dropped into his lap, he started laughing so hard that I could see tears leak from the corners of his eyes.

Before long, everybody at the table was laughing. Except the girl. She bowed her head, even lower than it already was, folded her hands, and started to pray. I imagined her prayer: "Dear God, please make these obnoxious louts go away. I don't mean banish them to the wilderness or swallow them up with an earthquake. Just move them to another table. Please."

But she was probably just blessing her food. Maybe even for the second time. With college cuisine, you can't be too careful.

Then the Senator appeared to have a brainstorm—or in his case, a light brain flurry. He nudged the two guys on either side of him, and the threesome stood up quietly. The four guys on the other side of the table—folding their hands in front of them in mock-prayer—followed suit.

Then they all crept away, looking back over their shoulder at Prayer Girl. As I saw what was unfolding, I urged myself, *Run, Coyote Boy, run! You do* not *want to see the hurt on Prayer Girl's face when she raises her head and opens her eyes.* But then a few seconds later, I found myself popping up from my table and moving quickly and quietly, just like the Coyote Boy I knew I'd always be.

I slid across from Prayer Girl in time to see her eyelids rise.

She looked down the table and shrugged one shoulder, puzzled. I smiled reassuringly at her. "Those guys don't like me," I say. "They kinda shun me, like the Amish do, you know?"

"That's not very kind," Prayer Girl said. I caught a trace of a Tennessee accent in her voice.

"No, it isn't," I agreed, adjusting my tray in front of me. "But what are you gonna do? My name is Griffin Smith."

"Melissa Shumate," she said, looking at her sandwich, not at me.

"I'm very glad to meet you, Melissa Shumate. Is that a peanut butter sandwich you have there?"

She smiled and nodded, and I raised my own PB&J sandwich in salute. I took a small bite and washed it down with my fat-free chocolate skim milk. That's right: It was both skim *and* chocolate. It's a wonder the dairy didn't call it Hey, We Know This Is Chocolate Milk, but It's Still Pretty Darn Good for You. At Least There's No Fat in Here! So Get Off Our Case Already!

"So, Melissa," I said, forcing myself to hold my reassuring smile, like a bodybuilder holding his pose, "when it comes to peanut butter, are you on the chunky or creamy side of the aisle?"

"Um, creamy?" she said. "How about you?"

Even if I had favored chunky peanut butter, packed with whole peanuts still in their shells, there was only one viable answer: "I'm with you, Melissa."

From there, I quizzed Melissa the Prayer Girl about her class schedule and discovered we had Friday morning World History together. I resolved in my mind and heart to sit next to her whenever I could. Unless she was one of those front-row eager learners. I'm more of a back-row lurker myself. That way, I can see when the really smart people are taking notes and follow their lead.

But while Prayer Girl and I might not be destined to be World History sidekicks, I resolved to be her cafeteria guardian angel. I figured Amanda Sandwich wouldn't mind. Before every meal, I would search the whole place—even those secluded tables in the corners—because Prayer Girl wasn't ever going to have to eat alone, unless she really wanted to. And she sure as heaven wasn't going to be a victim in any more Senatorial pranks. Not on my watch.

After Prayer Girl finished her sandwich, she dabbed the corners of her mouth with a napkin, then excused herself. "Maybe we can lunch again sometime," she offered.

"I would love that." I meant to say, "I would like that," but I decided I could live with the words the way they came out.

The words that started parading through my head as I watched Prayer Girl walk away couldn't technically be called a prayer, I don't think. More of a heaven-directed observation, perhaps: *I'm not ready to call that a sign. It could just as easily be a coincidence. But if it was a sign, I've gotta admit it was a good one. So, you know, nice job.*

At my first cross-country practice, I was taken aback at how much faster everything was. Warm-ups were faster, intervals were faster. Coach Freeman even talked faster than any coach I had in high school.

It was pretty much the same thing with the whole school year. Sitting here now, with my freshman year behind me—and waiting to muster the energy to start packing up my stuff—it's hard to believe nine months slid by so snake-quick. I guess that's what happens when one day is pretty much like another.

But there are a few that stand out—a handful that will make the Griffin Smith frosh year hall of fame, or hall of shame. Here they are:

SEPTEMBER 9

I'm sitting in the gym, recovering from a hard practice. Five one-mile repeats, all under 5:30. The girls' volleyball team is practicing, and I find watching them is aiding my recovery. Soon a dark-haired hitter limps over to the bleachers where I'm sitting and lowers herself gingerly. A trainer brings her an ice pack, which he holds on her knee.

"Patellar tendon has been bugging me since summer," she informs me.

"I'm sorry," I say.

"You on the cross-country team?"

I try not to nod too vigorously. "Track too."

"I really admire distance runners," she says. "I wish I had that kinda stamina."

I shrug. "I wish I had your hops. You looked good out there."

I proceed to make her laugh a half-dozen times over the next ten minutes, and with the last laugh, she leans toward me and puts a hand on my knee.

I know where this is going. I'm no Cole Sharp, but I have traveled this road a few times.

I learn that Emily the Hitter is a sophomore and that she lives off campus and that her roommate is in Bakersfield for the weekend and that she hates to cook for just one. I ask Emily what her major is, and she laughs, "You mean, besides volleyball? Seriously, Griffin, I have no idea. But what about you? What do you want to be someday?"

I smile, but I know it's a sad smile, because I know my answer will be a lie. But not a lie to impress Emily, the shamelessly flirting sophomore; rather, it will be a lie to protect her. You see, the answer that flashes in my brain is LCD-TV-clear and vivid: I *want to be the kind of person who deserves to be with Amanda Mackenzie.*

So instead of the truth, I tell Emily I'm just as in the dark as she is. Then I tell her, "You know, I really probably shouldn't join you for dinner and whatnot. We race tomorrow. It's a home meet, but I still need to get up really early."

Emily stares at me, eyes somewhere between disbelief- and utter-shock-wide. "Are you sure?" she coos.

"Yeah," I mutter, "I'm afraid so."

SEPTEMBER 12

I finally track down Cole, via his cell. The guy's been harder to find than bin Laden.

"Griff, I am so sorry," is the first thing out of his mouth. "I feel like I kind of abandoned you."

"It's cool, Sharp," I tell him. "It's weird: I did actually feel abandoned at first, but I understand about missing home. I've wanted to jump on a plane a few times myself already. And I've heard of at least ten Lewis students who have already headed back to their home country."

"Still, Griff, it's kind of embarrassing. Everybody's been asking me what happened. I don't want to tell them the truth. I wish I could be more mentally tough."

I have to let out a barking laugh at that one. "Well, I wish I could throw the disc a mile and be all-state in football and bench-press three hundred pounds. But we all have our little disappointments to deal with."

"Thanks for saying that. Thanks for not bustin' my chops the way Sal Ernst and some of those guys have been doing."

"Just threaten not to visit him in prison, Sharp. That'll shut him up."

"Thanks, Griff," Cole says when he stops chuckling. "It feels good to laugh again."

"It feels good to hear you laugh again."

SEPTEMBER 21

Mom calls to wish me a happy birthday—on my actual birthday. When the shock wears off, I tell her, "Thank you."

"I have something else to tell you," she says. "I'm sending you something—something of Dalton's. This grief counselor we've been seeing suggested it, so I've been picking out things for his friends. He really didn't have that many friends. But Griffin, I know that Dalton thought of you as a friend. And then there's what you wrote. Nothing that anybody else wrote has meant as much to Maxwell and me. I read your note at our Wednesday night grief recovery meeting. Almost everybody cried. I wish you could have been there. But anyway, I need your help. I'm not sure what to send you. He didn't have many books, and at least as far as I know, you're not into computer games the way he was."

I'm tempted to say, "Hey, I've an idea—did you find any of his drugs?" But I think of something I want even more than whatever pharmaceuticals Dalton might have tucked away in his sock drawer. Plus, there's the whole "Don't be a selfish, insensitive jerk" factor to consider.

"Mom," I say, "I know exactly what I want. And it will mean a lot to me to have it. It's kind of a way for me to honor his memory."

"Anything you want, Griffin . . . son. Just name it. I'll Fed-Ex it out tomorrow."

I reveal to my mom the desired Dalton memento, and I actually do a little Tiger Woods fist-pump when she says, "I know exactly where that is."

OCTOBER 28

I grab my prepaid calling card and head from my room to the hallway to call Amanda Mac. Our Friday night conversations have become something of a tradition.

I'm looking forward, even more than usual, to tonight's chat because I think I almost have her convinced to meet me someplace between her school and mine for Thanksgiving break.

She answers on the first half ring. A good sign. She's by the phone, waiting. "You doing okay?" she asks.

"Yeah," I answer lazily. "I didn't make the travel squad to regionals this weekend, but I'll still get my varsity letter. So that's pretty cool, you know."

"Yes. It is. Congratulations, Griff."

"Amanda? Is something wrong? You don't sound very good. You sick?"

"Well . . ." She sounds nervous. I have never heard Amanda Mac nervous before.

"Amanda? I'm worried about you. Are things okay with your family? I know your parents are having trouble. . . ."

"It's not that, Griffin. It's just that there is something I have been feeling I need to tell you for the past three weeks, but it's so hard. I'm afraid of how you'll react."

Tell me you're on drugs. We can deal with that. I'm kind of an expert on the subject, actually. Please just tell me you're on drugs. Or that you're flunking out of school. That's fixable too. Almost anything would be fixable, except—

"Okay, I'm just going to say it: Griff, listen. I have a, um, boyfriend. His name is Jeremy. He's from Parkville, kind of our neck of the woods. We've been going out since late September, but it's gotten pretty serious recently."

A boyfriend? Amanda Mackenzie has a boyfriend, and it's not me?! *But I should have known. A small Christian college filled with spiritual, well-scrubbed Christians, with their beatific smiles and fancy leather Bibles, quoting Calvin's* Institutes *and volunteering at soup kitchens and homeless shelters on the weekends. I hate every teetotaling, drug-free, no-sex-for-me-thanks-until-I'm-married one of 'em!*

"Griffin, are you still there? Are you okay? Please say something! You're so quiet."

Quiet? It's not quiet inside my head, baby. Not in my heart. It's like freakin' Baghdad in here.

"Griffin! Please talk to me. You're scaring me."

"Don't worry about me. I'm fine."

"Are you sure?"

Sure? I'm not sure about anything anymore. But why are you wasting your time talking to me? Why don't you go find your um-boyfriend and give him a big um-kiss. You can talk about how someday you're going to get married and have twelve adorable um-babies. One for each of the original twelve tribes of Israel. You can all learn to play a musical instrument, even little Timothy Silas-Barnabas, who'll master the glockenspiel. You can give concerts—excuse me—minister in music on the weekends to orphans and crack addicts. But enough about that. I'm going to find a big bottle of um-vodka and get so stupid um-drunk that I won't be able to walk for an um-week. Then I'm finding my um-lighters. Then the um-fun is really going to begin. Unleash the um-hounds!

"Griffin? Please, please, please. I am freaking out here!"

"Sorry, Amanda. There was just someone bugging me to use the phone. And you've certainly given me a lot to process here. But I'm fine. And hey, congrats on the new man. I'm not surprised you found somebody. You're the best, really. Look, I gotta go before this one guy yanks the receiver right outta my hand. I'll e-mail you later. Good night."

I leave the phone hanging from its cord like a lynched horse thief. I walk purposefully into my dorm room. Senator Thomas and Hartley are playing Splinter Cell, so they barely grunt at me, which is a good thing. I grab my cross-country travel bag and stuff a T-shirt into it, followed by three primary-color lighters and an unbreakable bottle of triple-distilled Smirnoff, which the previous week I had almost poured down the sink during a rare attack of conscience. Silly, silly me.

The five-minute walk to the weight room seems to take an hour. I open the weight room door and poke my head inside. (I don't want to get drunk *behind* the weight room if there is somebody *inside* working out. All of that grunting and exertion breathing will kill the buzz.)

The Carrot is sitting on a weight bench, dangerously close to Russ Barrington, who was third man on our cross-country team before succumbing to a high ankle sprain a week ago. Sitting this close never would have flown at summer church camp. The Carrot and Russ aren't "leaving room for Jesus."

"Hi, Griffin," The Carrot calls to me. She still acts embarrassed and quasi-guilty whenever I run into her, which isn't often. Because, unlike her, my major goal for the semester isn't to make out with every guy at Lewis who owns a jockstrap.

"You gonna hit a workout, Smith?" Barrington asks, and I can feel the disappointment dripping off of his words.

"In a few minutes," I tell him. "I just realized I forgot something. Russ Barrington, Amy *Korette*, a good evening to both of you, in case I don't see you later."

The Carrot starts giggling even before I close the door.

I run back to the dorm, where the Senator and his friendly giant are still bent over their controllers. I stab my hand into my sock drawer, and my fingers immediately find what I need. Then it's back to the weight room—no, wait—the cafeteria. It will be quieter behind there.

After scanning the garbage-strewn terrain behind the cafeteria,

I position myself between two giant green dumpsters. I wait for the voice in my head to shut up—the voice that keeps saying, "When you hurt, I hurt."

I'm not sure if it's Dad or God or James Earl Jones talking, but it's irksome. So irksome that I fish one lighter out of my bag and fire it like a fastball in the near-empty dumpster on my right.

"That must feel good," a voice says. But there is a major problem: This voice isn't coming from inside my head.

I wheel around. A short guy with stringy hair is wiping his hands on an apron. Where did *he* come from?

"Wuh-huh?" I say because I am a genius orator. I can't believe Lewis didn't offer me a forensics scholarship.

"You know," Apron Man says, "I smoked cigarettes too. For twenty-seven years—since I was fourteen years old. Planned my whole day around 'em. 'Do I have enough cigarettes for the drive to work? For my morning coffee break? For after lunch? For the drive home?' Those little death-sticks ruled me. So, young friend, you can believe me when I tell you how good it is to say goodbye to such a dangerous habit. To be free from something that was killin' you, little by little."

I force a chuckle. "I don't think you understand, sir."

This cook/dishwasher/whatever chuckles right back. "Don't be so sure, now. I know full well that it might not be *cigarettes* you've been smoking, but my advice holds, all the same. Now, don't you think you should toss in that other lighter too?"

I nod deferentially. "I gotta hand it to you on that one. How'd you know I carry a spare?"

"Let's just say I've been there."

Oh, I seriously doubt that, Apron Man. But you're good—I'll give you that. I'm down to my last lighter, but that's all I will need.

"Well," my reformed-smoker friend says, "I gotta get back inside. You gonna be okay?"

"Most definitely."

"Good. And good for you. I mean that. This is an important step you've taken tonight."

I wait for him to open, then close, a metal door that's almost invisible against the back of the building. Then I fire up my last living lighter and hold it up like a conductor's baton. My other hand finds The Carrot's letter in my back pocket. And let me tell you, when flame meets scented stationery, it's a beautiful thing. I drop the burning letter on the ground and watch it glow orange and start to collapse in on itself.

Then I drop the lighter, too. When my right heel crunches it, I imagine it's the nose of Amanda Mac's um-boyfriend. Freedom from self-abuse, with a helping of catharsis on the side. Maybe this night won't be so tragic after all. And I did still have the vodka.

NOVEMBER 19

Dad picks me up at the airport. He earned a bonus at his crappy job—something about being Troubleshooter of the Quarter—and wasted most of it on a plane ticket for me. (I staunchly refused the offer, by the way, until Dad put Colby on the phone and he said to me, between sniffs and sobs, "I *need* my big brother." That was cheating.)

On the way home from the airport, I devise a list of must-dos for Thanksgiving break.

Burn the rest of The Carrot's letters. (Must borrow lighter first.)

Lift weights with Cole. Watch ESPN with Cole. Eat ridiculous amounts of non-college-cafeteria food with Cole.

Structure at least one speed-workout to take me past Janine Fasson's house, just to show her that Coyote Boy has still got it.

Not think about Amanda and her Parkville um-boyfriend.

My first evening at home in almost four months goes great. Rhonda's speech is free of "yo's," "homies," and "peeps." Dad just can't stop smiling and shaking his head, and Colby cries, "Bro!" and grabs my arm like it's a rope swing approximately every 13.2 seconds.

The night is weird though. I find myself getting out of bed repeatedly, padding to Colby's room, and watching him breathe. I refuse to leave until I've seen his chest rise and fall at least twenty-five times. And I realize how much I'm not over what happened with Dalton. I wonder if I ever will be.

December 24

I'm home again. This time courtesy of one of Rhonda's credit cards. Colby is a shepherd in a Christmas Eve skit at Grace Fellowship. Amanda Mac isn't there to see it; she's attending a cantata in Parkville. And that's a good thing. Because I want no part of the internal tug-of-war pitting the forces of I Must See My Little Brother Sing Along with a Heavenly Host of Kindergarten Angels vs. I Must Not, Under Any Circumstances, See Amanda Mac Sharing a Pew in *My* Church with Her Wretched Parkville Um-Boyfriend.

Amanda calls our house no fewer than ten times during Christmas break. But somehow she fails to connect with me each time. Thank God and AT&T for caller ID.

March 27

I rap my knuckles on the open door of Coach Freeman's office. "Coach," I say, "you got a minute?"

"Come on in, Smith. Sit down. Good 1600 last week. A sub

4:40—not bad for this early in the season. 'Course, eventually, you're going to need to move to the 5,000 or the steeplechase if you want to keep a spot on varsity."

I realize I'm nibbling on my lower lip. "Well, Coach, that's kinda what I wanted to talk to you about. Here's the thing: I need to remove myself from the team."

Coach frowns thoughtfully. "Personal problems, Smith? I don't want to pry, but there are accommodations we can make."

"It's not really personal problems—well, it kinda is. Ah, man. I'm really messing this up. Here's the thing: I have broken a team rule. I'd rather not specify which one. But I signed my name to the rules, and now I broke one. So there's only one thing to do."

Coach's head starts bobbing gently. "I agree. And I'll respect your privacy on this, but I would like to know what compelled you to come in here and remove yourself from the team."

"It was Imaginary Ryun, sir. We were doing a tempo run a couple of days ago, and he told me, 'Griff, it doesn't matter how jacked up Amanda has you with this whole um-boyfriend situation and whatnot. You're not going to find true comfort in triple-distilled vodka. And besides, you're breaking team rules—rules you agreed to follow of your own free will. You never would have caught me breaking training rules—just formidable time barriers and world records.'"

Yeah, right. I couldn't tell Coach Freeman about Imaginary Ryun, any more than I could tell him about my soul mate, Robin, the Boy Wonder. So instead, I opt to simply shrug and say, "It was just the right thing to do."

As I'm leaving his office, Coach calls after me, "Smith, whatever this stumbling stone is, I suggest you remove it. I'd like to have you on my teams next year."

"I'll try," I call over my shoulder.

When I get back to the dorm, Senator Thomas is windmilling his stubby arms. "Can you believe how hot it is?" he says, punctuating his question with a deep belch. "Killer basketball weather. We're gonna hit the outdoor courts over in the park. You wanna come?"

"Nah," I say, "but thanks for asking."

"You should reconsider," he says. "You know, you're a decent athlete. If you played ball with me and the guys on a regular basis, we might be able to turn you into a real basketball player."

"Maybe next time," I say, demonstrating Job-like patience and long-suffering.

"Suit yourself," Senator says. Then he gestures to a plastic bottle of Gatorade on his chest of drawers. "I gotta whiz—watch that for me, will you? Don't let that big goof Hartley start quaffing it if he comes in."

"I'm on the job," I say, offering a salute that Senator does not see because he's already on his way down to the quad's communal bathroom to, as he so poetically put it, whiz.

I stand up and pluck the Gatorade from the dresser. Watermelon flavor. My favorite. I'm not really thirsty, but I down half the bottle in three mighty gulps. Then I grab my vodka from my sock drawer. There is almost enough of the fifth left to fill the Gatorade bottle to its previous level.

I bury the vodka bottle under my pillow just as Senator returns. "Okay, then, time to hoop," he announces.

"Hoop it up," I say, handing him his beverage. "And you know, it really did seem hot when I was out a while ago. Be sure to drink plenty of fluids."

Senator grips his Gatorade bottle like it's a trophy he's just won. "Got that covered, Smith."

Then he's gone.

It's all I can do not to follow him over to the courts. I know that Amanda Mac would disapprove of what I've just done. But she doesn't understand. If Elden Thomas were alive during New Testament times, he'd no doubt be a Philistine, a tax collector, or a Philistine tax collector—if there was such a thing. Besides, he said "quaffing." He's lucky I didn't "whiz" in his beverage.

Anyway, since Amanda's affections now lie with someone from across the Missouri River, in lovely Parkville, her opinion shouldn't really matter anymore.

APRIL 19

Amanda calls me at 10 p.m. "It's been almost a month since we've talked," she says after hearing my tentative "Hello?"

"How long is this childishness going to go on, Griffin?"

"I really can't say."

"Will you even talk to me, really talk? For just five minutes?"

I sigh wearily. "I guess I can handle that."

"Five Minutes of Truth. Can you handle *that*?"

I know it's a trap. She's questioning my manhood by asking me if I can handle it, if I can take the heat. But I'm not falling for it. "It's not a matter of being able to handle something," I explain patiently. "I'm just making a choice."

"So you say. Jeremy's not afraid of it."

"Okay, fine, Amanda, bring it. Five minutes. Heck, take six if you want."

"Five will be fine," she says, and I can almost hear her smiling, all the way up in Oregon. "First question: Have you, uh, *been* with anybody this school year?"

I hear myself groan. "Amanda, can't we start with favorite

color, favorite TV show, that kind of thing?"

"If I ask you that, sure. But that's not what I asked. Do you need me to repeat the real question?"

"No, no, no. Please don't. You freaked me out enough the first time."

"Well?"

"No, actually, I haven't."

"Okay, you do know that the name of the exercise is Five Minutes of *Truth*?"

"Yeah, I caught that. You heard my answer."

"You sound disappointed in yourself."

"I don't know what I am. Really."

"Okay. We'll move on, then. Griff . . . whoa, this is hard to ask. How do you feel about me? Right now."

"Well, the first words that come to mind are jealous, angry . . . and sorry."

"Sorry? Why sorry?"

"Because of the time I wasted. The opportunities. I mean, every time I think of you with Perry Parkville, I just wanna . . ."

"Jeremy. His name is Jeremy, not Perry."

"Good for him."

"Do you want to know his last name?"

"No. Please, no." *Doesn't this girl know* anything*? It's much easier to pretend someone doesn't really exist if he has only a first name.*

"Are you ready for the next thing?"

"Hit me."

"Why, Griffin? Why did you never even give us a chance?"

"You really want to know this?"

"The exercise is called Five Minutes of what, Griffin?"

"Okay, Amanda. If you really want this . . . I. Am. A. Mess.

And I don't mean a lovable, incorrigible ragamuffin with a cluttered closet and unkempt hair; I mean a person with a defective heart who just can't seem to keep his sweaty palm off the self-destruct button. If you knew the half of it, it would turn your stomach. You'd back away from me with fear and revulsion in your eyes, then run, run, run all the way to Parkville and into Perceville's waiting arms."

"That's not true."

"There's no way you can make that statement. Besides, my mom left, overcoming even maternal instinct to get away from me. You'd leave too, believe me. And you can't make a statement otherwise."

"I just did. But you're not luring me into an argument, because I'm not done with my questions. Do you believe you're going to heaven when you die?"

"Yes and no."

"Don't play games with me here."

"I'm dead serious. See, I have a philosophy about heaven. There's no way I'm getting inside the gates. With the mess that's inside of me, I'll set off the security alarms like crazy. They'll go nuts like a pinball machine. But on the other hand, I really don't think I'm evil. Weak, self-destructive, unreliable, and fickle—but not truly evil. So I'm hoping God will let me patrol the outer walls. Watch for fallen angels and congressmen trying to sneak in. Toss back the occasional errant Frisbee. Maybe do some light repair work. A bit of caulking. Give the walls a new coat of paint every millennium or so."

"Griffin, that's really tragic. Think of it, being on the outside, trying to look in. Forever."

"I don't think it's all that bad. As long as I can hear Colby laughing, as long as I know Cole made it in okay, I'll be fine. And you know, Cole's got a cannon arm, even without the resurrection body. We could probably chuck a football back and forth over the wall from time to time. And maybe there could be a trapdoor where you could slide out a leftover piece of pie once in a while."

I pause for a moment. "Okay, I got a question now: Are you laughing, Amanda, or crying?"

"Both. Because you really don't get it, do you?"

"What? You don't like my scenario? I'm not kidding about it. It's the best I can hope for."

"Really? What happens when it's time to sleep?"

"I just roll up by the wall and sleep. I won't get cold or anything. It *is* heaven, after all. And I won't need any bedding. I always end up kicking my blankets and sheets off, anyway."

I hear Amanda blow her nose delicately. "Let me tell you something, Griffin. The first time you fall asleep, I'm coming out there and carrying you inside. Where you belong."

"You can't carry me, Mackenzie. I weigh a solid buck-fifty. Actually, a buck-fifty-five. I've been hitting the weights pretty hard lately. I got, what, forty pounds on you?"

"Well, then, I'll get Jesus to help me. And we'll get Colby to hold the door."

"Hey, you leave him out of this! That's a cheap shot, and you know it."

"No, it isn't. Think about it: What person in this world will be more heartbroken if he's in heaven and you're not? And he won't be the only one."

"Look, I don't want to hurt Colby. I don't want to hurt anybody."

"Then you better start letting people love you. And I think you know where to start."

"I just don't understand how it can work, Amanda."

"That's the cool thing, Mr. Salutatorian, Mr. Studious. You don't have to understand it. You just let it happen to you, and you say thank you, thank you, thank you—about a bazillion times a day.

"Are we done now?"

"Five more seconds. But I think I'll let you slide."

"Wish I could say the same thing, but Amanda, do you love Jeremy?"

"Grif-fin!"

"I'm sorry. Let's refresh ourselves on the name of the game. Because I do believe my question beat the buzzer. Five minutes of . . . of . . ."

"No. The answer is no."

I decide not to go for the obvious follow-up. Instead, I say, "I hear ya. I don't love him either."

Amanda laughs politely, then says, "I need to go now. But I want to leave you with one final question—and you don't even have to answer it. Just think about it, okay?"

"Okay."

"Griffin, have you ever considered the possibility that the people who love you would rather live with you—and whatever pain and problems that brings—than *not* have you in their lives?

I say goodbye and, in deference to Amanda, start considering the aforementioned possibility. That lasts for about five seconds because this particular possibility is just too much to consider after a grueling session of Five Minutes of Truth. "Maybe tomorrow," I note to myself.

MAY 26

It's the finals for World History. Now, *there's* a lightweight class for you. All you have to do is burn into your brain about a bazillion names, dates, and events concerning the Entire Freakin' History of the Entire Freakin' World since the Dawn of Time.

I sit down next to Prayer Girl and nod at her. She stares at the test as the professor, Dr. Roberts, hands it to her, upside down. (Clarification: The test is upside down, not the prof.)

I think that Prayer Girl actually shudders. Behind me, I hear a few groans as fellow students realize the heft of this test.

Finally, when Roberts and his teaching assistant finish distributing the test, he faces the class. "Please turn your exams over and begin," he says.

I turn mine over and start scanning the first page. I see Magna Carta, Reformation, Sumerians . . . all of the stuff I expect. I grab my skinny rectangular bubble-paper form, wanting to start filling in those little ovals before Copernicus and all his friends—along with all of those numbers, both AD and BC—dash right out of my head.

But I'll be a monk's uncle (preferably champagne pioneer Dom Perignon, 1638–1716) if every last oval isn't neatly blacked in already.

Great, I think, *I got the answer key by mistake. Maybe I can memorize at least the first ten answers before I go up and inform Roberts that his T.A. must have screwed up.*

Prayer Girl's hand is already up, or at least halfway there. She acts as if she might pull a muscle if she extends her arm fully.

Then there is murmuring. Genuine post-Sunday service murmuring. It sounds like something spooked a bunch of corralled horses. I like to think it was a coyote.

Senator Thomas raises his voice above the din. "Sir," he says in a voice so officious that I wonder how much I could alter it by clasping my hands around his neck and squeezing mightily, "it appears there is some mistake here."

"What seems to be the problem?" Roberts asks innocently.

"Uh, well . . . it appears my test form is already completed."

"Hmmm. Interesting," Roberts notes. "Anyone else have a completed test?"

I look around and see heads bobbing and hands rising.

"Well," Roberts says with a yawn, "if all of your finals are completed, perhaps we should check the answers."

I wonder where this could be going. No place good, that's for sure. It could be that someone stole the answer key and Roberts found out about it. So maybe he's going to walk us through the stolen test, just to take up class time, then spring a new, surprise test on us.

However, as Roberts reads the first question, I see that the answer on my sheet is correct. Bach signed each piece of music, "Soli Deo Gloria" (for the glory of God alone). One of the choices is (E) Pluribus Unum. Give me a break. That one was a gimme.

Midway through the test, though, Roberts reads three straight questions that I would have missed. I never could keep all of those English kings straight, and I don't know, neither do I care, about the Bering Land Bridge. I see Prayer Girl wince on a few questions later in the test.

Roberts finishes, then he addresses the front row, starting on the far left and pointing at each student like he's Moses or something and asking, "What grade did you get on your final?"

The first couple of students answer "Uh, an A, I guess" and "An A . . . or something?"

"Please be more specific," Roberts scolds both of them. "What, precisely, did you get on your final?"

Soon everyone catches on: "An A, sir, one hundred percent" is the definitive answer.

When every last flabbergasted freshman has reported a grade, Roberts smiles—or rather, makes some kind of face denoting the closest thing *he'll* ever get to a smile.

"I love world history," he says. "It's my passion in life. And I'd love for each of you to learn a metric ton of world history and share at least a little of my passion. But each of you knows what this school is really all about. Lewis College wouldn't still be standing if not for God's grace, and I most surely wouldn't be standing here either."

Prayer Girl nudges my arm with her elbow. "Whoa," she whispers.

I almost respond with "Whoa, indeed," but realize just in time that this would solidify me as the most pathetic conversationalist in the history of male/female spoken-word communication.

Then Roberts is talking again: "So, as much as I would love to have each of you truly learn about world history, I'd rather have you learn about grace. There's just one problem: I don't think you *can* learn about grace; I think you have to experience it. Each of you has now experienced grace, just a little grace, just a droplet of grace. And I have only one question for you: How does it feel?"

Then he's gone.

Senator blurts, "Dude, what?! Sweet! Bring on the grace!"

The sycophants near him nod and chuckle in agreement. One even says, "Amen, brother!"

And another unnamed classmate agrees, "Wow. I've never experienced this kind of grace before."

It's funny, because for about a tenth of a second I feel the urge to concur with Senator too. Then I realize that, as usual, he's full of what the King James New Testament affectionately calls "dung." Senator has, no doubt, been awash in an ocean of grace all his life. It's pure grace that no one has beaten him to a pulp this year. Especially during the two weeks he marched around campus bellowing about how he was going to sue Gatorade for their "heinous yet unfunny prank."

As for me, Colby has shown me grace by forgiving me for all the names I've called him—names I wish to God I could take back. But even after all the name-calling and teasing and "Can't you see I'm busy right now?" brush-offs, he still wants to hang out with me more than with any person in the world. He sounds impossibly excited every time I call him on the phone. When I went home at Christmas, he bounded out the door and attached himself to me like an octopus—who got shorted on limbs. I thought they were going to have to pry him off with the Jaws of Life.

I close my eyes and start trying to divide polynomials in my head, because I know if I keep thinking about Colby and how purely good he is to me, I will start dripping tears all over my perfect test. And then, in shame and embarrassment, I'll have to transfer to a school far away, perhaps on the East Coast or in the United Arab Emirates. And that would be a pity, because Lewis has kind of grown on me. Especially since I heard The Carrot is transferring to Cal State Northridge next year.

After I get a grip on my emotions, I start thinking of Dad, the kind of guy who never misses a chance to put on his Good Samaritan hat—even if it makes him look like a dork.

Then there's Amanda Mac. Whenever she mentioned Jeremy

in an e-mail or during a phone conversation, I resolved to ignore her next three communication attempts, regardless of media. I don't know if she ever caught on to my system, but she kept trying. The girl is just relentless. I've hit a tennis ball against brick walls that were less relentless.

I'm still a little mad at her for that oratorical low blow that led to my succumbing to a rousing game of Five Minutes of Truth. But in the end, I'm grateful for those few truthful minutes—although I'm not sure I want to make a habit of it. It was a relief to finally tell somebody about my theory of heaven. I couldn't have told my dad, or I would probably be back in some counselor's office, and I think that Ms. Young-Thornton suffered enough on my account for all mental-health professionals, for all time. And I couldn't tell Youth Pastor Ted because I was sure that he'd kick my case up to the elders, who would insist on laying hands on me. And if any group of people is going to lay hands on me, it's going to be those elusive Burlington cheerleaders.

In short, Amanda did what she always does: listen a lot and judge not even a little—even after all I've done or, more accurately when it comes to her, haven't done. I swear, the girl couldn't hold a grudge if it was dipped in superglue.

Sometimes when I'm running, I'll stop hearing Clapton or Dylan or Reverend Al or U2 in my head, and it will be Amanda Mac singing that Shining Star song. Her voice is so clear that it's like she's living up there.

I can't wait to tell her about what's just happened in Roberts's class. And I'm curious if she'll agree with him about grace—that you can't learn about it, that you must experience it. Of course, she'll ask me what I think about grace. And I think I have an answer, though I'll have to give it in the form of a story:

The Smiths used to go on one big family vacation each summer—back when we were still a family. Once we picked out a destination, someone would send us a DVD, brochures, magazines, and so on to make us feel good about making such a wise decision about where to vacation. And if I got tired of the provided hype, I could always go to the Web and launch a hype hunt of my own. Bottom line: I always knew everything about where we were vacationing weeks before we got there.

I could tell you San Diego's average summer temperature, the typical July rainfall in Orlando, and the elevation of Pikes Peak's summit. I could even describe what our hotel room would look like and whether the pool was a rectangle or kidney-shaped. (Although, why anyone would want to create a pool in the shape of an organ that filters urine, I am not sure. That seems like asking for trouble to me.)

If I were asked to write a persuasive essay extolling the virtues of San Diego, Santa Fe, Orlando, Colorado Springs, and the like, I'm pretty sure I could have earned an A. (Especially if I threw in a "quintessence" or two.)

But I learned something each time we arrived at our locations: There's nothing like actually being there. A brochure can't make you feel warm sand under your bare feet when you're running along the beach at six minutes a mile. And even the most high-def DVD shots of the view from the top of Pikes Peak are a weak substitute for being up there yourself, feeling like you're on top of the world and hoping you don't pass out before you get a chance to take it all in.

That's how it was with me and grace. I learned about it, read about it, heard the sermons, did the Bible studies. My freshman year, I even memorized the official Grace Fellowship definition:

Grace is the unmerited favor of God bestowed on his beloved children. (Pure poetry, isn't it?) I could describe grace, define it, even teach a children's church lesson on it.

But here's what I'm thinking now, and this is, indeed, **Key Life Lesson #5**, if you're still counting along with me: You really *can't* learn about grace. You have to experience it, like we did in Roberts's class—and like I have pretty much my whole stupid life, but I've been too drunk, too depressed, too ashamed, and too *et cetera* to fully appreciate it.

So if you hear someone ask me what grace is, please drop-kick me if you hear me utter the term *unmerited favor*. Then remind me, please, that grace is a hardcore professor giving his whole class an A on a final exam purely because he wants to. Grace is a guy who'll lie on the floor all night with a dying dog so it won't have to die scared and alone. Grace is dodging SUVs—playing sure-enough life-and-death human Frogger—so that a little kid can have a remembrance of his puppy.

And maybe grace is God holding on to me even though I regularly bend his fingers back so far that I wonder if they'll snap. The dude must be double-jointed.

I'm hoping that God's grip will hold over the days immediately ahead, because I have a long trip home ahead of me—a trip far different, far longer, than the one I had planned. I don't get to fly home; I'm driving again, eventually. This news doesn't depress me, though, because life isn't just about where you're going or how you're getting there. Who you have beside you on the way can make all the difference. In a couple minutes, you'll understand.

You should also know one more thing: I really am Paying Attention now. Most of the time anyway. So if a coyote happens to bound into my path on the trip, this time I'll be ready.

Epilogue

Prayer Girl will be here any time. She's my ride to the airport. Of all the people I met this past year, she's probably my favorite. She's going to stay at Lewis for a while and knock out a couple required classes during summer semester. I worry about her eating alone, but she's assured me she'll be okay. And she's quick to add, "You're so sweet to worry."

She has told me that she'll pray for me over the summer and requested I do the same for her. I said I would. And I will. I mean, if you can't pray for someone you call Prayer Girl, you're really pretty pathetic.

I think she's going to be okay. She wants to be a social worker, and she seems like the kind of person who'd be good at that. Maybe if I'd had someone like her when I was a kid, I wouldn't be such a mess now.

It's weird: Thinking about Prayer Girl is making me, as Mr. Ross would want me to say, wistful—wistful about some of the other people I encountered on my journey from almost-nineteen to almost-twenty. Now, I don't expect you to be wistful like I am, but maybe you're at least curious. So here goes . . .

BRANDI THE REALITY GIRL

She graduated from being reality-show eye candy to crappy-horror-film eye candy. You be the judge if that's show-biz progress or not. She's starring in something called *Blood Drive*, which will be released later this summer. Last week, I heard her interviewed on one of those info-tainment shows that Rhonda loves so much. Here's my favorite part:

Info-tainment Hostess: "So, Brandi, like, I hear you meet your demise in this movie."

Brandi: "Oooh, I do, I do! And let me tell you, he is *so* hot!"

I almost fell out of my chair when I heard this. And all I could think was, *I wish Dalton and I could've witnessed this together. I don't know two people in the world who could have appreciated it more.* I know it's strange to miss someone you barely knew, but I started missing Dalton right then. I thought more about how we could have been good friends. We could have shared a lot more than a reluctant mom.

Sometimes I pray for his soul. I don't know how effective it is, but I figure it can't hurt. It's weird: I've never had much use for denominations. It seems like merely one more way for one group of humans to justify being better and smarter than the others. I just can't see Jesus being much of a denominational kind of person. (Besides, in our town, the Methodists and Lutherans feud like the Crips and the Bloods, ever since the unfortunate Gatorade-splashing incident during the summer softball tournament a couple years ago. The whole thing makes me sad—although grateful for an excuse not to play softball.) But when I pray for Dalton and his soul, I hope that this is one area in which the Catholics are right and we Protestants are wrong.

Mom and Maxwell

They are writing a book together, and I'm happy to report that it will be free of vampires and ravens, naked or clothed. They're writing nonfiction, about Dalton. "Some people will read this as a cautionary tale," Mom told me, "but it's more than that. Someone needs to tell Dalton's story. He can't just be forgotten. We need to do this, to help make things right with him. And when we're done with this, Griffin, I'm going to pour all of myself into making things right with you, your father, and little Colby."

I felt myself not believing her promises toward the three abandoned Smiths, but I did get a sense that she and Maxwell would finish their book. And it wouldn't surprise me (much) if it's a good book.

Amanda Sandwich

Perhaps full of too much eggnog, she went back to Carlton Tucker over Christmas break—which made me so sad that I lacked words to describe it. But a month later, he began cheating on her with a freshman at Talbot High, and that led to Tearful Breakup Number 3 or 4 in the Amanda/Carlton saga. Amanda is going to a local junior college, and Carlton is taking a year off, which is an intriguing choice for someone who slouched and scammed his way through high school.

Amanda e-mails me on occasion, and she promised to invite me to this mega-party she's hosting during the summer. I'll probably go, she'll probably pass out, and I can picture myself standing guard over her again—Amanda Sandwich's personal Nightwatchman, or is it Guardian Angel? Whatever the case, God have mercy on Carlton or any other little horndogs who try to sneak into her room. I've been lifting weights, and I've picked up a few moves watching Ultimate Fighting Competition with the jocks in Hill Hall. I've learned a move called a kimura, and I'm relatively certain I could dislocate Carlton's elbow with it. It would be fun to try, anyway. A guy's gotta have dreams.

COLE SHARP

He's living at home, attending nearby Pittsburg State. This fall, he'll play ball for the Pittsburg State Gorillas, the coolest team name in the history of intercollegiate athletics. During spring practices, he played mostly special teams but saw enough action to get a concussion in the big intersquad scrimmage. He is proud of that concussion. "It's my favorite," he told me, "because it's a college football concussion. It doesn't get much better than that."

During first semester, he sent me a few e-mails apologizing—again and again—about being Rhonda's make-out pawn. And when he picked me up at the airport when I went home for Christmas break, his first words were, "I really am sorry about the thing with Rhonda."

I looked at him, perplexed, which I'm quite good at due to many years of truly *being* perplexed. "What thing?" I shrugged.

He smiled at me, and he hasn't tried to apologize again since then. I guess that's the point.

B.T. AND RHONDA

They have yet to set a wedding date, but she's still wearing his ring—and given that it's summer, probably not much else. I'm not looking forward to seeing all *that* again. But Dad told me a couple of weeks ago that he honestly believed he'd "found a place of forgiveness" with Rhonda. And this time he didn't sound like he was facing the flag with his hand over his heart.

So I think I'll avoid the pool as much as I can this summer. There's nothing there I haven't already seen. But I gotta admit, I'm curious what this whole forgiveness thing looks like. Skeptical, but curious all the same.

COLBY

We talked all the time this past year. Reece, one of the guys in our quad, has unlimited cell minutes, so I borrowed his Nokia whenever I maxed out another prepaid calling card. I'm grateful to Reece, because there is no one I missed more than my little brother.

Last week, he told me he got "almost all X's" on his final kindergarten report card. In kindergarten, X's are king, the kinder-equivalent of an A. He got a few check marks, denoting adequate work. His report card was free of minus signs, the mark of shame.

I told him I was proud of him, but I added, "Colby, don't get too stressed out about getting all X's. Just do your best. Try to learn some cool stuff. A few check marks here and there is no big deal, okay?"

It was hard to believe those words were coming from me. I wondered how my life might have been different if a teacher or parent had said them to me. Or if I'd said them to myself. But that's water—actually, lots and lots of vodka—under the bridge now. All I care about is not letting the stress and pressure do to Colby what they did to me. If he stashes bottles of anything in his room, it better be root beer.

When we were saying goodbye, he told me, "I real-miss you and real-love you."

Then he asked me, "Hey, bro, will you tell me a story?"

I paused a minute, wondering where to begin. *If Reece's cell battery holds out,* I thought, *I'll tell my brother stories all night. Stories about coyotes, carjackers, and the perils of reasoning with a man holding a rifle. I'll tell him about standing guard for Amanda Sandwich and about the weirdest final exam I'll ever take. I'll tell him why I think the song title "Amazing Grace" is redundant because there is no other kind of grace. I'll tell him all of this and more, just as soon as I can find my voice.*

AMANDA MACKENZIE

As soon as I choked my way through a few stories for Colby, I called Amanda Mac, whom I will see in a few hours. That's because I'm flying from John Wayne Airport to lovely Redmond, Oregon, to help Amanda drive her Civic back to Talbot. Her original travel plans fell through. More specifically, Jeremy the um-boyfriend, scheduled Passenger #1, cheated on Amanda with Angie Gaylord, scheduled Passenger #2. And I thought my trip *out* to college got off to a weird start.

Amanda was crying when I announced that I was returning her call. "Griff," she said, "I just don't know what to do. My mom has moved out, and Zeke is out of school now, and my dad doesn't have any vacation time left because of all that's gone on. And his car is acting up, so he really, really needs mine but doesn't want me driving all that way by myself, and . . . everything's just such a mess."

"Amanda," I whispered, "I will drive you."

"But how will you get up here?"

"Airplane. Big airplane."

"But changing your ticket will be really expensive."

"Well, knowing my dad's credit card situation, this will just be like taking a guy riddled with bullet holes and knife wounds and giving him a paper cut."

"Well, if you're sure. Of course, I'll have to ask my dad. It is a long drive and all. You know what that's going to mean."

"Do you think your dad trusts me?"

"I'm not sure, Griff. But he knows he can trust *me*. What about your dad? Will he be okay with all of this?"

"When I lay out the situation, and my plan, he will probably say, 'Well, we certainly are facing a paucity of choices. If you'll give me your word that you'll be responsible and chaste, I guess we can proceed.' Then I'll get off the phone as quickly as I can, before he can change his mind."

"What about you, Griffin? Are you sure you're not going to change *your* mind? I mean, you could be home tomorrow. I don't even know for sure how long this is going to take us."

"I'm not changing my mind, Mackenzie. And I want you to know that I'm going to be the best driver in history. I will be like that dude in the Transporter movies, albeit without the charming accent. But I got more hair. Anyway, I will get you home safe. I promise."

"Okay, then. There's just one more thing. I feel bad about asking something of someone who's doing me such a huge favor, but . . ."

"But?" I asked, hearing the suspicion in my voice.

"If we're going to do this, travel this many miles together, I want to hear it all."

"Hear what all?"

"You know what I mean. I want more than Five Minutes of Truth; I want five thousand miles of truth. Because we have to figure this out—"this" meaning *us*. Look, I know you're not Jeremy, and that is a huge plus, a huge relief. But knowing who you're not isn't enough. I need to know who you really *are*. So, are you up for that?"

"I don't know if I'm up for it, but I'll do it. I won't duck anything."

"Really?"

"Really."

"How can I be sure you're not just blowing more smoke?"

"Because I want to figure out us just as bad as you do."

Through the window, I see Prayer Girl's car approaching, so there's time to ponder only one more thing: When will Amanda ask me about the shirt? The one that Mom mailed to me, just like she said she would.

It's possible Amanda Mac won't notice it right away. I'll be busy loading up her car and moving warily, ever on the lookout for the ex-um-boyfriend. (I would call it a blessing if I could put him in a kimura, as a little prelude to Carlton Tucker.)

Anyway, it could be that Amanda won't pop the question until we're settled into her car and on our way home:

"So, Griff, what's with the shirt? Who is the little emo girl, and why do you need her to smile?"

"I'm not exactly sure who the emo girl is, but I *am* sure that it's good for someone, anyone, to smile at you. I think it helps heal you."

"Mmm. Where did you buy it?"

"It was a gift from a friend."

"A friend from Lewis?"

"Nope. From someplace else. A place where coyotes run wild."

"Griff, are you okay? You look so sad all of the sudden."

"I'm fine. It's just that I get kinda bummed whenever I wear this shirt."

"Then why do you wear it?"

"I feel like I need to, so that no one will forget . . ."

"Griff, are you crying? I have never seen you cry."

"I guess I am."

"So . . ."

"Is it okay if I tell you?"

"Please, please. I have waited years for this."

"Me too. Here's the thing, Amanda . . ."

I'm absolutely convinced that nothing—nothing living or dead, angelic or demonic, today or tomorrow, high or low, thinkable or unthinkable—absolutely nothing can get between us and God's love because of the way that Jesus our Master has embraced us.

—Romans 8:38-39, MSG

RESOURCES

If you are struggling with substance abuse or another form of self-harm, the authors and publisher of this book encourage you to seek the help and support of a parent, pastor, youth leader, counselor, or other trusted adult. If, for some reason, you don't feel you have support locally, please consider contacting one of the following organizations:

- Teen Challenge (http://teenchallengeusa.com)
- The US. Department of Health & Human Services' Substance Abuse/Mental Health Services Administration (http://www.samhsa.gov/Treatment/treatment_public_i.aspx)
- The Children'sARK, P.O. Box 497, Green Mountain Falls, CO 80819. (www.childrensark.org; phone: 719-684-9511)

Also, if you know someone who struggles with self-harm, you may also find a helpful resource in *Inside a Cutter's Mind*, by Jerusha Clark and Dr. E. Henslin (June 2007).

About the Authors

TODD AND JEDD HAFER have authored many books, including *Snickers from the Front Pew: Confessions of Two Preacher's Kids*, *Wake Up and Smell the Pizza*, and *In the Chat Room with God*. Todd is an editorial director for Hallmark in Kansas City, Missouri, while Jedd is a director at The Children's ARK in Colorado Springs, Colorado, a home for troubled teens. Check out Todd and Jedd's website at www.haferbros.com.